CURSED FOREVER TO
SAIL THE SEVEN SEAS

THE TALES OF THE
FLYING DUTCHMAN

BY

VARIOUS AUTHORS

British Library Cataloguing-in-Publication Data
A catalogue record for this book is available from the
British Library

CONTENTS

SENTA

Sir Max Pemberton

The storm had menaced the ship since two bells of the first dog-watch; but its full fury was not to be experienced until darkness fell.

A fiery sun sank into clouds as black as thunder when the bells were heard; and anon, the wind came wailing from the west with such a note of utter melancholy that even the oldest among the sailors shuddered at their own prophecies; while the passengers of many nations lay huddled about the deck or sought the deep shelter of the profound cabin, where a crazy lamp but emphasised the darkness. There a Dutch pastor prayed that God would deliver them from the storm – while women clutched their children as though strong arms would protect them.

Now, this was a Dutch barque that had put out from Riga to sail to London; and among its passengers was a young musician with a lofty brow and a thinker's moods, who had set out from Russia to visit Paris, in the hope of having the first of his serious operas represented there.

Richard Wagner was twenty-six years old at that time. He had written much that was afterwards to be forgotten; had studied at Leipzig and at Vienna, where he composed the music of a romantic opera *Die Feen*, and subsequently heard that great singer, Schroder-Devrient, for whom he was to complete *Rienzi*, and so at last come into his own.

Unhappily, Germany did not yet know the genius in her midst – and poor, and at his wits' end for bread, the Master passed from one scene to another – always seeking a haven for his genius, but yet to find it. A post as musical director in the theatre at Riga did not satisfy him – and feeling that he was being too much influenced by the music of France and Italy, he conceived the idea that Paris might welcome him . . . and that, even from the least musical nation in Europe, the English, he might obtain a hearing.

He was very poor at that time, occupied a mean lodging in Riga and had the greatest difficulty in supporting himself and the wife, who subsequently was to suffer so much chagrin because of his infidelities.

But he managed, nevertheless, to secure a passage for them both upon the Dutch barque that was to sail for London – nor did he forget to take his Great Dane, Robber, who accompanied him at that time on all his voyages.

So the party set out and soon was faced by the difficulties of the passage.

A motley horde of Russians, Poles, Germans and Dutch crowded the mean ship to the point of danger. There were two or three English merchants, some sailors of the same race who had been shipwrecked on an island of the Baltic, a group of Jewish traders, and last, but by no means the least interesting to the romantic Master, there was Senta, the Norwegian girl, with her wide blue eyes and her plaintive songs and her weird stories of the sea, which the Vikings surely should have taught her in the great ages of adventure.

It was Robber, the Great Dane, who first discovered Senta, as she squatted by the round house amidships and recited her legends to the sailors. Somehow, the monster hound seemed a fit companion for the fragile little creature, whose mind was an index to the ages, but whose body was a mere wraith. He would curl up beside her and reward her ballads with no more than reproachful eyes – when her voice sank into the soft melancholy of some doleful fable of the sea, he would howl without shame and so rebuke her. Nevertheless, all felt that Senta was quite safe in the great dog's keeping – and when the captain, Darand, tried to make love to her, he cursed the day which brought such a ferocious beast aboard.

To a man of the romantic and amorous temperament of Richard Wagner, his discovery of a blue-eyed prophetess was a godsend.

Often he would pace the deck with her until the early hours of the morning; and always in her talk he discovered that profound note of melancholy which the drear seas and ghostly Northern lands inspire. Nevertheless, it was not always of the sagas that she spoke, but sometimes of the more earthly passion of love.

'I am to marry Erik of Bergen when he returns from his next voyage,' she confessed to the Master one day – and no sooner had the words been uttered than she fell into a profound melancholy, as though the tidings were of sorrow and not of joy.

'Does not marriage mean very much to you, then?' the Master asked her. 'Are you not in love with this sailor lover of yours?'

Senta looked up with eyes that burned.

'I am so much in love with him that we shall sail the seas together when all here are in their graves and this ship is but rotting wood on a forgotten shore.'

Wagner was not at all surprised. He knew what Norse imagery was and would not mock it.

'A very old woman you will be then, Senta.'

'A very, very old woman, Master, who now has but a few days to live. We go into the world of shadows, Erik and I, and we sail these seas for ever. Thus has sadness come to me, I shall perish, but this ship may be saved at last. The voices tell me so, and they have never lied to me.'

'But Senta, why should the ship be in danger? Was there ever a calmer sea than this upon which we sail? And if a storm comes, are there not many havens? Come, come, let us think of Erik and of love. I will make a song for you, and you shall sing it. We will call it Erik the Steersman – for I also have written of your sagas and you shall hear my verses when there is nobody round about to hear us.'

She told him in return that she had known both of him and his music when she had been in Riga, and his proper vanity swelled at her prophecies of his future greatness.

'All the world will acknowledge you for its Master,' she said, 'but there will be weary years of waiting. Count nothing upon the city to which you are going, for it is through your own Germany that success will come. The English will not understand you, for they know no music; and in Paris they will not hear you. No, no, Master, it is to Germany that you must look if the ship is saved!'

'Then even your voices are not sure about that, Senta. They think there is danger for us.'

'There is great danger, Master, and it is coming out of the west. Some will perish but some will live – while I, I shall ride upon the storm with my lover through all eternity – even as she who gave me her name and whose spirit hovers upon these waters even as we talk.'

She took up her guitar at the words and began to sing softly, as though addressing one unseen but waiting.

The Master, however, went back to his cabin wondering at this message of death and asking himself if the hour which should end all his dreams was at hand.

So the menace of the storm became apparent when the ship had rounded the North Cape and was heading to the south-west for the Port of Bergen.

The day had been fair enough with a clear light of an ungenerous sun and placid waters which were a solace to the emigrants. All, indeed, was life and laughter upon the crowded ship . . . and even Senta, the dreamer, could attune her song to the mood and remember the cry of her youth. They had all been dancing to her music when the dinner bell called them . . . and Richard Wagner himself was thinking in terms of a ballet, which, many years later on, was to ornament his opera of *Tannhäuser* as Paris first knew it. So the merry hours passed until the reddening sun sank beneath the ominous bank of the clouds and the dirge of the wind began to be heard in the rigging as a prelude to the dreadful night. Then, truly, Senta's laughter passed; and gathering the seamen about her, she told them stories of phantom ships and of shrieks from their stricken decks, above which the spirits hovered as the doomed vessels drove on to a penance of eternity.

'There was one named Darand, as this captain of yours is named,' she said, 'and he was in the southern seas, long, long years ago. There was also a wind such as blows upon us tonight . . . and the great Cape faced him and all his skill could not bring his ship into the western waters. Then he cared not for God or Devil, but called upon the spirits of evil to answer him, and they came up from the black waters and pestilence fell upon all that company, and it died horribly even while the storm was still raging. But the souls of those poor people came back again to Darand's barque from the blackness of death, and the steersman took his place at the wheel again, and now for ever the ship sails that southern sea and woe to those whose eyes look upon it, for they also shall surely perish . . .'

So much and much more fell from the lips of the little prophetess as she gathered the seamen about her, and together they watched the oncoming storm.

Darand, their captain, a lusty fellow with the courage of a rabbit, did not hear his name thus taken in vain . . . and for long he refused to believe that the storm was more than a passing squall; while he averred that midnight would show them a fine heaven of stars with a breeze so favourable that they would be half-way to Bergen at the same hour of the morrow. At the same time, he continued to hope that fear might yet drive the pretty Senta to his cabin . . . and he fixed wanton eyes upon her while she sang her plaintive little songs to the sailors, and even carried her a pannikin of wine, like a gallant lover who thinks first of his Dulcinea, whatever the peril of the hour. When she drank it, however, her toast was 'the Phantom Ship,' and that so scared this sawdust Nelson that he turned as white as one of his own sails and began to question her closely.

'How – you talk of phantom ships. Who, then, has put that nonsense into your head, my pretty? There are no phantom ships in these waters, as every sailor knows. Why, then, speak of what does not exist?'

'I speak, Captain, of that which my eyes have seen. A ship sails yonder in the loom of the cloud, and its crew are not of this world. Be warned, then, for the danger is upon us and God alone knows if any of us will be alive when the new day breaks.'

She pointed with a hand no bigger than that of a child away to the west, and to the gold and the deep crimson of its horizon. There was no ship there – but so had she hypnotised the devil-fearing seamen about her that more than one cried – 'Yonder, yonder on the starboard bow – don't you see her – a fore-and-aft schooner – no, no, a brig – I tell you she's a barque . . . there's a man on the quarter deck – no, two and two more at the wheel . . . I tell you it's nothing at all, just the shadows, that's what it is . . . and the wind rising – my

God, how long is the old man going to hold on like this . . . has he lost his senses then?'

Darand himself was at first too afraid to say anything at all, but presently he awoke to the realities and crying – 'All hands on deck to take in sail,' he began to prepare the ship for the ordeal which was upon her. In a twinkling, as it were, the topsails were down, the jibs bellowing on the boom, the mizzen lowered and the hatches battened down. All passengers were ordered below and sent there with little ceremony; and so it befell that Richard Wagner and Senta, neither of whom the Dutchman cared to provoke, sought the shelter of the cuddy beneath the quarter deck, where two men now stood at the wheel, and the great dog watched them as though his very presence might avail against the tempest.

'You spoke of a phantom ship,' said the Master presently. 'I saw none and there was none to see. Are these things then revealed to you in a vision, child, or do you desire to drive these good fellows crazy? That, surely, would not be worthy of you.'

She flushed at the rebuke, and for a little while did not know how to answer him.

'I see with my soul, but not with my eyes,' she said at last, 'since my childhood, the visions have come to me and I have heard voices which tell me of things hidden from those about me. To-night, I can hear the voices of Evil which come from the Phantom Ship, and so I speak of it. It is a warning that many of these poor people must die – that God is about to judge their souls. Why, then, should I be silent when the voices bid me speak? Have I not told you already the things that are true?'

'You have said that I shall live when many perish.'

'It is true, true,' she cried . . . and then with a voice of woe, she added, 'but I shall die and go to my love, and we shall sail these seas for ever.'

For ever!

Richard Wagner looked out on the storm-ridden ocean and the terror of her prophecy appalled him.

What an irony of his destiny if all his dreams should perish in these dark waters! He believed that he had a master message to deliver to the people of all countries and that the first notes of it would soon be heard. Now the raging sea threatened to obliterate all that he had planned and desired with such an earnest hope . . . and he knew for a truth that his grave might be there amidst the tumult of the surf which now drove the barque headlong.

Yet his was not a superstitious mind, and although its images were of the shadow world of gods and sirens and sagas of the remote past, his faith was merely negative; and he no more believed the story of a phantom ship than of the devil knocking on Luther's door at Weimar. Squatting there upon the deck of the barque he had become a materialist, weighing but his personal chance of safety in the balance, and yet content, almost as one driven to any consolation, to listen to this little dreamer and to take comfort in her words.

He would live; but she would perish.

Her youth, her spirituality fascinated him . . . and he looked at her with profound sorrow as he thought that to-morrow the same beautiful eyes might be gazing sightless at the angry heaven . . . the voice hushed, the poetry of her thoughts unsung. Then, almost in the same mood, he could rid himself of the spell and come back to reality. The ship and all its people might perish despite her prophecies. And, indeed, it soon seemed that such must be their fate, and that the end truly was at hand.

It was black dark by this time and all their light came from the loom of the scudding cloud, where the lightning found its curtain and cast back great aureoles of light down upon the frenzied breakers. All the terror of the storm would be revealed at one instant, to be blotted out the next and left but a memory of a menacing revelation. And all the time the wind howled and screeched in the flying rigging; sails were torn to ribbons; the decks washed by huge waves; the lanterns extinguished . . . and those below terrified by the waters which poured in among them as the backwash of that Styx they presently must cross.

Anon, panic arose.

Russians mad with terror forced their way to the decks and shouted wildly at a captain whom fear had already deprived of his wits. Drink was got from the purser's store, and a keg of brandy broached in the waist of the barque. Soon, weird figures staggered to the slippery decks and shook impotent fists at the skies which mocked them. Men were swept overboard now as flies from a board which is washed and women died in men's arms for very fear. There came a crescendo of terrifying sounds out of the void and the thunders crashed as though a myriad devils were clamouring for souls, while there was no longer steerage way upon the barque, nor any thought of a haven. She had become the sport of the tempest, and her hours appeared to be numbered.

Throughout it all, Senta and the Master watched from the shelter of the lower deck and rarely ventured a word in the momentary intervals of storm. Once, indeed, it became again apparent that she saw some vision of the sea, and that some figure of her subjective mind appeared to her. When the musician dared to ask her what that figure was, she declared without hesitation that Erik, her lover, was calling to her, and that he had told her that the ship would be saved.

'But only,' she said with unutterable sadness, '– only if I

go to him where he is waiting for me.'

'You do not fear to go, my dear – not to your lover, surely.'

'You do not understand,' she said, 'when Erik comes for me, then I must die. Oh, I know it, I know it!' and for the first time she began to weep, not for fear of the storm, but for the man's sake.

Wagner was well acquainted with moods such as this, and his own dreams were often the fruit of them.

Profound mysteries of the Unseen, the shadow-world peopled by unnumbered souls; gods fighting in the air and below the water, lovers who died because they had loved . . . of such fables were his mighty operas to be made. And here, surely, in this pathetic little oracle, whom the visions haunted, here, in truth, was just such a figure as he loved.

He believed no word of her story, it may be, and yet her words gave him consolation. The ship was to be saved, she said, though she might perish. He did not believe that she was to die, yet such argument as he could use seemed weak enough in view of his bias toward the dreamer.

'Believe no such thing,' he said, 'if this Erik of yours is the brave fellow I believe him to be, he will be the first to protect you – is he not a sailor also? I think that you have told me so, my dear. Then, surely, sailors do not come to do evil to those they love?'

The question intrigued her and turned her thoughts to other scenes.

'He is captain of the sloop *Christiana*,' she said, 'his father is the minister in the church of Molda. He was at Riga last year, and we spent many days together – such happy days they were, never to come again. We should have seen him this time at Bergen if God had let us go there. But now I know it must be in some other place . . . and if he finds me, it will be because he is sent to do so. Oh, do not think that I fear death with Erik – but we are both so young to leave the sunshine and the light; and at one time it seemed that we had many years before us. It cannot be now. I have seen the Phantom Ship, and none see it and live . . .'

'You think, then, that all these mad people who perished to-night, they all saw the vision with you?'

'I am sure of it. Did you not hear their words? "Yonder," they cried, and pointed at it. Then I knew how it would be with them – and you, Master, you have seen it happen with your own eyes.'

He had to confess that it was so.

The sea had claimed the price of folly and the dead already floated about the ship in the darkness.

It was the crisis of the storm; and none upon the barque believed that she could live.

Darand, the captain, had long given up any hope of saving

either vessel or cargo, and of his crew, few were sober. Some sang crazy songs of ancient mariners and of seamen who had gone to the devil; others lay about like logs, half insensible and wholly indifferent to the storm. Of them all but the Englishman, Barker, and the Scottish bo'sun, Atkinson, kept their wits, and did all that seamanship could do to keep the crazy ship afloat and the monster seas from engulfing her. Rousing such of the hands as were capable of any service at all, they got the torn jibs from the booms and stripped the aft rigging of all canvas. Almost under bare poles, the barque headed to the south-west and so toward that town of Bergen, which it now seemed impossible that she should ever see. And as though such courage merited reward, there was at last a breaking of the hurricane, a modulation in the raucous voices of winds and a sudden cleavage of the black cloud, which drove no longer across the heavens in unbroken mass but was riven to let the moon shine upon the raging water and to show them Ursa Major in all its majesty. Now, indeed, the mate began to tell them that there was hope . . . and as though to justify his words, the man at the wheel cried 'light on the port bow' – and instantly the whole company became alert as though this was the end of it and the port of their salvation already made.

Richard Wagner saw the light and Senta with him.

She knew that northern shore well, for she had often sailed

it with the seamen who came to her father's house; and her lover Erik had spent the best part of his young life in trading with the villages of the fjords and in piloting strange ships into them.

So, no sooner had she seen the beacon than she declared it to be that of the Hammerfest, and that if they could weather the great cape which sheltered the fjord, then indeed were they as surely saved as though they had dropped anchor in the harbour of Bergen.

'I know the place,' she cried wildly. 'I have sailed there often with Erik when he was taking English people to the North Cape. There is another light, a red one, when you pass the point of the island, and after that you can see the houses of the town, a very little town with very poor people, but there is an inn there, and we can all shelter there. Did I not tell you that the ship would be saved? Was I not right from the beginning, dear Master?'

He told her that she was and rejoiced to see that her other words had seemingly been forgotten. The joy of hope and life was as sure for her as any upon the ship – and in the new excitement of deliverance, she stood by the side of the Englishman telling him that this or that was the course he must follow, explaining the situation both of the island and the port and promising him water enough to float the greatest ship that ever sailed the seas.

'They say that the fjord is a mile deep even against the side of the mountain. I have seen Erik sail the *Christiana* so close to the rock that I could put my hand upon it. Now keep a little more to port and then you must put the helm hard over. Yes, yes, there is the red lantern, and those are the lights of the town. We are safe now and shall think of storm no more.'

The man obeyed, while Captain Darand, perceiving what had happened, came to his senses and again took charge of the barque.

Among the passengers, there was indescribable reaction. Women fainted for joy of their escape; men sang incoherendy or danced about or remembered the unfinished bottles. And gradually, as the vessel was steered amid the jagged rocks upon which great waves still broke into fountains of foam and swirling waters, even Richard Wagner suffered an intense emotion which even he could not control.

Music now came to his aid, and all its magic inspiration.

He has told us how, at that moment, the scheme of *The Flying Dutchman* came to him. How the music possessed his soul and would be heard. The thunder of storm; the tragic love (if it were to be tragic) of the litde prophetess; the great crags towering up in the first light of the coming dawn – all contributed to that elation of the spirit by which alone great masterpieces are born.

Yet there remained the doubt.

As he watched the frail Senta standing triumphantly at the helmsman's side, he could ask, what of to-morrow.

Was the fable of her end but a fable, or had she been truly warned?

Time alone would tell him whether this child of the dreams had dreamed truly – whether she would die or live, prove her prophecies true or deny them gloriously.

The ship was anchored to the rock just as the day broke – and even at that early hour, some townsmen waited on the shore to offer help to a company so miraculously saved.

A dreadful night it had been, they declared. More than one good barque would sail the seas no more. Dead men's faces had been seen from the cliff head and wreckage had been washed up against the barrier reefs outside. Fortunate was this fellow Darand; fortunate those who sailed with him. He should go to the church, they said, and give thanks – and for that the church stood open, and there were candles lighted upon its altar.

A few obeyed this injunction; but more thought of the inn and of hot food and drink there to be prepared.

Soon a procession was formed, the lanterns of the welcomers still lighted though the day had come. The pious sang hymns; the impious laughed and shouted and patted upon their broad backs the good folk who welcomed them.

It was natural at this time, that Richard Wagner should find himself walking side by side with Senta of the dark prophecies, and that he should wish to recall them to her. She, however, had the radiance of the new day upon her pretty face . . . and when it passed, it was some memory of the man Darand, and of his pursuit of her, which brought the cloud.

'I shall sail no more with him,' she said, 'you see how he insults me. It is well for him that Erik is not here. There would be no more Captain Darand, no surely,' and then with real anger she cried: 'But he shall yet repay – I will tell a tale of him at Bergen that many will hear – if ever I see Bergen again.'

'But, my dear, you don't doubt that now. What is to forbid you? We shall wait until the good weather comes, and then we shall sail – you cannot stop in a wild man's country like this. It might be months before any ship called to take you to your home.'

She laughed at that.

'They are my own people and none are kinder . . . I shall tell them how Darand has treated me, and they also may have something to say to him. I don't fear him here, and I will never sail with him again – even though I have seen the Phantom Ship, and may not have many days to live.'

So back to her premonitions and to their sorrow. She had

not forgotten the apparition, as Wagner hoped; and the old legend still could affright her.

'You must forget that,' the Master said, with a kindly hand laid upon her shoulder, 'think no more of it, Senta. I like to hear these old tales as well as anybody, but I know that they are all nonsense. They come out of the darkness of the blind ages when life was a terrible thing and men had no true perception of God or of His purpose. They are the fairy stories of people whose imagination dwelt often upon death because life itself was such a hazardous thing. We know that they are false now when we listen to them – and you are too wise to give them credence.'

She shook her head but was not convinced.

'I hope it may be so – I do not know,' she said, 'things have been revealed to me in dreams often, and I have never found them untrue. The days will tell us, Master, the days that are to come. If Erik comes here, then I shall know that all is true and that it is the end.'

He tried to laugh it away with kindly banter about her lover . . . and so they went to the hospitable inn and to the warm breakfast there prepared for them. Darand, the captain, it appeared had arrived there before them, and his stories of the adventure seemed to imply that his courage had been as high as the waves which so nearly overwhelmed them. Menacingly also, he declared that it all came of having a 'witch' woman aboard – and that true or false, he was convinced in his own mind that all their misfortunes had been brought upon them by a little strumpet, who pretended to see phantom ships and such like, and had frightened the seamen half out of their wits.

Ridiculous as these tales were, a lonely people listened to them with greedy ears. Many a superstition held its own triumphantly amid those dominating crags and angry seas, where life itself was a daily battle with want and darkness, and the loom of solitude. To such a hamlet no visitor was less welcome than one credited with occult powers, able to tell them of to-morrow and to prophesy of life and death. Senta, indeed, would have been thrust bodily out of the inn but for Wagner's presence and protection.

'You are fools to listen to any such stories,' he thundered, 'the child is to marry Erik of Bergen, and would he marry a witch? Ask that fellow Darand rather, how he has done his duty by her and then let us answer him. I will be responsible for her, good people. You need fear nothing while she is with me.'

That was well enough; but it was quite clear that no house in the little town would shelter her when night came again, and that she must, willy nilly, either sleep on the shore or go back to Darand and the ship. Wagner advised the latter course, being afraid of what would happen if she remained ashore. Indeed, he promised to accompany her, though much preferring a dry bed at the inn, and so they set out together at sundown and a fisherman rowed them back to the barque – almost deserted save for a few of its crew, and still showing shattered evidence of the storm.

The night was fair and the wind much moderated. Darand had not returned to the ship; and it appeared that he would not return; yet Senta was afraid to go to her cabin, and they made themselves snug in the old harbourage by the wheel house. A bribe to a somnolent cook brought them hot coffee from the galley, and afterwards there was the guitar for those songs which had so sure a hold upon the imagination of the seamen. Senta sang as sweetly as ever; but this time it was of the ancient heroes, of Vikings in armour who sailed the Southern seas and returned with women and booty as their prey. And while she sang, the tarry sailors gathered about her and tears of sentiment or of greed rolled down their unwashed cheeks.

Wagner found, as ever, this barbarous music much to his liking. The scheme of his life's work was already shaping in his mind, and he was preparing to abandon all those traditions of French and Italian art by which hitherto he had been bound. Soon he would teach the world the lessons it must learn and by those lessons his own fame would be won. So he listened patiently to Senta; and when at last she wearied and the sailors crept to their bunks, he still dwelt upon the immensity of his dream and all that realization would mean to him. Then sleep overtook him also – and the sunshine of a better day was shining when he awoke to hear a sailor tell him that Senta had left the ship and that the manner of her going had been miraculous.

'The ship passed us in the night – I saw the loom of her sails,' he said, a voice called out to her, and she sprang from yonder poop as the phantom went by us – in silence, sir, as a wisp of cloud that drifts down from the hills. No man will ever see or hear of her again, believe me. She has gone whence none return, and God deliver her soul.'

The Master thought upon it, pacing the deck in the chill air full of wonder at what he had heard.

Was the story of another world or of this?

Had Erik come after all in his ship the *Christiana*, and was her cry one of recognition as she leapt into the arms awaiting her? He believed it might be so – and yet, who shall fathom all the mystery of the sea and her phantoms?

One thing is sure.

The truth he never learned. Next day the barque set sail for London, and a few weeks after Richard Wagner was in Paris.

But he never forgot Senta nor her songs; *The Flying Dutchman* bore witness to that as all the world knows. He would never have written so great a masterpiece, he has confessed, but for the little prophetess, who believed that death awaited her and yet may have found life in her lover's arms.

THE MEMOIRS OF HERR VON SCHNABELEWOPSKI

Heinrich Heine

It was a charming spring day when I first left Hamburg. I can still see how in the harbour the golden sunrays gleamed on the tarry bellies of the ships, and think I still hear the joyous, long-drawn *Ho-i-ho!* of the sailors. Such a port in spring-time has a pleasant similarity with the feelings of a youth who goes for the first time out into the world on the great ocean of life. All his thoughts are gaily variegated, pride swells every sail of his desires – *ho-i-ho!* But soon a storm rises, the horizon grows dark, the tempest howls, the planks crack, the waves break the rudder, and the poor ship is wrecked on romantic rocks, or stranded on damp, prosaic sandbanks; or perhaps, brittle and broken, with its masts gone, and without an anchor of hope, it returns to its old harbour, and there moulders away, wretchedly unrigged, as a miserable wreck.

But there are men who cannot be compared to common ships, because they are like steamboats. They carry a gloomy fire within, and sail against wind and weather; their smoky banner streams behind, like the black plume of the Wild Huntsman; their zigzagged wheels remind one of weighty spurs with which they prick the ribs of the waves, and the obstinate, resistant elements must obey their will like a steed; but sometimes the boiler bursts, and the internal fire burns us up!

But now I will escape from metaphor, and get on board a real ship bound from Hamburg to Amsterdam. It was a Swedish vessel, and besides the hero of these pages, was also loaded with iron, being destined probably to bring as a return freight a cargo of cod-fish to the aristocracy of Hamburg, or owls to Athens.

The banks of the Elbe are charming, especially so behind Altona, near Rainville. There Klopstock lies buried. I know of no place where a dead poet could more fitly rest. To exist there as a *living* poet is, of course, a much more difficult matter. How often have I sought thy grave, oh Singer of the Messiah, thou who hast sung with such touching truthfulness the sufferings of Jesus. But thou didst dwell long enough on the Königstrasse behind the Jungfernsteig to know how prophets are crucified.

On the second day we came to Cuxhaven, which is a colony from Hamburg, The inhabitants are subjects of the Republic, and have a good time of it. When they freeze in winter woollen blankets are sent to them, and when the summer is all too hot they are supplied with lemonade. A high or well-wise senator resides there as pro-consul. He has an income of twenty thousand marks, and rules over five thousand subjects. There is also a sea-bath, which has the great advantage over all others, that it is at the same time an Elbe-bath. A great dam, on which one can walk, leads to Ritzebuttel, which also belongs to Cuxhaven. The term is derived from the Phoenician, as *Ritze* and *Buttel* signify in it the mouth of the Elbe. Many historians maintain that Charlemagne only enlarged Hamburg, but that the Phoenicians founded it about the time that Sodom and Gomorrah were destroyed, and it is not unlikely that fugitives from these cities fled to the mouth of the Elbe. Between the Fuhlentwiete and the coffee factory men have found old money, coined during the reign of Bera XVI and Byrsa X. I believe that Hamburg is the old Tarsus whence Solomon received whole shiploads of gold, silver, ivory, peacocks, and monkeys. Solomon, that is, the king of Judah and Israel, always had a special fancy for gold and monkeys.

This my first voyage can never be forgotten. My old grand-aunt had told me many tales of the sea, which now rose to new life in my memory. I could sit for hours on the deck recalling the old stories, and when the waves murmured it seemed as if I heard my grand-aunt's voice. And when I closed my eyes I could see her before me, as she twitched her lips and told the legend of the *Flying Dutchman*.

I should have been glad to see some mermaids, such as sit on white rocks and comb their sea-green hair; but I only heard them singing.

However earnestly I gazed many a time down into the transparent waters, I could not behold the sunken cities, in which mortals enchanted into fishy forms lead a deep, a marvellous deep, and hidden ocean life. They say that salmon and old rays sit there, dressed like ladies, at their windows, and, fanning themselves, look down into the street, where cod-fish glide by in trim councillors' costume, and dandy young herrings look up at them through eye-glasses, and crabs, lobsters, and all kinds of such common crustaceans, swarm swimming about. I could never see so deep; I only heard the faint bells of the sunken cities peal once more their old melodious chime.

Once by night I saw a great ship with outspread blood-red sails go by, so that it seemed like a dark giant in a scarlet cloak. Was that the *Flying Dutchman*?

But in Amsterdam, where I soon arrived, I saw the grim Mynheer bodily, and that on the stage. On this occasion, in the theatre of that city, I also had an opportunity to make the acquaintance of one of those fairies whom I had sought in vain in the sea. And to her, as she was particularly charming,

I will devote a special section.

You certainly know the fable of the *Flying Dutchman*. It is the story of an enchanted ship which can never arrive in port, and which since time immemorial has been sailing about at sea. When it meets a vessel, some of the unearthly sailors come in a boat and beg the others to take a packet of letters home for them. These letters must be nailed to the mast, else some misfortune will happen to the ship – above all if no Bible be on board, and no horse-shoe nailed to the foremast. The letters are always addressed to people whom no one knows, and who have long been dead, so that some late descendant gets a letter addressed to a far away great-great-grandmother, who has slept for centuries in her grave. That timber spectre, that grim grey ship, is so called from the captain, a Hollander, who once swore by all the devils that he would get round a certain mountain, whose name has escaped me, in spite of a fearful storm, though he should sail till the Day of Judgement. The devil took him at his word, therefore he must sail for ever, until set free by a woman's truth. The devil in his stupidity has no faith in female truth, and allowed the enchanted captain to land once in seven years and get married, and so find opportunities to save his soul. Poor Dutchman! He is often only too glad to be saved from his marriage and his wife-saviour, and get again on board.

The play which I saw in Amsterdam was based on this legend. Another seven years have passed; the poor Hollander is more weary than ever of his endless wandering; he lands, becomes intimate with a Scottish nobleman, to whom he sells diamonds for a mere song, and when he hears that his customer has a beautiful daughter, he asks that he may wed her. This bargain also is agreed to. Next we see the Scottish home; the maiden with anxious heart awaits the bridegroom. She often looks with strange sorrow at a great, time-worn picture which hangs in the hall, and represents a handsome man in the Netherlandish-Spanish garb. It is an old heirloom, and according to a legend of her grandmother, is a true portrait of the Flying Dutchman as he was seen in Scotland a hundred years before, in the time of William of Orange. And with this has come down a warning that the women of the family must beware of the original. This has naturally enough had the result of deeply impressing the features of the picture on the heart of the romantic girl. Therefore, when the man himself makes his appearance, she is startled, but not with fear. He too is moved at beholding the portrait. But when he is informed whose likeness it is, he with tact and easy conversation turns aside all suspicion, jests at the legend, laughs at the Flying Dutchman, the Wandering Jew of the Ocean, and yet, as if moved by the thought, passed into a pathetic mood, depicting how terrible the life must be of one condemned to endure unheard-of tortures on a wild waste of waters – how his body itself is his living coffin, wherein his soul is terribly imprisoned – how life and death alike reject him, like an empty cask scornfully thrown by the sea on the shore, and as contemptuously repulsed again into the sea – how his agony is as deep as the sea on which he sails – his ship without anchor, and his heart without hope.

I believe that these were nearly the words with which the bridegroom ends. The bride regards him with deep earnestness, casting glances meanwhile at his portrait. It seems as if she had penetrated his secret; and when he afterwards asks, 'Katherine, wilt thou be true to me?' she answers, 'True to death.'

I remember that just then I heard a laugh, and that it came not from the pit but from the gallery of the gods above. As I glanced up I saw a wondrous lovely Eve in Paradise, who looked seductively at me, with great blue eyes. Her arm hung over the gallery, and in her hand she held an apple, or rather an orange. But instead of symbolically dividing it with me, she only metaphorically cast the peel on my head. Was it done intentionally or by accident? That I would know! But when I entered the Paradise to cultivate the acquaintance, I was not a little startled to find a white soft creature, a wonderfully womanly tender being, not languishing, yet delicately clear as crystal, a form of home-like propriety and fascinating amiability. Only that there was something on the left upper lip which curved or twined like the tail of a slipper gliding lizard. It was a mysterious trait, something such as is not found in pure angels, and just as little in mere devils. This expression comes not from evil, but from the *knowledge* of good and evil – it is a smile which has been poisoned or flavoured by tasting the Apple of Eden. When I see this expression on soft, full, rosy, ladies' lips, then I feel in my own a cramp-like twitching – a convulsive yearning – to kiss those lips: it is our Affinity.

I whispered into the ear of the beauty:

'Young lady, I will kiss thy mouth.'

'*Bei Gott, Mynheer!* that is a good idea,' was the hasty answer, which rang with bewitching sound from her heart.

But – no. I will here draw a veil over, and end the story or picture of which the Flying Dutchman was the frame. Thereby will I revenge myself on the prurient prudes who devour such narratives with delight, and are enraptured with them to their heart of hearts, *et plus ultra*, and then abuse the narrator, and turn up their noses at him in society, and decry him as immoral. It is a nice story, too, delicious as preserved pine-apple or fresh caviare or truffles in Burgundy, and would be pleasant reading after prayers; but out of spite, and to punish old offences, I will suppress it. Here I make a long dash ———————— Which may be supposed to be a black sofa on which we sat as I wooed. But the innocent must suffer with the guilty, and I dare say that many a good soul looks bitterly and reproachfully at me. However, unto these of the better kind I will admit that I was never so wildly kissed as by this Dutch blonde, and that she most triumphantly destroyed the prejudice which I had hitherto held against blue eyes and fair hair. *Now* I understand why an English poet has compared such women to frozen champagne. In the icy crust lies hidden the strongest extract. There is nothing more piquant than the contrast between external cold and the inner fire which, Bacchante-like, flames up and irresistibly intoxicates the happy carouser. Ay, far more than in brunettes does the fire of passion burn in many a sham-calm holy image with golden-glory hair, and blue angel's eyes, and pious lily hands. I knew a blonde of one of the best families in Holland who at times left her beautiful chateau on the Zuyder-Zee and went incognito to Amsterdam, and there in the theatre threw orange-peel on the head of any one who pleased her, and gave herself up to the wildest debauchery, like a Dutch Messalina! . . .

When I re-entered the theatre, I came in time to see the last scene of the play, where the wife of the Flying Dutchman on a high cliff wrings her hands in despair, while her unhappy husband is seen on the deck of his unearthly ship, tossing on the waves. He loves her, and will leave her lest she be lost with him, and he tells her all his dreadful destiny, and the cruel curse which hangs above his head. But she cries aloud, 'I was ever true to thee, and I know how to be ever true unto death!'

Saying this she throws herself into the waves, and then the enchantment is ended. The Flying Dutchman is saved, and we see the ghostly ship slowly sink into the abyss of the sea.

The moral of the play is that women should never marry a Flying Dutchman, while we men may learn from it that one can through women go down and perish – under favourable circumstances!

THE STORY OF THE HAUNTED SHIP

Wilhelm Hauff

My father kept a small shop at Balsora. He was neither poor nor rich, and one of those people who are afraid of venturing anything lest they should lose the little they possess. He brought me up plainly and virtuously, and soon I was enabled to assist him in his trade. Scarcely had I reached my eighteenth year, and hardly had he made his first large speculation, when he died, probably from grief at having confided a thousand pieces of gold to the sea.

I could not help thinking him lucky afterwards on account of his death, for a few weeks later the news arrived that the ship to which my father had entrusted his goods had sunk. This mishap, however, did not curb my youthful courage. I converted everything that my father had left into money, and set forth to try my fortune abroad, accompanied only by my father's old servant, who from long attachment would not separate himself from me and my fate.

We took ship at Balsora and left the haven with a favourable wind. The ship in which we embarked was bound for India.

When we had sailed some fifteen days over the ordinary track, the Captain predicted a storm. He looked very serious, for it appeared that he was not sufficiently acquainted with the course in these parts to await a storm with composure. He had all sail furled, and we drifted along quite gently. The night had fallen. It was cold and clear, and the Captain began to think he had been deceived by false indications of the storm. All at once a ship which we had not observed before drove past at a little distance from our own. Wild shouts and cheers resounded from her deck; at which, in such an anxious hour before a tempest, I wondered not a little. The Captain, who stood by my side, turned as pale as death. 'My ship is doomed!' he cried; 'yonder sails death.' Before I could question him as to the meaning of this strange exclamation, the sailors came running towards us, howling and crying. 'Have you seen it?' they cried. 'It is all over with us.'

But the Captain caused some consolatory verses to be read out of the Koran, and placed himself at the helm. All in vain! Visibly the storm increased in fury, and before an hour had passed the ship crashed and stuck fast. The boats were lowered, and scarcely had the last sailors saved themselves, when the ship sank before our eyes, and I was launched on the sea, a beggar. Further miseries yet awaited us. The storm raged more furiously, our boat became unmanageable. I had clasped my old servant tightly, and we vowed never to part from one another. At length day broke. But at the first dawn of morning a squall caught the boat in which we were seated and capsized it. I never saw my shipmates again. I was stunned by the shock; and when I awoke, I found myself in the arms of my old and faithful servant, who had saved himself on the overturned boat and dragged me after him. The tempest had subsided. Nothing more was seen of our ship. We discovered, however, not far from us another ship, towards which the waves were drifting us. As we drew near I recognized it as the same ship that had dashed past us on the preceding night, and which had terrified our Captain so much. I was inspired with a singular horror at the sight of this vessel. The expression of the Captain which had been so terribly fulfilled, the desolate aspect of the ship, on which, near as we were and loudly as we shouted, no one appeared, frightened me. However, this was our only means of safety, therefore we praised the Prophet who had so wonderfully preserved us.

Over the ship's bow hung a long cable. We paddled with hands and feet towards it in order to grasp it. At length we succeeded. Loudly I raised my voice, but all was silent on board. We then climbed up by the rope, I as the youngest going first. Oh, horror! What a spectacle met my gaze as I stepped upon the deck! The planks were reddened with blood; twenty or thirty corpses in Turkish dresses lay on the deck. Close to the mainmast stood a man, richly attired, a sabre in his hand, but with features pale and distorted; a great nail driven through his forehead pinning him to the mainmast. He also was dead.

Terror shackled my steps. I scarcely ventured to breathe. At last my companion had also come up. He too was struck at the sight of the deck, on which nothing living was to be seen, only so many frightful corpses. After a time we ventured, after having invoked the aid of the Prophet in anguish of heart, to go forward. At each step we glanced around expecting to discover something new and yet more terrible. But all was the same. Far and wide nothing was living but ourselves and the ocean. We dared hot even speak aloud, lest the dead Captain spitted to the mast should turn his ghastly eyes upon us, or one of the corpses move its head. At last we reached a hatchway which led to the ship's hold. There we both stopped, involuntarily, and looked at each other, for neither dared to speak his thoughts.

'O Master,' said my faithful servant, 'something awful has happened here! Yet, though the hold below be full of murderers, I would rather give myself up to their mercy than remain here any longer among these corpses.' I thought the same. We grew bold and, full of expectation, descended. But here likewise all was still as death, and only our steps sounded on the ladder. We stood at the door of the cabin. I placed my ear against it and listened. Nothing could be heard. I opened it, and the cabin presented a disorderly appearance. Dresses, weapons; and other things lay in confusion. Everything was out of its place. The crew, or at least the Captain, must have been carousing not long since, for all was still lying about.

We went from place to place and from cabin to cabin, and everywhere found splendid stores of silk, pearls, sugar, and the like. I was beside myself with joy at this sight, for since no one was on board, I thought I had a right to appropriate all to myself; but Ibrahim reminded me that we were doubtless far from land, which we could never reach without the help of man.

We refreshed ourselves with the meats and drinks, of which we found an ample supply, and finally ascended again to the deck. But here we shuddered at the sight of the ghastly corpses. We resolved upon freeing ourselves from them by throwing them overboard. But how awful was the dread which we felt when we found that not one could be moved from his position! So firmly fixed were they to the flooring, that we should have had to take up the planks of the decks in order to remove them, and for this purpose we had not tools. Neither could we loose the Captain from the mainmast, nor wrest his sabre from his rigid grasp.

We passed the day in sad contemplation of our position, and when night began to fall I allowed old Ibrahim to lie down to sleep, while I kept watch on deck spying for some means of deliverance. But when the moon had come out, and I reckoned by the stars that it was about eleven o'clock, such an irresistible sleep took possession of me that I involuntarily fell behind a cask that stood on the deck. However, this was more stupefaction than sleep, for I distinctly heard the sea beating against the side of the ship, and the sails creaking and whistling in the wind. All of a sudden I thought I heard voices and men's footsteps on the deck. I endeavoured to get up to see what it was, but an invisible power held my limbs fettered; I could not even open my eyes. The voices, however, grew more distinct, and it appeared to me as if a merry crew was rushing about on the deck. Now and then I thought I heard the sonorous voice of a commander, and also distinctly the hoisting and lowering of cordage and sails. But by degrees my senses left me, I sank into a deeper sleep, in which I only thought I could hear a clatter of arms, and only awoke when the sun was far above the horizon and scorching my face.

I stared about in astonishment. Storm, ship, the dead, and what I had heard during the night, appeared to me like a dream, but when I glanced around I found everything as on the previous day. Immovable lay the dead, immovable stood the Captain spitted to the mast. I laughed over my dream, and rose up to seek the old man.

He was seated, absorbed in reflection in the cabin. 'Oh, Master,' he exclaimed, as I entered. 'I would rather lie at the bottom of the sea than pass another night in this bewitched ship.' I inquired the cause of his trouble, and he thus answered me: 'After I had slept some hours, I awoke and heard people running about above my head. I thought at first it was you, but there were at least twenty, rushing to and fro, aloft, and I also heard calling and shouting. At last heavy steps came down the cabin. Upon this I became insensible, and only now and then my consciousness returned for a few moments, and then I saw the same man who is nailed to the mast overhead, sitting there at that table, singing and drinking, while the man in the scarlet dress, who is close to him on the floor, sat beside him and drank with him.' Such was my old servant's narrative.

Believe me, my friends, I did not feel at all at ease, for it was no illusion. I had also heard the dead men quite plainly. To sail in such company was gruesome to me. My Ibrahim, however, relapsed into profound meditation. 'I have just hit it!' he exclaimed at last. He recalled a little formula, which his grandfather, a man of experience and a great traveller, had taught him, which was a charm against ghosts and sorcery. He likewise affirmed that we might ward off the unnatural sleep during the coming night, by diligently saying verses from the Koran.

The proposal of the old man pleased me. In anxious expectation we saw the night approach. Adjoining the cabin was a narrow berth, into which we resolved to retire. We bored several holes through the door, large enough to overlook the whole cabin; we then locked the door as well as we could inside, and Ibrahim wrote the name of the Prophet in all four corners. Thus we awaited the terrors of the night. It might be about eleven o'clock when I began to feel very drowsy. My companion therefore advised me to say some verses from the Koran, which indeed helped me. All at once everything grew animated above, the cordage creaked, feet paced the deck, and several voices became clearly heard. We had thus sat for some time in intense expectation, when we heard something descending the steps of the cabin stairs. The old man on hearing this commenced to recite the formula which his grandfather had taught him against ghosts and sorcery:

If you are spirits from the air,
Or come from depths of sea,
Have in dark sepulchres your lair,
Or if from fire you be.
Allah is your God and Lord,
All spirits must obey His word.

I must confess I did not quite believe in this charm, and my hair stood on end as the door opened. In stepped that tall majestic man whom I had seen nailed to the mainmast. The nail still passed through his skull, but his sword was sheathed. Behind him followed another person less richly dressed; him also I had seen stretched on deck. The Captain, for there was no doubt it was he, had a pale face, a large black beard and fiery eyes, with which he looked around the whole cabin. I could see him quite distinctly as he passed our door; but he did not seem to notice the door at all, which hid us. Both seated themselves at the table which stood in the middle of the cabin, speaking loudly and almost shouting to one another in an unknown tongue. They grew more and more hot and excited, until at last the Captain brought his fist down upon the table, so that the cabin shook. The other jumped up with a wild laugh and beckoned the Captain to follow him. The latter rose, tore his sabre out of its sheath, and both left the cabin.

After they had gone we breathed more freely, but our alarm was not to terminate yet. Louder and louder grew the noise on deck. We heard rushing backwards and forwards, shouting, laughing and howling. At last a most fiendish noise was heard, so we thought the deck together with all its sails was coming down on us, clashing of arms and shrieks – and suddenly a dead silence followed. When, after many hours, we ventured to ascend, we found everything as before; not one had shifted his place; all lay as stiff as wood.

Thus we passed many days on board this ship, and constantly steered on an eastern course, where according to my calculation land should be found; but although we seemed to cover many miles by day, yet at night it seemed to go back, for we were always in the same place at the rising of the sun. We could not understand this, except that the dead crew each night navigated the ship in a directly opposite course with full sails. In order to prevent this, we furled all the sails before night fell, and employed the same means as we had used on the cabin door. We wrote the name of the prophet, and the formula prescribed by Ibrahim's grandfather upon a scroll of parchment, and wound it round the furled sails. Anxiously we awaited the result in our berths. The noise now seemed to increase more violently than ever; but behold, on the following morning, the sails were still furled, as we had left them. By day we only hoisted as many sails as were needed to carry the ship gently along, and thus in five days we covered a considerable tract.

At last on the sixth morning we discovered land at a short distance, and thanked Allah and his Prophet for our miraculous deliverance. This day and on the following night we sailed along a coast, and on the seventh morning we thought at a short distance we saw a town. With much difficulty we dropped our anchor, which at once struck ground, lowered a little boat, which was on deck, and rowed with all our strength towards the town. After the lapse of half-an-hour we entered a river which ran into the sea, and landed. On entering the gate of the town we asked the name of it, and learnt that it was an Indian town, not far from where I had intended to land at first. We went towards a caravanserai and refreshed ourselves after our adventurous journey. I also inquired there after some wise and intelligent man, intimating to the landlord that I wished to consult one on matters relating to sorcery. He led me to some remote street to a mean-looking house and knocked. I was allowed to enter, and simply told to ask for Muley.

In the house I met a little old man, with a grey beard and a long nose, who asked me what I wanted. I told him I desired to see the wise Muley, and he answered me that he was Muley. I now asked his advice what I should do with the corpses, and how I was to set about to remove them from the ship. He answered me that very likely the ship's crew were spell-bound on the ocean on account of some crime; and he believed the charm might be broken by bringing them on land, which, however, could only be done by taking up the planks on which they lay. The ship, together with all its goods, by divine and human law belonged to me, because I had, as it were, found it. I was, however, to keep all very secret, and make him a little present of my abundance in return for which he and his slaves would assist me in removing the dead. I promised to reward him richly, and we set forth followed by five slaves provided with saws and hatchets. On the road the magician Muley could not sufficiently laud the happy thought of tacking the Koran verses upon the sails. He said that this had been the only means of our deliverance.

It was yet early morning when we reached our vessel. We all set to work immediately, and in an hour four lay already in the boat. Some of the slaves had to row them to land to bury them there. They related on their return that the corpses had saved them the trouble of burial, for hardly had they been put on the ground when they crumbled into dust. We continued sawing off the corpses, and before evening all had been removed to land except one, namely he who was nailed to the mast. In vain we endeavoured to draw the nail out of the wood. Every effort could not displace it a hair's-breadth. I did not know what to do, for it was impossible to cut down the mast to bring him to land. Muley, however, devised an expedient. He ordered a slave quickly to row to land, in order to bring him a pot filled with earth. When it was brought, the magician pronounced some mystic words over it, and emptied the earth upon the head of the corpse. Immediately he opened his eyes, heaved a deep sigh, and the wound of the nail in his forehead began to bleed. We now extracted the nail easily, and the wounded man fell into the arms of one of the slaves.

'Who has brought me hither?' he said, after having slightly recovered. Muley pointed to me, and I approached him. 'Thanks be to thee, unknown stranger, for thou hast rescued me from a long martyrdom. For fifty years has my corpse been floating upon these waves, and my spirit was condemned to reanimate it each night; but now earth having touched my head, I can return to my fathers reconciled.' I begged him to tell us how he had fallen into this awful condition, and he answered: 'Fifty years ago I was a man of power and rank, and lived in Algiers. The longing after gain induced me to fit out a vessel in order to engage in piracy. I had already carried on this business for some time, when one day I took on board at Zante a Dervish, who asked for a free passage. My companions and myself were wild fellows, and paid no respect to the sanctity of the man, but rather mocked him. But one day, when he had reproached me in his holy zeal with my sinful mode of living, I became furious at night, after having drunk a great deal with my steersman in my cabin. Enraged at what a Dervish had told me, and what I would not even allow a Sultan to tell me, I rushed upon deck, and plunged my dagger in his breast. As he died, he cursed me and my crew, that we might neither live nor die till our heads should touch the earth. The Dervish died, and we threw him into the sea, laughing at his menaces; but in the very same night his words were fulfilled.

'Some of my crew mutinied against me. We fought with insane fury until my adherents were defeated, and I was nailed to the mainmast. But the mutineers also expired of their wounds, and my ship soon became but an immense tomb. My eyes also grew dim, my breathing ceased, I thought I was dying. But it was only a kind of numbness that seized me. The very next night, and at the precise hour that we had thrown the Dervish into the sea, I and all my companions awoke, we were alive, but we could only do and say what we had said and done on that night. Thus we have been sailing these fifty years unable to live or die: for how could we reach land? It was with a savage joy that we sailed many times with full sail in the storm, hoping that at length we might strike some rock, and rest our wearied heads at the bottom of the sea. We did not succeed. But now I shall die. Thanks once more, to my unknown deliverer, and if treasures can reward thee, accept my ship as a mark of my gratitude.'

After having said this, the Captain's head fell upon his breast, and he expired. Immediately his body also, like the crew's, crumbled to dust. We collected it in a little urn and buried him on shore. I engaged, however, workmen from the town, who repaired my ship thoroughly. After having bartered the goods which I had on board for others at a great profit, I collected a crew, rewarded my friend Muley handsomely, and set sail towards my native place. I made, however, a detour, and landed on many islands and countries where I sold my goods. The Prophet blessed my enterprise. After a lapse of nine months, twice as wealthy as the dying Captain had made me, I reached Balsora. My fellow citizens were astonished at my riches and my fortune, and did not believe anything else but that I must have found the diamond valley of the celebrated traveller Sinbad. I left their belief undisturbed, but henceforth the young people of Balsora, when they were scarcely eighteen years old, were obliged to go out into the world in order like myself to seek their fortune. But I lived quietly and peacefully, and every five years undertook a journey to Mecca, in order to thank the Lord for His blessing at this sacred shrine, and pray for the Captain and his crew that He might receive them into His Paradise.

AN ENCOUNTER WITH A GHOST

W. Clark Russell

It is a great many years now since the Phantom Ship was last sighted; so long indeed that one might fairly suppose Vanderdecken had got to windward at last, doubled the Cape, and settled down somewhere in his native land to enjoy a well-earned repose after his centuries of conflict with the Pacific gales. It turns out, however, that the poor old skipper is still afloat. His vessel has not only been sighted, but boarded – a quite unprecedented incident in the history of this marine apparition. The countenance of Vanderdecken has been surveyed by human eyes, and, what is of some importance, the vexed question of the rig of his craft has been set at rest once and for good. She is not a ship, it seems, but a brig with stump topgallantmasts and single topsail yards. The yarn of one of the crew of the barque who sighted the *Flying Dutchman* and boarded her is curious, rather graphic, and full of singular particulars. Perhaps were an engraving of the mariner who related the story to accompany this account the interest would be heightened –

for so queer a looking sailor I never before set eyes on. He is what the young ladies of Limehouse and Poplar would call a 'shell-back,' his shoulders being as round as the shell of a turtle; his hair hangs over his forehead and down the back of his neck in masses of minute ringlets; he broke the bridge of his nose when a youth by falling down the main hold of a ship, and that feature submits but little more to the eye than a pair of nostrils; his small eyes are lodged very deep, and twinkle in their caverns like glowworms, and under his chin stands a lump of coarse black hair. He masticated a large junk of tobacco as he gave me his story, which may have added a deeper note to his hoarse and wheezing voice. He began thus:

'The *Sally G.*'s an American barque; Captain Prodgers was the master, Mr Anderson chief mate, and there were sixteen hands. We was bound from Palermo to New London with a cargo of fruit, and on the 11th of April last we reckoned ourselves to be somewhere near about 1500 miles to the east'ards of Montauk Point. We was rather a mixed company. I'm an Englishman myself, and there was Tom, a Gravesend man. Us two made all the Englishmen aboard. But there was three Scotchmen and six Irishmen; so Britannia mustered middling strong. There was likewise a Swede, and chaps we call 'Dagos', Mediterranean scowbanks, the right word is, who'll pass for Portuguese, or Spaniards, or Hi-talians, just as they're wanted.

'The 11th of April was a werry fine morning: a light breeze from the south'ard and east'ard, sea calm, and sky blue. I was in the port watch, and came on deck at eight o'clock. The barque was under all plain sail; and soon after we had turned out, Mr Anderson, the chief mate, sings out to some of us to jump aloft and get the stun'sail booms rigged out. I lay aloft, and got on to the foretopsail yard; but, as I was stepping from the rigging on to foot-ropes, I caught sight of a bit of white shining upon the horizon about two points on the starboard bow. I turned my head and bawled down "Sail ho!" and pointed, and the mate crossed the deck to look; but he had to wait a bit to see her; for it required half-an-hour more of sailing to heave the stranger up wisible from the deck. You may reckon no one took much notice of the wessel ahead while she remained small. Having set the stun'sails, we went on quiedy with our different jobs, and the mate walked up and down the weather side o' the deck, sometimes squinting aloft, sometimes taking a look at the compass, and now and again casting his eyes upon the stranger. But the *Sally G.*'s a quick boat in smooth water; the stun'sails were helping her along, and we came up with the old sawed-off square wagon ahead as though she had been a lighthouse. I thought she'd h'ist her ensign as we came along, but she never showed no colours.

'When we was close enough to see her plain we all stood lookin' and wonderin'. I don't know as ever I saw a queerer-looking wessel. Her stern was up and down in the water; she'd a great sheer aft that made her look sagged: her sides were as rusty as an old kettle; her rigging was grey; she had short topgallant masts, and a man named Maloney told me the canvas was so thin that he could see the sky looking blue through it. This might ha'been, but I took no notice o' that myself, I saw the mate working away at the brig's stern with a spyglass, and then he turns to the captain, who had come on deck, and says, "Captain," says he, "I can't see no name." "Here, give me hold," says the captain, and he took the glass and looked himself, and then says, "No; there's no name. But I'll tell 'ee what, Mr Anderson, there's *bin* a name there, but the water's washed the letterin' away." "Well," says the mate, "I reckon she must be a diving job. They've fished her up out o' deep water, and ye may take her to be a showman's speculation, sir." The cook was standing near the pumps looking at her, and he says to me who was anigh him, "Bill," he says, "d'ye notice her deck-house is green?" "Yes," says I, "I see that, cook," I says. "That means, Bill," says he in a slow way, and looking strange, "that she's a Dutchman." "She ought to be," says I. "I don't know that we ought to be glad that we met her, Bill," says the cook. "I'd as lief be shipmates with a Fin as keep that wessel company." "Why,

what ails ye, cook?" says I. "What's the matter with the brig?"
"Look at her," says he, shaking his head and speaking hollow
like. I thought he wasn't worth while paying attention to.
The cook, sir, was a man as believed in ghosts, and was a
werry ignorant person. He couldn't read nor write, but he
was extraordinary positive. He'd quote things wrong, and
'ud refuse to be corrected, saying he knew better, and that
books was full o' lies. Yet he was a good cook, and there was
more conscience in the duff he biled for the men than I can
recollect meeting with in any sea-mess. Well, I let him shake
his head, and stood watchin' the brig.

'As we came up with her she backed her main yards and
lowered a boat. This was a pretty strong hint to us to stop;
so we boom-ended our stun'sails, brought the barque to the
wind, and hove her to. Two men got into the boat, and a
man squatted hisself in the stern sheets, and the boat headed
for us. It were difficult to guess what they could want, for the
vessel looked right enough aloft, nothin' wanting up there,
and if they was in distress it was queer they didn't signalize
us in the morning, when we hove in sight.

'All hands knocked off work to see the Dutchman, as the
cook called him, come aboard. The boat hooked on, and
the man in charge of her climbed over the side. He was a
shortish man with a werry Dutch face on him, and there
was no getting at his age by staring. His skin had the greyish,

washed-out look o' the brig's rigging. He'd got on a bell-shaped fur cap with a peak to it, that lay flat on his forehead, sea-boots, a round jacket, big breeches which he filled out handsomely, and the stem of a long Dutch pipe sticking out of his coat pocket werry strangely ornamented. I noticed a sort o' eagerness in the way some of our men – 'specially the Swede and two o' the Scotchmen – stared at him as if he wan't a wholesome sight. The cook never took his eyes off him for an instant.

'Arter gazing slowly round at us, he singled out the captain with ne're a man to tell him who was skipper, and going up to Captain Prodgers, he makes a long speech. While he talked, the captain and Mr Anderson twisted their heads about like hens trying to look aloft, first bringing one ear to bear and then another, but they couldn't understand him no more than if he had spoke Chinaman's lingo. He spoke to'em for ten minutes, never stoppin', goin' along slow and regular, without e'er a movement in his face, and his arms hanging up and down alongside of him without a stir. I see him now, and I likewise see the skipper and Mr Anderson a listenin' and lookin' just as they'd appear if they was trying to see into the bottom of a well. At last he stopped, and then nobody spoke, and all hands looked at each other, savin' the cook, who wouldn't take his eyes away from the Dutchman. Suddenly the skipper sings out, "Call the watch below on deck." I ran forward and bawled down the scuttle for the men to rouse up smartly, and presently all the crew were on deck looking at the Dutchman.

' "Look ye, men," says Captain Prodgers, "among you all there's enough of you, to make out seven languages; Irish, Scotch, English, Swedish Portugee, Spanish, and Hi-talian. Let all hands turn to and listen their hardest whilst I make this man say his speech over again. Now, then, fix your hattentions, bullies." And with that he signs to the Dutchman to begin again. He didn't seem to know what was wanted at first, but after the skipper and Mr Anderson had motioned and flourished to him like a pair of windmills for about five minutes, he gravely nods his head and goes through his speech, all hands listening hard, bobbing their noses together as they leans forward, and all o' them werry anxious to make out the man's meaning. In ten minutes he made an end; and then Captain Prodgers, looking at us, says, "Well?" Nobody answered. "Is it Irish?" says he. "No, it isn't Irish, sor," says Micky O'Connor. "Is it English or Scotch?" says he. "No, sir," says I. "Is it, Swedish?" says Captain Prodgers. The Swede says; "Not it," and the scowbanks said it wasn't Portuguese, nor Hi-talian, nor any lingo that's spoke down in their part o' Europe. "Then, what the deuce can it be?" says Captain Prodgers. "A languidge," answers the cook, in a faint voice, "as is buried and forgot."

'Well, sir, this being the sitiwation, what was to be done? Some skippers, I daresay, would ha'waved the Dutchman into his boat, filled the main topsail, and stood on. But Captain Prodgers is a humane man. "Look here, Mr Anderson," says he, "it's pretty clear that whatever may be the matter with that there brig, this Dutch sailor man, if so be he *is* a Dutchman, can't tell us what's wrong. So," says he, "get that starboard quarter boat manned and go aboard the brig yourself, and see if you can make out what's amiss."

'No sooner said than done. The boat was lowered, and me and two o' the scowbanks and one o' the Scotchmen, makin' four men, tumbled into her, and we rowed Mr Anderson on board the brig. I took notice of Mr Anderson looking and looking werry hard at the wessel as we went along, as a man might who didn't much fancy the job he was put upon. We had our backs to the brig, but when we threw in our oars and got alongside, I'm blessed if the sight o' that old hull and the queer appearance o' the rigging didn't give me a kind o' crawling sensation. It might ha' been what the cook had said, or it might ha' been the faded paint and the brig's sides, that looked like a man's face arter he's cured o' the smallpox, or like a bit of French cheese I once saw, that might ha' passed for a muffin. But whatever it was, I didn't like the feeling, and rather wished I had let Sammy Saunders shove in front of me and get my place when we all run to man the boat.

However, there I was, and bein' there I thought I might as well see all that was going to happen, so I followed the mate aboard, he taking no notice. Indeed, I reckon he wished me to come, not liking to be the only one o' us 'twixt the rails of that strange old brig.

'I took a look forward and saw four men standing together, and leaning against the side o' the galley, where the sun shone. I didn't like their appearance at all. They hung there like coves fairly wore out. They all seemed middlin' old, but for that matter their faces was just as puzzling as the Dutchman's who had boarded us; ye might ha' called them old or young as you please, and both 'ud ha' been right. They all stared at us as we got over the side, but barring this twisting of their eyes round they was quite lifeless, and a melancholy row of men they seemed. There was a dim and grey-lookin' old man at the tiller, and him that was the skipper stood at the gangway to meet Mr Anderson. Did ye ever see a dried apple – a werry old 'un, sir? Well, that skipper's face were like that. It was all brownness and wrinkles, with a bit of a withered nose amidships, and under it a slit that stood for a mouth, and a pair of eyes that I calculate 'ud shine red in the dark. He'd a fur cap on, and an old coat that came down to the calves of his legs, and I never see skinnier fingers nor legs with such a sheer at the joints as though his body stood on a hoop. His boots was like a pair of shovels. He bobbed to

the mate and smiled away like clockwork and then droppin'
his arms down as t'other Dutchman had done, he up and
spoke a speech that must ha' lasted eight minutes by any
man's watch.

'When he began to talk the mate looked round and was
glad enough to see me standing close astern of him, I believe;
he fell back a step to draw nearer to me, and listened with
his head dropped. But the strange bosh, sir, were harder to
follow than t'other man's had been; this old man's pipes were
cracked, and he made a noise like a saw. The men forrards
never moved; there they stood sunning themselves, and the
dim old cove as steered looked at nothin' but the leech o' the
topgallant sail, though the wessel was hove-to, mind.

'As soon as the skipper had done, Mr Anderson he says
in a loud strong voice, "Mister," says he, "all that you've bin
saying is no doubt past contradicting of, but I'm bound to
tell 'ee I don't understand your lingo. Yonder barque's the
Sally G., Captain Prodgers, and I'm her mate. If ye'll tell
me what you want, we'll try to do it for you;" and here he
stopped and looked at the little man, who made no answer,
but kept on smilin' away as if somebody was tickling of him.
"What's the name o' this wessel?" says Mr Anderson in a
werry powerful woice. The skipper only smiled. The mate
looked forrards at the men, and sings out sternly, "Anybody
understand me there?" Says he, "I say, what's the name o'

this wessel, and what d'ye want?" Ne'er a one took notice, and the skipper he kept on smiling. "Come you along with me," says Mr Anderson, after takin' a long look round, and speaking to me. "We'll overhaul his old sugar-box for ourselves, and see what's wrong."

'So away we went to the harness-cask, the old skipper arter us, smiling all the time, and we looks into it, and sees it full o' pieces of meat. The mate he smelt of these wittles, and says, "They're sweet enough. Nothin' wrong in here." Then we goes over to the scuttle-butts and drops the dipper in, and finds 'em full o' fresh water. "Well, they can't be in want o' water," says the mate. Then, stopping a minute, he pulls out a piece o' chalk and stoops down and writes down the latitood and longitood in big letters, and then gets up and points to the marks, looking at the skipper. But this wasn't it either, for the skipper, always smiling, shakes his head so quickly that I thought it would ha' dropped off. Then we sounded the well, but that was right enough; no water there to take notice of. "Come along with me," says the mate, and down we bundles into the cabin, the skipper behind us. A strange old place it was, with a smell of snuff about. It looked to me to be wisibly decayin'. It made me feel as a diver does when he finds hisself in the cabin of a wessel that's been under water for years and years. I wondered to see no barnacles. We opens a door or two until we comes to the pantry, looks in, and sees plenty o' grub knocking about the shelves. "Well, they ain't starvin'," says the mate. "An' there's no water comin' in," says I. "And they don't want our reckonin'," says the mate. "Perhaps they've got the cholera aboard," says I. "Let's go forrard and see," says the mate.

'We went up the companion steps, the skipper followin' of us like a shadder, and walks to the fore hatch, and drops into the forecastle. A rummier place even than the cabin: full of ancient bunks covered with a wild flourish o' carving, and scores o' cockroaches blackening the timbers, with three or four sea-chests and an odd boot or two, and the likes o' that. "If the cholera's aboard," says the mate, "it ain't in this fo'cs'le, for there's nobody here." With that we scrambles on deck again. The skipper lay in wait for us at the fore scuttle, and when he sees us he falls a-smiling. "Capt'en," says Mr Anderson, "we've overhauled your wessel fore and aft, and can't find anything wrong. There's plenty o' meat and water aboard, the wessel's tight, ye don't want our reckonings, and there ain't no disease perceptible. That bein' so, I don't see what good we can do by stopping."

'The skipper looked at him narrowly and smilingly as he said this, and when he were done, he began another speech; but this Mr Anderson cut short by saying that there was nothing to thank him for, and that what we had done wasn't worth mentioning, and then calling to me, we drops into our boat and returns to the *Sally G*. None of us spoke as we rowed back, no man feelin' comfortable. On reaching the barque, I went forrard, followed by all hands, who wanted to know what we had seen; but their questions was stopped by the order being given to swing the main yards and get the stunsails on her agin.

'No sooner was this done than the cook tailed on to me and wouldn't let me go. "What did ye see?" says he. "A brig," says I. "And what else," says he. "Four strange men standing in the sun," says I, "and a dim old man at the tiller, and a skipper like a marmozeet," says I. "And what was his langwidge," says the cook. "Unbeknown," says I. "Bill," says he, in a low woice, which made the others, who stood listening, lean forrards to hear, "Bill," says he, "I'm sorry for you," says he, "I don't want to alarm you, Bill, but you've been aboard the *Flying Dutchman*," says he, "and take notice of what I'm going to say," says the cook; "and if I'm wrong I'll give any man leave to bile me in my own coppers. There'll be a gale o' wind," he says, "within the next twenty-four hours."

'D'ye see this hand, sir,' said the mariner who favoured me with this narrative, laying his large paw upon his knee, with the tar-stained palm uppermost. 'Well, as true as that there hand of mine is a-lying on my leg at this minute, did a wiolent gale o' wind bust down upon us heigh teen hours arter we parted company with that Dutch brig. It blew from the west'ards, and drove us one hundred mile out o' our course. So there ye have it, sir. That's the naked truth. I don't ask you to mind what the cook said. You may forget him. Here's a fact to speak for itself. Heigh teen hours arter we left that brig, a hurricane bust down upon us. If that ain't conclusive there's nothin' more to say'.'

THE TRUE FATE OF THE FLYING DUTCHMAN

George Griffith

There is nothing original about the following story as far as I am concerned, and therefore I cannot of course be expected to vouch for the truth of it. I merely retail it to you as nearly as possible as I had it from the man who gave it to me, an ancient shellback very much on his beam ends, as the nautical saying goes, to whom I once had an opportunity of doing a good turn, as a set-off to which, like the ancient mariner in Gilbert's burlesque of Coleridge's masterpiece, 'he spun me this painful yarn'.

'As I was telling you, Sir,' taking a fresh nip of the grog wherewith I had loosened his tongue, 'until three or four year ago, when I got laid by for good, I'd been following the sea, man and boy, for something going on for sixty years, and, as you rightly guessed, I've seen one or two queer sorts of things in my time.

'It's the fashion nowadays for folk to turn up their eddicated noses at things that isn't plain for 'em to see in all their bearings with the naked eye a fathom in front of them, but for all that there's things as true as any that ye reads in the papers, and a bit truer, some of 'em, that happens away out there in the big wide sea that few folks ever 'ears of, and when they do 'ear of'em, as I say, they just turns their noses up at 'em in a superior sort of way and calls 'em lies.'

'Like the story of the *Flying Dutchman* for instance?' I said, drawing a sympathetic bow at a venture, and, as it happened, hitting the mark.

The old man's jaw dropped for a moment and the wrinkles round his still bright grey eyes contracted. Then he rapped gently on the table with the little blackened stump of a clay pipe that he was smoking, and said in a half-startled, half-dreamy sort of voice:

'You've hit it, Mister. I don't know how you've come to do it, but it's just about that that I'm going to spin you this yarn you asked for. It's no lie that story about Vanderdecken and the old galliot that he boxed about the Cape in for pretty near three hundred years, because, mister, as true as I'm sitting here' – and again he rapped on the table with his pipe – 'I've seen him, and, what's more, I believe I'm the only man living, ashore or afloat, that saw the last of him and his old broad-bottomed hooker, or what was left of him.'

To have expressed doubt at such a juncture would have been fatal, so I simply said:

'Then if that's so you must have as queer a yarn to spin as ever man told. Help yourself and reel it out.'

He accepted the invitation and got under weigh again.

'It's getting on for five-and-forty years now that I, a British-born boy hailing from Falmouth, had the bad luck to find myself cabin-boy and general knock-about on the *Prairie Flower*, a Yankee China tea-clipper, sailing out of Baltimore. I say "bad luck" because if ever a harmless, willing lad led a dog's life on board a floating workhouse that was me on the *Prairie Flower*.

'The Skipper, Dave Schuyler was his name, was a good seaman of the old driving sort, but as big a brute as ever thought himself the Lord Almighty because he had command of a smart ship. He was a half-Yankee, half-Dutchman, as you might guess from his name, and he was wicked enough to sink a ship twice the tonnage of the *Prairie Flower*.

'There was another boy on board beside me, a little fellow with a spirit of a lion and a body of a mouse, so to speak, and we hadn't been at sea a week before the skipper took a deadly hate against him because he answered him back once instead of cringing to him like a kicked dog as he expected everyone aboard the ship to do. After that he never lost a chance of hazing the poor lad – that's the sea term for 'sitting on him' you know, Sir – and at last one bitter cold night down in the Forties he found some fault with him and for a punishment

70

sent him up to the foretop-gallant yard and told him to stop there till he told him to come down.

'He never did come down, leastways not in the regular way, for when it got daylight there was no one on the yard and I was the only boy on board the ship. Of course the poor little chap had either been jerked off the yard by the rolling of the ship or else he'd got half-frozen and half-stupid with the cold and just dropped overboard. It was put down against his name in the log-book "Fallen overboard from aloft", and it was an accident for all anyone knew except the skipper and me and a young long-shoreman named Frank Peters, who had been sent by the owners as supercargo or ship's husband, as we used to call 'em in those days.

'The skipper didn't know that I knew anything about it; he didn't see that I wasn't below when he sent Slim Jim aloft to sit on the yard. If he had done I shouldn't have seen the end of the voyage, but Mr Peters heard him give the order and saw the kick that he helped him off the poop with, and the next morning when he was missing he up and told him that it was nothing less than manslaughter and he should report him at the first port the ship touched at. The skipper didn't say much, but he thought a lot, and what he thought wasn't very healthy for Mr Peters.

'We had a rough baddish lot in the fo'castle – just such a lot as yer might expect to sail with such a skipper – and as we had a lot of bad luck one way and another after the lad fell overboard, he hadn't much trouble in persuading them that the super-cargo was an out-and-out Jonah and was bringing all the bad time on to 'em. We hadn't got many days' runs behind us before poor Peters was hated fore and aft, and there were a good many of the chaps for'ard and who'd have helped him overboard for an extra tot of grog.

'We went hammering away down the Forties and at last got round the Cape, and one bright windy moonlight night the lookout sung out:

' "A sail on the starboard bow – and a queer one she looks too."

'Queer she did look, I can tell you, lying right in the track of the moon's light over the water, rising and falling to the waves with a slow heavy motion that showed she was a dull sailor, whatever else she was. You've seen those square-bowed square-sterned slab-sided Dutchmen that used to sail out of Rotterdam and Amsterdam a few years ago?

'Well, build up a great high sort of castle on the stern with galleries running out aft at the sides and big square lanterns like they have now in the streets stuck up at the corners, cut the bow down low, run the bowsprit up about as steep again as we have them now, and put a square sail underneath it on the martingale and rig the masts and yards in the most antediluvian style you can think of – and that's the sort of craft that we saw lying between us and the moonlight that night.

'There was a flag hanging half-mast high from his foremast and his sails were flapping about just as though there wasn't a catspaw of wind, and yet we were beating up under short sail against a ten-knot breeze from the nor'east. The skipper got his glass on him in a minute, and when he took it down from his eye he said with words that I won't repeat to you, Sir:

' "If that's not old Vanderdecken himself may I be drowned with my head in a slush bucket. Haul round the fore-yard there, and let her fall off a bit. We'll see if the old Dutchman has anything to say. P'raps he can tell us what to do with this ————— Jonah that we've got aboard."

'It wasn't a job that any man aboard the ship liked, but Dave Schuyler was in a mood that it wouldn't do to fool with. When the yards were round he called the boat's crew aft, ordered the steward to serve out a double tot of rum, and then told them to lower away the quarter-boat, as he wanted to take Jonah to pay a visit to Vanderdecken.

' "We'll send bad luck to bad luck, boys," he said, "and then p'raps we'll be rid of it. What do you say? He might be able to show old Vanderdecken the way into Table Bay."

'It was a horrible cruel ghastly sort of notion, but as soon as they'd got the grog into them the men jumped at it and went to clear away the boat, swearing that Jonah had better sink the Dutchman than them. The skipper had a word or two with the mate, nearly as big a brute and bully as himself, and by the time the boat was clear poor Peters was brought up on deck out of his bunk, and Schuyler showed him the queer craft that was bobbing about under half a mile from us and said in a mocking politeful sort of voice:

' "There, Mr Peters, Sir, allow me to introduce you to an old pal and countryman of mine, Philip Vanderdecken, better known as the Flying Dutchman. You've brought us a blamed sight of bad luck since you've been on board the *Prairie Flower*, and as I think we shall get to China better without you than with you I am going to take you aboard in the boat and ask Vanderdecken to give you a passage home."

'The poor chap looked at the strange uncanny craft abeam and then at the skipper in a mute beseeching sort of way. Then he lost his nerve, as any other man might have done in the same fix, and fell on his knees and started out to beg for mercy, but Schuyler wasn't that sort.

'He sung out to a couple of the chaps at the davits and they picked up poor Peters, whipped a line round his hands and feet and bundled him into the boat without any more fuss. Then he sent me down into the supercargo's cabin to fetch up some of his clothes, saying with a laugh that he might find it cold and want them before he got home. I went down and fetched up all I could lay my hands on.

'Now I ought to have said that this Peters was a Roman Catholic, and on his table I found a little silver crucifix with a silver chain to it. Something told me to take this up too, I thought it might sort of comfort him. When I got on deck the boat was in the water and the skipper pretty nearly frightened the life out of me by telling me to shin down the tackles and take the gentleman his clo'es, as he said.

'I had to go, though I think I'd sooner have jumped overboard than get into a boat going to that ghostly-looking ship; but when I got down and showed poor Peters his crucifix, his face lit up so that I was almost glad I'd come. He asked me to hang it round his neck, and I did.

'As we approached, the most awful-looking faces mortal eyes ever looked at showed themselves over the bulwarks staring down at us, but there was never a word or a sound out of any of 'em. On the big high stern there was a tall figure with long white hair and a long ragged white beard, and he was dressed just like the sailors you see in some of the old pictures at Grinnidge Hospital.

'When we ran alongside under her high quarter the faces of the boat's crew were almost as white as the ghostly things that were looking at us over the side, but the skipper didn't seem to have a bit of fear about him. He stood up in the stern sheets and hailed in Dutch, and there came back something that sounded like the same language, only far away as though the voice had dropped from the clouds.

'The tall figure came down from the quarter-deck and then a crazy old rope ladder all covered with dried green slime, like the ship's sides were, tumbled out of the gangway port. All he could do the skipper couldn't persuade one of the men to go up that ladder. They told him straight they'd see him further first, only in a lot stronger words than that, and so he cursed them for a lot of white-livered chicken-hearted swabs and swarmed up himself.

'We held our breath and heard him saying something to the old fellow with the white hair and beard that we knew by this time must be Vanderdecken himself. Then he came to the gangway and slung a rope over and told us to make it fast round the supercargo's shoulders. The men wanted to be away again, and they did it without any more telling, in spite of the poor fellow's shrieks and prayers for mercy. Then the skipper, and maybe some of them on board, toiled on the rope and hauled poor Peters, struggling and yelling like a madman, up over the side. They had scarcely got him on deck when Schuyler called to me and told me to bring his clothes up.

'I was so struck with fright that I couldn't move, and when the skipper saw this he swore that if I didn't come up sharp he'd haul me up after Peters and leave me with him. Then one of the chaps in the boat told me to hurry up and hoist myself aboard, or they'd sling me up, for they didn't want to stop there all night, and the end of it was that I slung the bundle of Peter's clothes round my neck and swarmed up, feeling every moment as I should drop into the water again.

'It's no use telling you what I saw on deck, because if I did you wouldn't believe me. If ever there was a ghost-ship with real timbers, and cordage, and sails, and a crew of ghosts, that was her. The skipper had untied Peters's legs and arms and was just telling him that he might like to walk about a bit and get acquainted with his new shipmates as I reached the deck. Then he slung his bag of clothes at him with a horrible oath, knocking the poor chap over like a nine-pin he was that weak with fright, and after he'd done it he did what I couldn't have believed even he'd do if I hadn't seen it – he held out his hand to Vanderdecken's ghost and said what I expect was good-bye in Dutch.

'Vanderdecken took it, and said something in his queer, far-away voice that made Schuyler drop his hand as if it had been red-hot instead of ice-cold as I expect it was, and he was almost as white as Vanderdecken himself when he stumbled to the gangway and scrambled down the ladder as hard as he could go. I needn't tell you I followed him as sharp as I could, Peters cursing Schuyler from the bulwarks.

'As we were pulling away from the side those queer ghostly faces came and looked over at us, and among them was poor Peters's, and it was as white and ghostly as any of 'em, but they were quiet and he wasn't. He shook his fists above his head and screamed out words that were a lot awfuller than swearing from the way he said 'em, and the last words we heard were:

' "We'll meet again yet, David Schuyler, and when we do I'll take you with me to the judgment of God. Remember that."

'And then there came a long scream like the whistle of the wind through cordage in a living gale, and we all shut our eyes and the chaps at the oars pulled as if old Vanderdecken himself was coming after 'em to fetch 'em back.

'By the time we got to the ship again and had her under weigh the Dutchman had got all his sails drawing and was bumping away over the short seas to the nor'ard and west'ard heading straight for Table Bay. The *Prairie Flower* never got to China, but that's not in the story so I can make it short. We ran ashore on one of the islands in the Malacca Straights one dark night when it was blowing fit to blow the beard off a Turk. Not a soul of the crew were saved but the skipper and me.

'It was nearly fifteen years after we parted company that time that I saw Dave Schuyler again. It was on the wharf at Hoboken and he knew me at once, although I had grown from a boy to a man. He wasn't much changed except he looked a good bit soberer and quieter. He came and spoke to me quite friendly like and we soon got into conversation, and he told me he'd got converted and found religion, or something of that sort, and had repented of his past life and was doing very well.

'Then he told me that he had a great scheme on hand, that there was millions in it if it could only be worked proper like, and he asked me to go to his house that night and he'd tell me all about it. I was out of a job just then, although I'd got my master's certificate, and to tell you the truth I was mortal hard up. I'd almost forgotten, not the *Flying Dutchman*, but what took us on board of him, for I'd seen so many other queer things done at sea since then that it didn't seem anything particular, so I said yes, and when I got to Schuyler's house that evening he spread out a chart of the middle Atlantic on his table, clapped his fore-finger down on it and said:

' "There, Tom lad, that's where we're going."

'I looked down and saw that he'd put his finger on the big patch in the centre of the North Atlantic that's called the Sargasso Sea.

' "I never knew there were any millions in seaweed before," I said looking up at him with a bit of a grin.

' "No," he said, "no more there aren't, and it isn't seaweed we're goin' for. You know enough not to need me to tell you that's a patch of still water made by the meeting of a lot of currents. No ship ever goes there, leastways if it can help it, but lot's go there as can't help it. Don't yer see that pretty near all the derelicts and missing ships in the North Atlantic that don't go down there must get taken there by the currents some time or other? Some of 'em have good cargoes that won't spoil by water. Most of 'em have money and valuables aboard and some of 'em have hundredweights of specie and bullion – and that's what we're going after."

' "That looks as if there might be money in it," I said after thinkin' a bit quietly and really it did seem very reasonable when you came to look at it. "How are you goin' to get there?" I said, looking at it all practical like.

' "Well, I've had this scheme in my head some years and now I've got a little three-hundred-ton steamer and we're going to drive her slap into the middle, seaweed or no seaweed, and if you like to be first officer of that steamer, well you can be and you shall have your share of the plunder if there is any and good wages as well."

' "I'm with you, Schuyler," says I. And so it was settled.

'I needn't tell you how long we were getting the *Gold*

Seeker – that was the name of our steamer – into the middle of those hundreds of miles of seaweed or what day-and-night labour we had to shove her through it, for it was about time I was hauling in the slack of this yarn, so I'll get on to the end.

'Never did mortal eyes look on such a collection of old weather-battered hulks and rusty iron floating coffins as we found jammed up together in that patch of sea and weed. We sighted 'em first at night and for all the world they looked in the gloom like a lot of ghost-ships that had started out to sail to the other world and never got there.

'We lay to for the light, and when it came what should be the first ship that I clapped eyes on lying broad abeam of us and only two or three hundred yards away but old Vanderdecken's craft, the *Flying Dutchman*. He'd got round the Cape at last, and this was the end of his three-hundred-year voyage.

'There was no mistaking him, although the ropes and chains had rotted and rusted through, and the yards had fallen down on deck, and the fore and aft sails were falling in tatters, and the timbers were that full of worm holes that they might have been riddled with small shot. As I was standing looking at her Schuyler came up from below.

'I didn't turn to look at him; I daren't, but I felt a trembling hand laid on my shoulder and heard his voice say in a hoarse shaking whisper:

' "My God, Tom, that's her again! You remember what Peters said when we left him on board of her. I knew it'd come – I've dreamt of it and I've heard his voice calling to me when I've been broad awake. It's got to be and I've got to go. Lower the boat, Tom, and come with me."

'I tried to persuade him out of it but it was no good. He swore he'd jump overboard and swim to her; so at last I gave in, hoping that after all it might be some other old craft like the Dutchman that had got fastened up here for hundreds of years. We had the gig out with a couple of men to pull her, and in a few minutes we were once more standing on the deck where we'd left poor Peters.

'There was no mistake about it, it was the same ship, only there was this difference, there was no captain and no crew. A few grey crumbling bones were lying about the cracked curled up decks and that was all. Schuyler gave one look round and then made straight for the cabin under the high quarter-deck. I followed him, and there, sitting at each end of the table with their heads bent forward on their folded arms were the bodies of Philip Vanderdecken and poor Frank Peters.

'They were dried to mummies, but still horribly life-like, and round Frank's neck was hanging the little silver chain with the crucifix lying on the table in front of him.

We stared at 'em speechless with horror and then Schuyler gasped out:

' "I knew it, Tom, he's fetched me here and here I'll have to die. What's that?"

'As he spoke a shiver seemed to run through the old hulk and we heard a queer crackling creaking noise and the sound of something falling on deck. Then Schuyler turned to me and whispered, for fear hadn't left him any better voice:

' "Run, Tom, run for the boat! She's breaking up at last."

'I took him by the arm and tried to drag him out with me, but as soon as I got him to the door he broke away and ran back and threw himself on his knees at the table. Just then the old craft gave a heave and my own fear got the best of me and I ran on deck.

'The fellows in the boat were shouting for us and I shouted back to 'em to come and help me bring the Skipper out. But before one of 'em could get up the side the main-mast fell aft crashing through the rotten timbers of the quarter-deck and blocking the way to the cabin. Then a great split opened right across the deck and I bundled into the boat and we pulled away as fast as the weed would let us.

'We hadn't got twenty yards off when the old craft broke up as though a broadside of big guns had been fired into her. She seemed to go right to pieces where she lay and the last of her that we saw was the high stern heeling over and going down, dragging the weeds with it. That was the last that any man, saw or ever will see of the *Flying Dutchman*.'

'And what about the *Gold Seeker*?' I asked. 'Did you get your millions?'

'Yes. The men wouldn't go back when we'd taken so much trouble to get there, and in less than a fortnight we got tons of treasure; but it never did us any good. No ship ever sighted the *Flying Dutchman* and got back safe to port. We broke our shaft getting out of the weed and knocked about for a month under what sail we could carry, then we drifted into the hurricane area and the last of the *Gold Seeker* was that she was smashed to pieces on one of the Keys of the Bahamas. I was the only one of her crew that was saved, and that's why I'm the only man alive that knows the true story of the fate of the *Flying Dutchman*.'

A PRIMER OF IMAGINARY GEOGRAPHY

James Brander Matthews

'Ship ahoy!'

There was an answer from our barque – for such it seemed to me by this time – but I could not make out the words.

'Where do you hail from?' was the next question.

I strained my ears to catch the response, being naturally anxious to know whence I had come.

'From the City of Destruction!' was what I thought I heard; and I confess that it surprised me not a little.

'Where are you bound?' was asked in turn.

Again I listened with intensest interest, and again did the reply astonish me greatly.

'Ultima Thule!' was the answer from our boat, and the voice of the man who answered was deep and melancholy.

Then I knew that I had set out strange countries for to see, and that I was all unequipped for so distant a voyage. Thule I knew, or at least I had heard of the king who reigned there once and who cast his goblet into the sea. But Ultima Thule! was not that beyond the uttermost borders of the earth?

'Any passengers?' was the next query, and I noted that the voice came now from the left and was almost abreast of us.

'One only,' responded the captain of our boat.

'Where bound?' was the final inquiry.

'To the Fortunate Islands!' was the answer; and as I heard this my spirits rose again, and I was glad, as what man would not be who was on his way to the paradise where the crimson-flowered meadows are full of the shade of frankincense-trees and of fruits of gold?

Then the boat bounded forward again, and I heard the wash of the waves.

All this time it seemed as though I were in darkness; but now I began dimly to discern the objects about me. I found that I was lying on a settee in a state-room at the stern of the vessel. Through the small round window over my head the first rays of the rising sun darted and soon lighted the little cabin.

As I looked about me with curiosity, wondering how I came to be a passenger on so unexpected a voyage, I saw the figure of a man framed in the doorway at the foot of the stairs leading to the deck above.

How it was I do not know, but I made sure at once that he was the captain of the ship, the man whose voice I had heard answering the hail.

He was tall and dark, with a scant beard and a fiery and

piercing gaze, which penetrated me as I faced him. Yet the expression of his countenance was not unfriendly; nor could any man lay eyes upon him without a movement of pity for the sadness written on his visage.

I rose to my feet as he came forward.

'Well,' he said, holding out his hand, 'and how are you after your nap?'

He spoke our language with ease and yet with a foreign accent. Perhaps it was this which betrayed him to me.

'Are you not Captain Vanderdecken?' I asked as I took his hand heartily.

'So you know me?' he returned, with a mournful little laugh, as he motioned to me to sit down again.

Thus the ice was broken, and he took his seat by my side, and we were soon deep in talk.

When he learned that I was a loyal New Yorker, his cordiality increased.

'I have relatives in New Amsterdam,' he cried; 'at least I had once. Deidrich Knickerbocker was my first cousin. And do you know Rip Van Winkle?'

Although I could not claim any close friendship with this gentleman, I boasted myself fully acquainted with his history.

'Yes, yes,' said Captain Vanderdecken, 'I suppose he was before your time. Most people are short-lived nowadays;

it's only with that Wandering Jew now that I ever have a chat over old times. Well, well, but you have heard of Rip? Were you ever told that I was on a visit to Hendrik Hudson the night Rip went up the mountains and took a drop too much?'

I had to confess that here was a fact I had not before known.

'I ran up the river,' said the Hollander, 'to have a game of bowls with the Englishman and his crew, nearly all of them countrymen of mine; and, by-the-way, Hudson always insists that it was I who brought the storm with me that gave poor Rip Van Winkle the rheumatism as he slept off his intoxication on the hillside under the pines. He was a good fellow, Rip, and a very good judge of schnapps, too.'

Seeing him smile with the pleasant memories of past companionship, I marvelled when the sorrowful expression swiftly covered his face again as a mask.

'But why talk of those who are dead and gone and are happy?' he asked in his deep voice. 'Soon there will be no one left, perhaps, but Ahasuerus and Vanderdecken – the Wandering Jew and the Flying Dutchman.'

He sighed bitterly, and then he gave a short, hard laugh.

'There's no use talking about these things, is there?' he cried. 'In an hour or two, if the wind holds, I can show you the house in which Ahasuerus has established his museum, the only solace of his lonely life. He has the most extraordinary gathering of curiosities the world has ever seen – truly a virtuoso's collection. An American reporter came on a voyage with me fifty or sixty years ago, and I took him over there. His name was Hawthorne. He interviewed the Jew, and wrote up the collection in the American papers, so I've been told.

'I remember reading the interview,' I said, 'and it was indeed a most remarkable collection.'

'It's all the more curious now for the odds and ends I've been able to pick up here and there for my old friend,' Vanderdecken declared; 'I got him the horn of Hernani, the harpoon with which Long Tom Coffin pinned the British officer to the mast, the long rifle of Natty Bumppo, the letter A in scarlet cloth embroidered in gold by Hester Prynne, the banner with the strange device "Excelsior," the gold bug which was once used as a plummet, Maud Muller's rake, and the jack-knives of Hosea Biglow and Sam Lawson.'

'You must have seen extraordinary things yourself,' I ventured to suggest.

'No man has seen stranger,' he answered, promptly. 'No man has ever been witness to more marvellous deeds than I – not even Ahasuerus, I verily believe, for he has only the land, and I have the boundless sea. I survey mankind from China to Peru. I have heard the horns of elfland blowing, and I could tell you the song the sirens sang. I have dropped anchor at the No Man's Land, and off Lyonesse, and in Xanadu, where Alph the sacred river ran. I have sailed from the still-vexed Bermoothes to the New Atlantis, of which there is no mention even until the year 1629.'

'In which year there was published an account of it written in the Latin tongue, but by an Englishman,' I said, desirous to reveal my acquirements.

'I have seen every strange coast,' continued the Flying Dutchman. 'The Island of Bells and Robinson Crusoe's Island and the Kingdoms of Brobdingnag and Lilliput. But it is not for me to vaunt myself for my voyages. And of a truth there are men I should like to have met and talked with whom I have yet failed to see. Especially is there one Ulysses, a sailor-man of antiquity who called himself Outis, whence I have sometimes suspected that he came from the town of Weissnichtwo.'

Just to discover what Vanderdecken would say, I inquired innocently whether this was the same person as one Captain Nemo of whose submarine exploits I had read.

'Captain Nemo?' the Flying Dutchman repeated scornfully. 'I never heard of him. Are you sure there is such a fellow?'

I tried to turn the conversation by asking if he had ever met another ancient mariner named Charon.

'Oh, yes,' was his answer. 'Charon keeps the ferry across

the Styx to the Elysian Fields, past the sunless marsh of Acheron. Yes – I've met him more than once. I met him only last month, and he was very proud of his new electric launch with its storage battery.'

When I expressed my surprise at this, he asked me if I did not know that the underworld was now lighted by electricity, and that Pluto had put in all the modern improvements. Before I had time to answer, he rose from his seat and slapped me on the shoulder.

'Come up with me! – if you want to behold things for yourself,' he cried. 'So far, it seems to me, you have never seen the sights!'

I followed him on deck. The sun was now two hours high, and I could just make out a faint line of land on the horizon.

'That rugged coast is Bohemia, which is really a desert country by the sea, although ignorant and bigoted pedants have dared to deny it,' and the scorn of my companion as he said this was wonderful to see. 'Its borders touch Alsatia, of which the chief town is a city of refuge. Not far inland, but a little to the south, is the beuatiful Forest of Arden, where men and maids dwell together in amity, and where clowns wander, making love to shepherdesses. Some of these same pestilent pedants have pretended to believe that this forest of Arden was situated in France, which is absurd, as there are no serpents and no lions in France, while we have the best of evidence as to the existence of both in Arden – you know that, don't you?'

I admitted that a green and gilded snake and a lioness with udders all drawn dry were known to have been seen there both on the same day. I ventured to suggest further that possibly this Forest of Arden was the Wandering Wood where Una met her lion.

'Of course,' was the curt response; 'everybody knows that Arden is a most beautiful region; even the toads there have precious jewels in their heads. And if you range the forest freely you may chance to find also the White Doe of Rylstone and the goat with the gilded horns that told fortunes in Paris long ago by tapping with his hoof on a tambourine.'

'These, then, are the Happy Hunting Grounds?' I suggested with a light laugh.

'Who would chase a tame goat?' he retorted with ill-concealed contempt for my ill-advised remark.

I thought it best to keep silence; and after a minute or two he resumed the conversation, like one who is glad of a good listener.

'In the outskirts of the Forest of Arden,' he began again, 'stands the Abbey of Thelema – the only abbey which is bounded by no wall and in which there is no clock at all nor any dial. And what need is there of knowing the time when one has for companions only comely and well-conditioned men and fair women of sweet disposition? And the motto of the Abbey of Thelema is *Fais ce que voudra* – Do what you will; and many of those who dwell in the Forest of Arden will tell you that they have taken this also for their device, and that if you live under the greenwood tree you may spend your life – as you like it.'

I acknowledged that this claim was probably well founded, since I recalled a song of the foresters in which they declared themselves without an enemy but winter and rough weather.

'Yes,' he went on, 'they are fond of singing in the Forest of Arden, and they sing good songs. And so they do in the fair land beyond where I have never been, and which I can never hope to go and see for myself, if all that they report is true – and yet what would I not give to see it and to die there.'

And as he said this sadly, his voice sank into a sigh.

'And where does the road through the forest lead, that you so much wish to set forth upon it?' I asked.

'That's the way to Arcady,' he said – 'to Arcady where all the leaves are merry. I may not go there, though I long for it. Those who attain to its borders never come back again – and why should they leave it? Yet there are tales told, and I have heard that this Arcady is the veritable El Dorado, and that in it is the true Fountain of Youth, gushing forth unfailingly for the refreshment of all who may reach it. But no one may find the entrance who cannot see it by the light that never was on land or sea.'

'It must be a favoured region,' I remarked.

'Of a truth it is,' he answered; 'and on the way there is the orchard where grow the golden apples of Hesperides, and the dragon is dead now that used to guard them, and so any one may help himself to the beautiful fruit. And by the side of the orchard flows the river Lethe, of which it is not well for man to drink, though many men would taste it gladly.' And again he sighed.

I knew not what to say, and so waited for him to speak once more.

'That promontory there on the weather bow,' he began again after a few moments' silence, 'that is Barataria, which was long supposed to be an island by its former governor, Don Sancho Panza, but which is now known by all to be connected with the mainland. Pleasant pastures slope down to the water, and if we were closer in shore you might chance to see Rozinante, the famous charger of Don Quixote de la Mancha, grazing amicably with the horse that brought the good news from Ghent to Aix.'

'I wish I could see them!' I cried, enthusiastically; 'but there is another horse I would rather behold than any – the winged steed Pegasus.'

Before responding, my guide raised his hand and shaded his eyes and scanned the horizon.

'No,' he said at last. 'I cannot descry any this afternoon. Sometimes in these latitudes I have seen a dozen hippogriffs circling about the ship, and I should like to have shown them to you. Perhaps they are all in the paddock at the stock-farm, where Apollo is now mating them with night-mares in the hope of improving the breed from which he selects the coursers that draw the chariot of the sun. They say that the experiment would have more chance of success if it were easier to find the night-mares' nests.'

'It was not a hippogriff I desired to see especially,' I returned when he paused, 'although that would be interesting, no doubt. It was the renowned Pegasus himself.'

'Pegasus is much like the other hippogriffs,' he retorted, 'although perhaps he has a little better record than any of them. But they say he has not won a single aerial handicap since that American professor of yours harnessed him to a one-hoss shay. That seemed to break his spirit, somehow; and I'm told he would shy now even at a broomstick train.'

'Even if he is out of condition,' I declared, 'Pegasus is still the steed I desire to see above all.'

'I haven't set eyes on him for weeks,' was the answer, 'so he is probably moulting; this is the time of year. He has a roomy boxstall in the new Augean stable at the foot of

Mount Parnassus. You know they have turned the spring of Castaly so that it flows through the stable-yard now, and so it is easy enough to keep the place clean.'

'If I may not see Pegasus,' I asked, 'is there any chance of my being taken to the Castle of the Sleeping Beauty?'

'I have never seen it myself,' he replied, 'and so I cannot show it to you. Rarely indeed may I leave the deck of my ship to go ashore; and this castle that you ask about is very far inland. I am told that it is in a country which the French travellers call *La Scribie*, a curious land, wherein the scene is laid of many a play, because its laws and its customs are exactly what every playwright has need of; but no poet has visited it for many years. Yet the Grand Duchess of Gerolstein, whose domains lie partly within the boundaries of Scribia, is still a subscriber to the *Gazette de Hollande* – the only newspaper I take himself, by the way.'

This last remark of the Captain's explained how it was that he had been able to keep up with the news of the day, despite his constant wanderings over the waste of waters; and what more natural in fact than that the Flying Dutchman should be a regular reader of the *Holland Gazette*?

Vandercken went forward into the prow of the vessel, calling to me to follow.

'Do you see those peaks afar in the distance?' he asked, pointing over the starboard bow.

I could just make out a saw-like outline in the direction indicated.

'Those are the Delectable Mountains,' he informed me; 'and down in a hollow between the two ranges is the Happy Valley.'

'Where Rasselas lived?'

'Yes,' he replied, 'and beyond the Delectable Mountains, on the far slope, lies Prester John's Kingdom, and there dwell anthropophagi, and men whose heads do grow beneath their shoulders. At least, so they say. For my part, I have never seen any such. And I have now no desire to go to Prester John's Kingdom, since I have been told that he has lately married Pope Joan. Do you see that grove of trees there at the base of the mountains?'

I answered that I thought I could distinguish weirdly contorted branches and strangely shivering foliage.

'That is the deadly upas-tree,' he explained, 'and it is as much as a man's life is worth to lie down in the shade of its twisted limbs. I slept there, on that point where the trees are the thickest, for a fortnight a century or so ago – but all I had for my pains was a headache. Still I should not advise you to adventure yourself under the shadow of those melancholy boughs.'

I confessed at once that I was little prompted to a visit so dangerous and so profitless.

'Profitless?' he repeated. 'As to that I am not so certain, for if you have a mind to see the rarest animals in the world, you could there sate your curiosity. On the shore, between the foot-hills and the grove of upas, is a park of wild beasts, the like of which no man has looked upon elsewhere. Even from the deck of this ship I have seen more than once a drove of unicorns, or a herd of centaurs, come down to the water to drink; and sometimes I have caught a pleasant glimpse of satyrs and fauns dancing in the sunlight. And once indeed – I shall never forget that extraordinary spectacle – as I sped past with every sail set and a ten-knot breeze astern, I saw the phoenix blaze up in its new birth, while the little salamanders frisked in the intense flame.'

'The phoenix?' I cried. 'You have seen the phoenix?'

'In just this latitude,' he answered, 'but it was about nine o'clock in the evening and I remember that the new moon was setting behind the mountains when I happened to come on deck.'

'And what was the phoenix like?' I asked.

'Really,' he replied, 'the bird was almost as Herodotus described her, of the make and size of the eagle, with a plumage partly red and partly golden. If we go by the point by moon, perhaps you may see her for yourself.'

'Is she there still?' I asked, in wonder.

'Why not?' he returned. 'All the game of this sort is

carefully preserved and the law is off on phoenixes only once in a century. Why, if it were not for the keepers, there soon would not be a single griffin or dragon left, not a single sphinx, not a single chimaera. Even as it is, I am told they do not breed as freely now as when they could roam the whole world in safety. That is why the game laws are so rigorous. Indeed, I am informed and believe that it is not permitted to kill the were-wolves even when their howling, as they run at large at night, prevents all sleep. It is true, of course, that very few people care to remain in such a neighbourhood.'

'I should think not,' I agreed. 'And what manner of people are they who dare to live here?'

'Along the shore there are a few harpies,' he answered; 'and now and then I have seen a mermaid on the rocks combing her hair with a golden comb as she sang to herself.'

'Harpies?' I repeated, in disgust. 'Why not the sea-serpent also?'

'There was a sea-serpent which lived for years in that cove yonder,' said the Captain, pointing to a pleasant bay on the starboard, 'but I have not seen it lately. Unless I am in error, it had a pitched battle hereabouts with a kraken. I don't remember who got the better of the fight – but I haven't seen the snake since.'

As I scanned the surface of the water to see if I might not detect some trace of one or another of these marvellous beasts of the sea, I remarked a bank of fog lying across our course.

'And what is this that we are coming to?' I inquired.

'That?' Captain Vanderdecken responded, indicating the misty outline straight before us. 'That is Altruria — at least it is so down in the charts, but I have never set eyes on it actually. It belongs to Utopia, you know; and they say that, although it is now on the level of the earth, it used once to be a flying island — the same which was formerly known as Laputa, and which was first visited and described by Captain Lemuel Gulliver about the year 1727, or a little earlier.'

'So that is Altruria,' I said, trying in vain to see it more clearly. 'There was an Altrurian in New York not long ago, but I had no chance of speech with him.'

'They are pleasant folk, those Altrurians,' said the Captain, 'although rather given to boasting. And they have really little enough to brag about, after all. Their climate is execrable — I find it ever windy hereabouts, and when I get in sight of that bank of fog, I always look out for squalls. I don't know just what the population is now, but I doubt if it is growing. You see, people talk about moving there to live, but they are rarely in a hurry to do it, I notice. Nor are the manufactures of the Altrurians as many as they were said to be. Their chief export now is the famous Procrustean bed; although the old house of Damocles & Co still does a good business in swords. Their tonnage is not what it used to be, and I'm told that they are issuing a good deal of paper money now to try and keep the balance of trade in their favour.'

'Are there not many poets among the inhabitants of Altruria?' I asked.

'They are all poets and romancers of one kind or another,' declared the Captain. 'Come below again into the cabin, and I will show you some of their books.'

The sky was now overcast and there was a chill wind blowing, so I was not at all loath to leave the deck, and to follow Vanderdecken down the steps into the cabin.

He took a thin volume from the table. 'This,' he said, 'is one of their books – *News from Nowhere*, it is called.'

He extended it towards me, and I held out my hand for it, but it slipped through my fingers. I started forward in a vain effort to seize it.

As I did so, the walls and the floor of the cabin seemed to melt away and to dissolve in air, and beyond them and taking their place were the walls and floor of my own house. Then suddenly the clock on the mantelpiece struck five, and I heard a bob-tail car rattling and clattering past the door on its way across town to Union Square, and thence to Greenwich Village, and so on down to the Hoboken Ferry.

Then I found myself on my own sofa, bending forward to pick up the volume of *Cyrano de Bergerac*, which lay on the carpet at my feet. I sat up erect and collected my thoughts as best I could after so strange a journey. And I wondered why it was that no one had ever prepared a primer of imaginary geography, giving to airy nothings a local habitation and a name, and accompanying it with an atlas of maps in the manner of the *Carte du Pays de Tendre*.

THE FATE OF THE 'SENEGAMBIAN QUEEN'

Wardon Allan Curtis

It was off the east coast of Madagascar, seat of pirate lairs, where no honest vessel ever ventured voluntarily, yet the clumsy little Dutch brig, labouring slowly southward before a fair north wind, with the mangrove swamps of the shore not three miles off its starboard quarter, could hardly be a vessel which storms had driven into that neighbourhood, for fair weather had prevailed for several weeks. Storm driven she was not, honest she could not but be, for no pirate would sail in such a wagon of the deep, and so the pirate lookout in the tall tree at the entrance of the cove where lay ambushed the *Senegambian Queen*, Captain William Avery, conjectured that it was in search of water that the stranger had approached the pirate-haunted coast. So little had the crew of the *Senegambian Queen* expected any quarry to come their way while they were on the island, and so little did they fear the advent of warships, that it was a full three hours after the brig was sighted before they were collected from the retreats to which they had scattered. Slowly the *Senegambian Queen* poked her black nose out from behind the forest-covered point of the cove, like some lank beast of prey reconnoitering the fat little vessel in the offing. Then, catching the wind, she began to skim the water. Such a poor prize the brig looked to be. The men cursed Captain Avery for calling them from their naps and sports to the pursuit of this little square-nosed Dutchman. But as they overhauled it, a languid interest and finally a keen surprise took the place of their complaining, for on the doomed vessel no preparations for flight or fight were being made. Indeed, there was no sign of alarm, and the crew of the brig were apparently oblivious to the existence of aught but themselves. Through a glass could be seen the captain sitting on the deck, reading a big tome. Along the bulwarks leaned a score of men, gazing at the coast. Not a glass, not an eye, even, was turned on the pursuing *Senegambian Queen*.

'Wake them up, quartermaster,' said Captain William Avery. 'Send a shot through their rigging and let them show that they are alive, or know that we are.'

The long twelve spoke, the shot passed harmlessly through the rigging of the brig, and then, like puppets in a show, the men leaning on the bulwarks turned about, the captain closed his book, and all gazed at the pirate ship, calmly and in no alarm.

'Well, the shot half awakened them,' said Captain William Avery. 'We will see if we cannot drive all the drowsiness from their eyes by boarding them. Ready for boarders!'

As if to aid the design of the captain, came a sudden freshening of the breeze, carrying the *Senegambian Queen* almost to the stranger before it shook the latter's sails at all. And then the eyes of the pirates fell upon what deprived them of speech, and the misgivings that invaded their minds would have made them turn tail and away, but that they were deprived of the power of motion, too. From the open mouth of Captain William Avery came naught but a gasp, the helmsman stood frozen at the wheel, and like statues stood the boarders with their gleaming cutlasses and pikes, while swiftly closed the distance between the well-groomed *Senegambian Queen* and the decaying hulk, along which ran phosphorescent gleams down near the water in the shadow that the two vessels made. On weather-blackened masts hung yellow, tattered, mildewed sails, and over the crumbling bulwarks looked a crew of ancient, hoary men, clad in ragged, faded garments of a past century. It was not the crew of the *Senegambian Queen* that sprang to lash the two vessels together as they touched, but the greybeard crew of the stranger, whose agility and strength belied their age-worn appearance:

'The *Flying Dutchman*! Cut the lashings! Port the helm!'

cried Captain William Avery, finding his voice at last, and at last spun the wheel in the helmsman's hands, and a dozen men sprang to do their commander's bidding, but leaped back in dread as a venerable old man appeared, drawing himself over the bulwarks and dropped upon the deck of the *Senegambian Queen.*

'Who is it that thus rudely lies aboard of the ship of Vanderdecken?' he cried in a quavering, yet deep and powerful voice. Not an answer had he save in the clanging of arms dropped by the pirates nearest him as they scurried back into the ranks of their comrades. 'But whatever your errand, I am ready to forgive the first men who have not fled from us in a century. Pirates you may be, but you are also men, and the first we have seen face to face in an hundred years. Like lords shall you be treated. Come aboard of us. Malvoisie, Chianti, sherry and the juices of the Rhine, mellowed by the flight of time until there is nowhere its like in this terrestrial globe, shall be yours. Not even kings can drink such wine as you shall have with us. Come, we bear you no ill-will, but love you like brothers, so pleasant it is to see the faces and hear the voices of men once more. Afar off in storms, afar off in fair weather, but always fleeing from our accursed ship, have we seen other ships, so unreal that we have wondered if time had not slain all mankind and we alone be left in the world in the midst of flitting spectres. Blessed be your dishonesty, your temerity, whatever has made you board us to-day. Pursue a ship we cannot, so slow are we. You are the first who have pursued us. Come, the good cheer waits.'

The pirates stood astonished for a time, silent and amazed, but at length Captain William Avery raised his voice and said: 'These men be preserved beyond their natural span by a curse, and nothing that is of this world has ever harmed them, but I do not believe that they are by reason of this curse more enabled to injure other men than before. They are weak old men. I fear them not. Let us cheer their cold hearts by accepting their hospitality, doing one good deed in our lives. Moreover, the marvels they can tell us will indeed be strange and pleasant to hear.'

The breeze lay dead on the water, the sun shone out of a cloudless sky and need of a watch on the *Senegambian Queen* there was none, and all of her crew save Sanchez at the wheel and Scipio and Libya, the two blacks, swarmed on to the vessel of Vanderdecken. That so old a ship should keep the seas caused them much astonishment, yet her frame seemed stout and sound withal, despite the gnawings of worms and time that were evident in the outer sheathings of her hull and decks. And her company, too, had in like manner been used by the years that had rolled over them. White were their hair and beards, ragged their garments, yet ruddy were their cheeks, bright their eyes, firm their step, straight their backs, and sonorous their voices. Indeed, Captain William Avery remarked upon these incongruities to Mynheer Vanderdecken, who eyed him narrowly, coughed once or twice and ordered that the wine be brought. Sorely were the pirates disappointed in the wine. Good it was and that was all. The flavour that the years had imparted to it was to be told in a slight suspicion of mawkishness, yet this was not what the rovers had found in other old wines, nor did they think it pleasant. Yet they quaffed it copiously, for after all it was wine, and as their spirits rose, they glanced at the silver flagons in the cabin and began to whisper among themselves that it would be but an act of charity to knock the Dutchmen on the head and send them out of the world of which they must be so weary, and, in default of any who could prove kinship, become their heirs. Such thoughts, ere long, Captain William Avery put into jocose words and addressed to Mynheer Vanderdecken, who for a moment grew grave, and then jolly, and cried:

'Done! But have one more cup of wine to our release,' and telling all of his men what Captain Avery had proposed, he ordered that the very oldest cask of wine be broached. The rovers gaily drained their beakers, though the sweet mawkishness was more than ever to be tasted in this, the oldest wine.

'Again,' shouted Mynheer Vanderdecken, and some of the

pirates held forth their beakers, but others lolled against the masts and bulwarks, or fell dozing to the deck.

'Let the stroke fall,' said Vanderdecken, but no stroke fell, only the last of the pirates, down to the deck among his prone comrades, sleeping heavily all, snoring and snorting, hard at it, as if striving to compress the slumbers of a week into a few hours' space.

'Van Steenwyck, do you shoot down the Spaniard at the wheel,' whispered the Dutch captain. 'Marnitz and Wynkoop, level your blunderbusses at the heads of the blacks, and bid them throw up their hands. We will spare them. As for these swine on the deck, tie weights to their feet and roll them into the sea before they begin to arouse.'

Into the quiet depths, one after another shot the crew of the *Senegambian Queen*, and when the last one had sunk beneath the glassy rollers, off came white beards and wigs and ragged coats and the Dutch crew piled aboard the pirate ship and took stock of the great treasure that was now theirs.

'Mynheer Van Oosterzee,' said the Dutch captain, addressing a richly dressed man who had not been visible while the pirates were on the brig, 'the two years for which I engaged with you are up. Play acting on the seas is more profitable than in Amsterdam, but I yearn for the boards once more. The promise I made you that this slow brig, under my direction, should bring more fortune than the swiftest keel ever laid in England or France, has been made good. The ragged sails and worm-eaten sheathing of the hull have brought more prey to us than ever this sea greyhound, with all of its top-hamper and its clean lines, overtook in like time. These white beards were more protection than coats of mail, superstition kept all cannon shot from our sides, and the wine with mandragora made easy the slaying of those who found it in their hearts to slay others. We have cleared the Indian Ocean of its last pirate. The robbers of England and France, with their jibes at the slow-going Dutch, have been overcome. Now for home.'

THE BRUTE

Joseph Conrad

Dodging in from the rain-swept street, I exchanged a smile and a glance with Miss Bank in the bar of the Three Crows. This exchange was effected with extreme propriety. It is a shock to think that, if still alive, Miss Bank must be something over sixty now. How time passes!

Noticing my gaze directed inquiringly at the partition of glass and varnished wood, Miss Blank was good enough to say, encouragingly:

'Only Mr Jermyn and Mr Stonor in the parlour with another gentleman I've never seen before.'

I moved towards the parlour door. A voice discoursing on the other side (it was but a matchboard partition), rose so loudly that the concluding words became quite plain in all their atrocity.

'That fellow Wilmot fairly dashed her brains out, and a good job, too!'

This inhuman sentiment, since there was nothing profane or improper in it, failed to do as much as to check the slight yawn Miss Blank was achieving behind her hand. And she remained gazing fixedly at the window-panes, which streamed with rain.

As I opened the parlour door the same voice went on in the same cruel strain:

'I was glad when I heard she got the knock from somebody at last. Sorry enough for poor Wilmot, though. That man and I used to be chums at one time. Of course that was the end of him. A clear case if there ever was one. No way out of it. None at all.'

The voice belonged to the gentleman Miss Blank had never seen before. He straddled his long legs on the heathrug. Jermyn, leaning forward, held his pocket-handkerchief spread out before the grate. He looked back dismally over his shoulder, and as I slipped behind one of the little wooden tables, I nodded to him. On the other side of the fire, imposingly calm and large, sat Mr Stonor, jammed tight into a capacious Windsor armchair. There was nothing small about him but his short, white side-whiskers. Yards and yards of extra superfine blue cloth (made up into an overcoat) reposed on a chair by his side. And he must just have brought some liner from sea, because another chair was smothered under his black waterproof, ample as a pall, and made of three-fold oiled silk, double-stitched throughout. A man's hand-bag of the usual size looking like a child's toy on the floor near his feet.

I did not nod to him. He was too big to be nodded to in that parlour. He was a senior Trinity pilot and condescended to take his turn in the cutter only during the summer months. He had been many times in charge of royal yachts in and out of Port Victoria. Besides, it's no use nodding to a monument. And he was like one. He didn't speak, he didn't budge. He just sat there, holding his handsome old head up, immovable, and almost bigger than life. It was extremely fine. Mr Stonor's presence reduced poor old Jermyn to a mere shabby wisp of a man, and made the talkative stranger in tweeds on the hearthrug look absurdly boyish. The latter must have been a few years over thirty, and was certainly not the sort of individual that gets abashed at the sound of his own voice, because gathering me in, as it were, by a friendly glance, he kept it going without a check.

'I was glad of it,' he repeated, emphatically. 'You may be surprised at it, but then you haven't gone through the experience I've had of her. I can tell you, it was something to remember. Of course, I got off scot free myself – as you can see. She did her best to break up my pluck for me tho'. She jolly near drove as fine a fellow as ever lived into a madhouse. What do you say to that – eh?'

Not an eyelid twitched in Mr Stonor's enormous face. Monumental! The speaker looked straight into my eyes.

'It used to make me sick to think of her going about the world murdering people.'

Jermyn approached the handkerchief a little nearer to the grate and groaned. It was simply a habit he had.

'I've seen her once,' he declared, with mournful indifference. 'She had a house –'

The stranger in tweeds turned to stare down at him, surprised.

'She had three houses,' he corrected, authoritatively. But Jermyn was not to be contradicted.

'She had a house, I say,' he repeated, with dismal obstinacy. 'A great, big ugly, white thing. You could see it from miles away – sticking up.'

'So you could,' assented the other readily. 'It was old Colchester's notion, though he was always threatening to give her up. He couldn't stand her racket any more, he declared; it was too much of a good thing for him; he would wash his hands of her, if he never got hold of another – and so on. I daresay he would have chucked her, only – it may surprise you – his missus wouldn't hear of it. Funny, eh? But with women, you never know how they will take a thing, and Mrs Colchester, with her moustaches and big eyebrows, set up for being as strong-minded as they make them. She used to walk about in a brown silk dress, with a great gold cable flopping about her bosom. You should have heard her snapping out: "Rubbish!" or "Stuff and nonsense!" I daresay she knew when she was well off. They had no children, and had never set up a home anywhere. When in England she just made shift to hang out anyhow in some cheap hotel or boarding-house. I daresay she liked to get back to the comforts she was used to. She knew very well she couldn't gain by any change. And, moreover, Colchester, though a first-rate man, was not what you may call in his first youth, and, perhaps, she may have thought that he wouldn't be able to get hold of another (as he used to say) so easily. Anyhow, for one reason or another, it was "Rubbish" and "Stuff and nonsense" for the good lady. I overhead once young Mr Apse himself say to her confidentially: "I assure you, Mrs Colchester, I am beginning to feel quite unhappy about the name she's getting for herself." "Oh," says she, with her deep little hoarse laugh, "if one took notice of all the silly talk," and she showed Apse all her ugly false teeth at once. "It would take more than that to make me lose my confidence in her, I assure you," says she.'

At this point, without any change of facial expression, Mr Stonor emitted a short, sardonic laugh. It was very impressive, but I didn't see the fun. I looked from one to another. The stranger on the hearthrug had an ugly smile.

'And Mr Apse shook both Mrs Colchester's hands, he was so pleased to hear a good word said for their favourite.

All these Apses, young and old you know, were perfectly infatuated with that abominable, dangerous . . .'

'I beg your pardon,' I interrupted, for he seemed to be addressing himself exclusively to me; 'but who on earth are you talking about?'

'I am talking of the Apse family,' he answered, courteously.

I nearly let out a damn at this. But just then the respected Miss Blank put her head in, and said that the cab was at the door, if Mr Stonor wanted to catch the eleven three up.

At once the senior pilot arose in his mighty bulk and began to struggle into his coat, with awe-inspiring upheavals. The stranger and I hurried impulsively to his assistance, and directly we laid our hands on him he became perfectly quiescent. We had to raise our arms very high, and to make efforts. It was like caparisoning a docile elephant. With a 'Thanks, gentlemen,' he dived under and squeezed himself through the door in a great hurry.

We smiled at each other in a friendly way.

'I wonder how he manages to hoist himself up a ship's side-ladder,' said the man in tweeds; and poor Jermyn, who was a mere North Sea pilot, without official status or recognition of any sort, pilot only by courtesy, groaned.

'He makes eight hundred a year.'

'Are you a sailor?' I asked the stranger, who had gone back

to his position on the rug.

'I used to be till a couple of years ago, when I got married,' answered this communicative individual. 'I even went to sea first in that very ship we were speaking of when you came in.'

'What ship?' I asked, puzzled. 'I never heard you mention a ship.'

'I've just told you her name, my dear sir,' he replied. 'The *Apse Family*. Surely you've heard of the great firm of Apse & Sons, shipowners. They had a pretty big fleet. There was the *Lucy Apse*, and the *Harold Apse*, and *Anne, John, Malcolm, Clara, Juliet*, and so on – no end of *Apses*. Every brother, sister, aunt, cousin, wife – and grandmother, too, for all I know – of the firm had a ship named after them. Good, solid, old-fashioned craft they were, too, built to carry and to last. None of your new-fangled, labour-saving appliances in them, but plenty of men and plenty of good salt beef and hard tack put aboard – and off you go to fight your way out and home again.'

The miserable Jermyn made a sound of approval, which sounded like a groan of pain. Those were the ships for him. He pointed out in doleful tones that you couldn't say to labour-saving appliances: 'Jump lively now, my hearties.' No labour-saving appliance would go aloft on a dirty night with the sands under your lee.

'No,' assented the stranger, with a wink at me. 'The Apses didn't believe in them either, apparently. They treated their people well – as people don't get treated nowadays, and they were awfully proud of their ships. Nothing ever happened to them. This last one, the *Apse Family*, was to be like the others, only she was to be still stronger, still safer, still more roomy and comfortable. I believe they meant her to last for ever. They had her built composite – iron, teak-wood, and green heart, and her scantling was something fabulous. If ever an order was given for a ship in a spirit of pride this one was. Everything of the best. The commodore captain of the employ was to command her, and they planned the accommodation for him like a house on shore under a big, tall poop that went nearly to the mainmast. No wonder Mrs Colchester wouldn't let the old man give her up. Why, it was the best home she ever had in all her married days. She had a nerve, that woman.

'The fuss that was made while that ship was building! Let's have this a little stronger, and that a little heavier; and hadn't that other thing better be changed for something a little thicker. The builders entered into the spirit of the game, and there she was, growing into the clumsiest, heaviest ship of her size right before all their eyes, without anybody becoming aware of it somehow. She was to be 2,000 tons register, or a little over; no less on any account. But see what happens. When they came to measure her she turned out 1,999 tons and a fraction. General consternation! And they say old Mr Apse was so annoyed when they told him that he took to his bed and died. The old gentleman had retired from the firm twenty-five years before, and was ninety-six years old if a day, so his death wasn't, perhaps, so surprising. Still Mr Lucian Apse was convinced that his father would have lived to a hundred. So we may put him at the head of the list. Next comes the poor devil of a shipwright that brute caught and squashed as she went off the ways. They called it the launch of a ship, but I've heard people say that, from the wailing and yelling and scrambling out of the way, it was more like letting a devil loose upon the river. She snapped all her checks like pack-thread, and went for the tugs in attendance like a fury. Before anybody could see what she was up to she sent one of them to the bottom, and laid up another for three months' repairs. One of her cables parted, and then, suddenly – you couldn't tell why – she let herself be brought up with the other as quiet as a lamb.

'That's how she was. You could never be sure what she would be up to next. There are ships difficult to handle, but generally you can depend on them behaving rationally. With *that* ship, whatever you did with her you never knew how it would end. She was a wicked beast. Or, perhaps, she was only just insane.'

He uttered this supposition in so earnest a tone that I could not refrain from smiling. He left off biting his lower lip to apostrophize me.

'Eh! Why not? Why couldn't there be something in her build, in her lines corresponding to – What's madness? Only something just a tiny bit wrong in the make of your brain. Why shouldn't there be a mad ship – I mean mad in a ship-like way, so that under no circumstances could you be sure she would do what any other sensible ship would naturally do for you. There are ships that steer wildly, and ships that can't be quite trusted always to stay; others want careful watching when running in a gale; and, again, there may be a ship that will make heavy weather of it in every little blow. But then you expect her to be always so. You take it as part of her character, as a ship, just as you take account of a man's peculiarities of temper when you deal with him. But with her you couldn't. She was unaccountable. If she wasn't mad, then she was the most evil-minded, underhand, savage brute that ever went afloat. I've seen her run in a heavy gale beautifully for two days, and on the third broach to twice in the same afternoon. The first time she flung the helmsman clean over the wheel, but as she didn't quite manage to kill him she had another try about three hours afterwards. She swamped herself fore and aft, burst all the canvas we had set, scared all hands into a panic, and even frightened Mrs

Colchester down there in these beautiful stern cabins that she was so proud of. When we mustered the crew there was one man missing. Swept overboard, of course, without being either seen or heard, poor devil! and I only wonder more of us didn't go.

'Always something like that. Always. I heard an old mate tell Captain Colchester once that it had come to this with him, that he was afraid to open his mouth to give any sort of order. She was as much of a terror in harbour as at sea. You could never be certain what would hold her. On the slightest provocation she would start snapping ropes, cables, wire hawsers, like carrots. She was heavy, clumsy, unhandy – but that does not quite explain that power for mischief she had. You know, somehow, when I think of her I can't help remembering what we hear of incurable lunatics breaking loose now and then.'

He looked at me inquisitively. But, of course, I couldn't admit that a ship could be mad.

'In the ports where she was known,' he went on, 'they dreaded the sight of her. She thought nothing of knocking away twenty feet or so of solid stone facing off a quay or wiping off the end of a wooden wharf. She must have lost miles of chain and hundreds of tons of anchors in her time. When she fell aboard some poor unoffending ship it was the very devil of a job to haul her off again. And she never got hurt herself – just a few scratches or so, perhaps. They had wanted to have her strong. And so she was. Strong enough to ram Polar ice with. And as she began so she went on. From the day she was launched she never let a year pass without murdering somebody. I think the owners got very worried about it. But they were a stiff-necked generation all these Apses; they wouldn't admit there could be anything wrong with the *Apse Family*. They wouldn't even change her name. "Stuff and nonsense," as Mrs Colchester used to say. They ought at least to have shut her up for life in some dry dock or other, away up the river, and never let her smell salt water again. I assure you, my dear sir, that she invariably did kill someone every voyage she made. It was perfectly well-known. She got a name for it, far and wide.'

I expressed my surprise that a ship with such a deadly reputation could ever get a crew.

'Then, you don't know what sailors are, my dear sir. Let me just show you by an instance. One day in dock at home, while loafing on the forcastle head, I noticed two respectable salts come along, one a middle-aged, competent, steady man, evidently, the other a smart, youngish chap. They read the name on the bows and stopped to look at her. Says the elder man: "*Apse Family*. That's the sanguinary female dog' (I'm putting it in that way) 'of a ship, Jack, that kills a man every voyage. I wouldn't sign in her – not for Joe, I wouldn't." And the other says: "If she were mine, I'd have her towed on the mud and set on fire, blamme if I wouldn't." Then the first man chimes in: "Much do they care! Men are cheap, God knows." The younger one spat in the water alongside. "They won't have me – not for double wages."

'They hung about for some time and then walked up the dock. Half an hour later I saw them both on our deck looking about for the mate, and apparently very anxious to be taken on. And they were.'

'How do you account for this?' I asked.

'What would you say?' he retorted. 'Recklessness! The vanity of boasting in the evening to all their chums: "We've just shipped in that there *Apse Family*. Blow her. She ain't going to scare us." Sheer sailor-like perversity! A sort of curiosity. Well – a little of all that, no doubt. I put the question to them in the course of the voyage. The answer of the elderly chap was:

' "A man can die but once." The younger assured me in a mocking tone that he wanted to see "how she would do it this time." But I tell you what; there was a sort of fascination about the brute.'

Jermyn, who seemed to have seen every ship in the world, broke in sulkily:

'I saw her once out of this very window towing up the river; a great black ugly thing, going along like a big hearse.'

'Something sinister about her looks, wasn't there?' said the man in tweeds, looking down at old Jermyn with a friendly eye. 'I always had a sort of horror of her. She gave me a beastly shock when I was no more than fourteen, the very first day – nay, hour – I joined her. Father came up to see me off, and was to go down to Gravesend with us. I was his second boy to go to sea. My big brother was already an officer then. We got on board about eleven in the morning, and found the ship ready to drop out of the basin, stern first. She had not moved three times her own length when, at a little pluck the tug gave her to enter the dock gates, she made one of her rampaging starts, and put such a weight on the check rope – a new six-inch hawser – that forward there they had no chance to ease it round in time, and it parted. I saw the broken end fly up high in the air, and the next moment that brute brought her quarter against the pier-head with a jar that staggered everybody about her decks. She didn't hurt herself. Not she! But one of the boys the mate had sent aloft on the mizzen to do something, came down on the poop-deck – thump, right in front of me. He was not much older than myself. We had been grinning at each other only a few minutes before. He must have been handling himself carelessly, not expecting to get such a jerk. I heard his startled cry – Oh! – in a high treble as he felt himself going, and looked up in time to see him go limp all over as he fell. Ough! Poor father was remarkably white about the gills when we shook hands in Gravesend. "Are you all right?" he, says, looking hard at me. "Yes, father." "Quite sure?" "Yes, father." "Well, then good-bye, my boy." He told me afterwards that for half a word he would have carried me off home with him there and then. I am the baby of the family – you know,' added the man in tweeds, stroking his moustache with an ingenuous smile.

I acknowledged this interesting communication by a sympathetic murmur. He waved his hand carelessly.

'This might have utterly spoiled a chap's nerve for going aloft, you know – utterly. He fell within two feet of me, cracking his head on a mooring-bitt. Never moved. Stone dead. Nice looking little fellow, he was. I had just been thinking we would be great chums. However, that wasn't yet the worst that brute of a ship could do. I served in her three years of my time, and then I got transferred to the *Lucy Apse*, for a year. The sailmaker we had in the *Apse Family* turned up there, too, and I remember him saying to me one evening, after we had been a week at sea: "Isn't she a meek little ship?" No wonder we thought the *Lucy Apse* a dear, meek, little ship after getting clear of that big, rampaging savage brute. It was like heaven. Her officers seemed to me the restfullest lot of men on earth. To me who had known no ship but the *Apse Family*, the *Lucy* was like a sort of magic craft that did what you wanted her to do of her own accord. One evening we got caught aback pretty sharply from right ahead. In about ten minutes we had her full again, sheets aft, tacks down, decks cleared, and the officer of the watch leaning against the weather rail peacefully. It seemed simply marvellous to me. The other would have stuck for half-an-hour in irons, rolling her decks full of water, knocking the men about – spars cracking, braces snapping, yards taking charge, and a confounded scare going on aft because of her beastly rudder, which she had a way of flapping about fit to raise your hair on end. I couldn't get over my wonder for days.

'Well, I finished my last year of apprenticeship in that jolly little ship – she wasn't so little either, but after that other heavy devil she seemed but a plaything to handle. I finished my time and passed; and then just as I was thinking of having three weeks of real good time on shore I got at breakfast a letter asking me the earliest day I could be ready to join the *Apse Family* as third mate. I gave my plate a shove that shot it into the middle of the table; dad looked up over his paper; mother raised her hands in astonishment, and I went out bare-headed into our bit of garden, where I walked round and round for an hour.

'When I came in again mother was out of the dining-room, and dad had shifted berth into his big armchair. The letter was lying on the mantelpiece.

' "It's very creditable to you to get the offer, and very kind of them to make it," he said. "And I see also that Charles has been appointed chief mate of that ship for one voyage."

'There was, overleaf, a P.S. to that effect in Mr Apse's own handwriting, which I had overlooked. Charley was my big brother.

' "I don't like very much to have two of my boys together in one ship," father goes on, in his deliberate, solemn way. "And I may tell you that I would not mind writing Mr Apse a letter to that effect."

'Dear old dad! He was a wonderful father. What would you have done? The mere notion of going back (and as an officer, too), to be worried and bothered, and kept on the jump night and day by that brute, made me feel sick. But she wasn't a ship you could afford to fight shy of. Besides, the most genuine excuse could not be given without mortally offending Apse & Sons. The firm, and I believe the whole family down to the old unmarried aunts in Lancashire, had grown desperately touchy about that accursed ship's character. This was the case for answering "Ready now" from your very death-bed if you wished to die in their good graces. And that's precisely what I did answer – by wire, to have it over and done with at once.

'The prospect of being shipmates with my big brother cheered me up considerably, though it made me a bit anxious, too. Ever since I remember myself as a little chap he had been very good to me, and I looked upon him as the finest fellow in the world. And so he was. No better officer ever walked the deck of a merchant ship. And that's a fact. He was a fine, strong, upstanding, sun-tanned, young fellow, with his brown hair curling a little, and an eye like a hawk. He was just splendid. We hadn't seen each other for many years, and even this time, though he had been in England three weeks already, he hadn't showed up at home yet, but had spent his spare time in Surrey somewhere making up to Maggie Colchester, old Captain Colchester's niece. Her father, a great friend of dad's, was in the sugar-broking business, and Charley made a sort of second home of their house. I wondered what my big brother would think of me. There was a sort of sternness about Charley's face which never left it, not even when he was larking in his rather wild fashion.

'He received me with a great shout of laughter. He seemed to think my joining as an officer the greatest joke in the world. There was a difference of ten years between us, and I suppose he remembered me best in pinafores. I was a kid of four when he first went to sea. It surprised me to find how boisterous he could be.

' "Now we shall see what you are made of," he cried. And he held me off by the shoulders, and punched my ribs, and hustled me into his berth. "Sit down, Ned. I am glad of the chance of having you with me. I'll put the finishing touch to you, my young officer, providing you're worth the trouble. And, first of all, get it well into your head that we are not going to let this brute kill anybody this voyage. We'll stop her racket."

'I perceived he was in dead earnest about it. He talked grimly of the ship, and how we must be careful and never allow this ugly beast to catch us napping with any of her damned tricks.

'He gave me a regular lecture on special seamanship for the use of the *Apse Family*; then changing his tone, he began to talk at large, rattling off the wildest, funniest nonsense; till my sides ached with laughing. I could see very well he was a bit above himself with high spirits. It couldn't be because of my coming. Not to that extent. But, of course, I wouldn't have dreamt of asking what was the matter. I had a proper respect for my big brother, I can tell you. But it was all made plain enough a day or two afterwards, when I heard that Miss Maggie Colchester was coming for the voyage. Uncle was giving her a sea-trip for the benefit of her health.

'I don't know what could have been wrong with her health. She had a beautiful colour, and a deuce of a lot of fair hair. She didn't care a rap for wind, or rain, or spray, or sun, or green seas, or anything. She was a blue-eyed, jolly girl of the very best sort, but the way she cheeked my big brother used to frighten me. I always expected it to end in an awful row. However, nothing decisive happened till after we had been in Sydney for a week. One day, in the men's dinner hour, Charley sticks his head into my cabin. I was stretched out on my back on the settee, smoking in peace.

' "Come ashore with me, Ned," he says, in his curt way.

'I jumped up, of course, and away after him down the gangway and up George Street. He strode along like a giant, and I at his elbow, panting. It was confoundedly hot. "Where on earth are you rushing me to, Charley?" I made bold to ask.

' "Here," he says.

' "Here" was a jeweller's shop. I couldn't imagine what he could want there. It seemed a sort of mad freak. He thrusts under my nose three rings, which looked very tiny on his big, brown palm, growling out –

' "For Maggie! Which?"

'I got a kind of scare at this. I couldn't make a sound, but I pointed at the one that sparkled white and blue. He put it in his waistcoat pocket, paid for it with a lot of sovereigns, and bolted out. When we got on board I was quite out of breath. "Shake hands, old chap," I gasped out. He gave me a thump on the back. "Give what orders you like to the boatswain when the hands turn-to," says he; "I am off duty this afternoon."

'Then he vanished from the deck for a while, but presently he came out of the cabin with Maggie, and these two went over the gangway publicly, before all hands, going for a walk together on that awful, blazing hot day, with clouds of dust flying about. They came back after a few hours looking very staid, but didn't seem to have the slightest idea where they had been. Anyway, that's the answer they both made to Mrs Colchester's question at tea-time.

'And didn't she turn on Charley, with her voice like an old night cabman's. "Rubbish. Don't know where you've been! Stuff and nonsense. You've walked the girl off her legs. Don't do it again."

'It's surprising how meek Charley could be with that old woman. Only on one occasion he whispered to me, "I'm jolly glad she isn't Maggie's aunt, except by marriage. That's no sort of relationship." But I think he let Maggie have too much of her own way. She was hopping all over that ship in her yachting skirt and a red tam o'shanter like a bright bird on a dead black tree. The old salts used to grin to themselves when they saw her coming along, and offered to teach her knots or splices. I believe she liked the men, for Charley's sake, I suppose.

'As you may imagine, the fiendish propensities of that cursed ship were never spoken of on board. Not in the cabin, at any rate. Only once on the homeward passage Charley said, incautiously, something about bringing all her crew home this time. Captain Colchester began to look uncomfortable at once, and that silly, hard-bitten old woman flew out at Charley as though he had said something indecent. I was quite confounded myself; as to Maggie, she sat completely mystified, opening her blue eyes very wide. Of course, before she was a day older she wormed it all out of me. She was a very difficult person to lie to.

' "How awful," she said, quite solemn. "So many poor fellows. I am glad the voyage is nearly over. I won't have a moment's peace about Charley now."

'I assured her Charley was all right. It took more than that ship knew to get over a seaman like Charley. And she agreed with me.

'Next day we got the tug off Dungeness; and when the tow-rope was fast Charley rubbed his hands and said to me in an undertone –

' "We've baffled her, Ned."

' "Looks like it," I said, with a grin at him. It was beautiful weather, and the sea as smooth as a millpond. We went up the river without a shadow of trouble except once, when off Hole Haven, the brute took a sudden sheer and nearly had a barge anchored just clear of the fairway. But I was aft, looking after the steering, and she did not catch me napping that time. Charley came up on the poop, looking very concerned. "Close shave," says he.

' "Never mind, Charley," I answered, cheerily. "You've tamed her."

'We were to tow right up to the dock. The river pilot boarded us below Gravesend, and the first words I heard him say were: "You may just as well take your port anchor inboard at once, Mr Mate."

'This had been done when I went forward. I saw Maggie on the forecastle head enjoying the bustle and I begged her to go aft, but she took no notice of me, of course. Then Charley, who was very busy with the head gear, caught sight of her and shouted in his biggest voice: "Get off the forecastle head, Maggie. You're in the way here." For all answer she made a funny face at him, and I saw poor Charley turn away, hiding a smile. She was flushed with the excitement of getting home again, and her blue eyes seemed to snap electric sparks as she looked at the river. A collier brig had gone round just ahead of us, and our tug had to stop her engines in a hurry to avoid running into her.

'In a moment, as is usually the case, all the shipping in the reach seemed to get into a hopeless tangle. A schooner and a ketch got up a small collision all to themselves right in the middle of the river. It was exciting to watch, and, meantime, our tug remained stopped. Any other ship than that brute could have been coaxed to keep straight for a couple of minutes – but not she! Her head fell off at once, and she began to drift down, taking her tug along with her. I noticed a cluster of coasters at anchor within a quarter of a mile of us, and I thought I had better speak to the pilot. "If you let her get amongst that lot?" I said, quietly, "she will grind some of them to bits before we get her out again."

' "Don't I know her!" cries he, stamping his foot in a perfect fury. And he out with his whistle to make that bothered tug get the ship's head up again as quick as possible. He blew like mad, waving his arm to port, and presently we could see that the tug's engines had been set going ahead. Her paddles churned the water, but it was as if she had been trying to tow a rock – she couldn't get an inch out of that ship. Again the pilot blew his whistle, and waved his arm to port. We could see the tug's paddles turning faster and faster away, broad on our bow.

'For a moment tug and ship hung motionless in a crowd of moving shipping, and then the terrific strain that evil, stony-hearted brute would always put on everything, tore the towing-chock clean out. The tow-rope surged over, snapping the iron stanchions of the head-rail one after another as if they had been sticks of sealing-wax. It was only then I noticed that in order to have a better view over our heads, Maggie had stepped upon the port anchor as it lay flat on the forecastle deck.

'It had been lowered properly into its hardwood beds, but there had been no time to take a turn with it. Anyway, it was quite secure as it was, for going into dock; but I could see directly that the tow-rope would sweep under the fluke in another second. My heart flew up right into my throat, but not before I had time to yell out: "Jump clear of that anchor!"

'But I hadn't time to shriek out her name. I don't suppose she heard me at all. The first touch of the hawser against the fluke threw her down; she was up on her feet again quick as lightning, but she was up on the wrong side. I heard a horrid, scraping sound, and then that anchor, tipping over, rose up like something alive; its great, rough iron arm caught Maggie round the waist, seemed to clasp her close with a dreadful hug, and flung itself with her over and down in a terrific clang of iron, followed by heavy ringing blows that shook the ship from stem to stern – because the ring stopper held!'

'How horrible!' I exclaimed.

'I used to dream for years afterwards of anchors catching hold of girls,' said the man in tweeds, a little wildly. He shuddered. 'With a most pitiful howl Charley was over after her almost on the instant. But, Lord! he didn't see as much as a gleam of her red tam o' shanter in the water. Nothing!

Nothing whatever! In a moment there were half-a-dozen boats around us, and he got pulled into one. I, with the boatswain and the carpenter, let go the other anchor in a hurry and brought the ship up somehow. The pilot had gone silly. He walked up and down the forecastle head wringing his hands and muttering to himself: "Killing women, now! Killing women, now!" Not another word could you get out of him.

'Dusk fell, then a night black as pitch; and peering upon the river I heard a low, mournful hail, "Ship, ahoy!" Two Gravesend watermen came alongside. They had a lantern in their wherry, and looked up the ship's side, holding on to the ladder without a word. I saw in the patch of light a lot of loose, fair hair down there.'

He shuddered again.

'After the tide turned poor Maggie's body had floated clear of one of them big mooring buoys,' he explained. 'I crept aft, feeling half-dead, and managed to send a rocket up – to let the other searchers know, on the river. And then I slunk away forward like a cur, and spent the night sitting on the heel of the bowsprit so as to be as far as possible out of Charley's way.'

'Poor fellow!' I murmured.

'Yes. Poor fellow,' he repeated, musingly. 'That brute wouldn't let him – not even him – cheat her of her prey.

But he made her fast in dock next morning. He did. We hadn't exchanged a word – not a single look for that matter. I didn't want to look at him. When the last rope was fast he put his hands to his head and stood gazing down at his feet as if trying to remember something. The men waited on the main deck for the words that end the voyage. Perhaps that is what he was trying to remember. I spoke for him. "That'll do, men."

'I never saw a crew leave a ship so quietly. They sneaked over the rail one after another, taking care not to bang their sea chests too heavily. They looked our way, but not one had the stomach to come up and offer to shake hands with the mate as is usual.

'I followed him all over the empty ship to and fro, here and there, with no living soul about but the two of us, because the old ship-keeper had locked himself up in the galley – both doors. Suddenly poor Charley mutters, in a crazy voice: "I'm done here," and strides down the gangway with me at his heels, up the dock, out at the gate, on towards Tower Hill. He used to take rooms with a decent old landlady in America Square, to be near his work.

'All at once he stops short, turns round, and comes back straight at me. "Ned," says he, "I am going home." I had the good luck to sight a four-wheeler and got him in just in time. His legs were beginning to give way. In our hall he fell down on a chair, and I'll never forget father's and mother's amazed, perfectly still faces as they stood over him. They couldn't understand what had happened to him till I blubbered out "Maggie got drowned, yesterday, in the river."

'Mother let out a little cry. Father looks from him to me, and from me to him, as if comparing our faces – for, upon my soul, Charley did not resemble himself at all. Nobody moved; and the poor fellow raises his big brown hands slowly to his throat, and with one single tug rips everything open – collar, shirt, waistcoat – a perfect wreck and ruin of a man. Father and I got him upstairs somehow, and mother pretty nearly killed herself nursing him through a brain fever.'

The man in tweeds nodded at me significantly.

'Ah! there was nothing that could be done with that brute. She had a devil in her.'

'Where's your brother?' I asked, expecting to hear he was dead. But he was commanding a smart steamer on the China coast, and never came home now.

Jermyn fetched a heavy sigh, and the handkerchief being now sufficiently dry, put it up tenderly to his red and lamentable nose.

'She was a ravening beast,' the man in tweeds started again. 'Old Colchester put his foot down and resigned. And would you believe it? Apse & Sons wrote to ask whether he wouldn't reconsider his decision! Anything to save the good name of the *Apse Family*! Old Colchester went to the office then and said that he would take charge again but only to sail her out into the North Sea and scuttle her there. He was nearly off his chump. He used to be darkish iron-grey, but his hair went snow-white in a fortnight. And Mr Lucian Apse (they had known each other as young men) pretended not to notice it. Eh? Here's infatuation if you like! Here's pride for you!

'They jumped at the first man they could get to take her, for fear of the scandal of the *Apse Family* not being able to find a skipper. He was a festive soul, I believe, but he stuck to her grim and hard. Wilmot was his second mate. A harum-scarum fellow, and pretending to a great scorn for all the girls. The fact is he was really timid. But let only one of them do as much as lift her little finger in encouragement, and there was nothing that could hold the beggar. As apprentice, once, he deserted abroad after a petticoat, and would have gone to the dogs then, if his skipper hadn't taken the trouble to find him and lug him by the ears out of some house of perdition or other.

'It was said that one of the firm had been heard once to express a hope that this brute of a ship would get lost soon. I can hardly credit the tale, unless it might have been Mr Alfred Apse, whom the family didn't think much of. They had him in the office, but he was considered a bad egg altogether, always flying off to race meetings and coming home drunk. You would have thought that a ship so full of deadly tricks would run herself ashore some day out of sheer cussedness. But not she! She was going to last for ever. She had a nose to keep off the bottom.'

Jermyn made a grunt of approval.

'A ship after a pilot's own heart, eh?' jeered the man in tweeds. 'Well, Wilmot managed it. He was the man for it, but even he, perhaps, couldn't have done the trick without the green-eyed governess, or nurse, or whatever she was to the children of Mr and Mrs Pamphilius.

'Those people were passengers in her from Port Adelaide to the Cape. Well, the ship went out and anchored outside for the day. The skipper – hospitable soul – had a lot of guests from town to a farewell lunch – as usual with him. It was five in the evening before the last shore boat left the side, and the weather looked ugly and dark in the gulf. There was no reason for him to get under way. However, as he had told everybody he was going that day, he imagined it was proper to do so anyhow. But as he had no mind after all these festivities to tackle the straits in the dark, with a scant wind, he gave orders to keep the ship under lower topsails and foresail as close as she would lie, dodging along the land till the morning. Then he sought his virtuous couch. The mate was on deck, having his face washed very clean with hard rain squalls. Wilmot relieved him at midnight.

'The *Apse Family* had, as you observed, a house on her poop . . .'

'A big, ugly white thing, sticking up,' Jermyn murmured, sadly, at the fire.

'That's it: a companion for the cabin stairs and a sort of chart-room combined. The rain drove in gusts on the sleepy Wilmot. The ship was then surging slowly to the southward, close hauled, with the coast within three miles or so to windward. There was nothing to look out for in that part of the gulf, and Wilmot went round to dodge the squalls under the lee of that chart-room, whose door on that side was open. The night was black, like a barrel of coal-tar. And then he heard a woman's voice whispering to him.

'That confounded green-eyed girl of the Pamphilius people had put the kids to bed a long time ago, of course, but it seems couldn't get to sleep herself. She heard eight bells struck, and the chief mate come below to turn in. She waited a bit, then got into her dressing-gown and stole across the empty saloon and up the stairs into the chart-room. She sat down on the settee near the open door to cool herself, I daresay.

'I suppose when she whispered to Wilmot it was as if somebody had struck a match in the fellow's brain. I don't know how it was they had got so very thick. I fancy he had met her ashore a few times before. I couldn't make it out, because, when telling the story, Wilmot would break off to swear something awful at every second word. We had met on the quay in Sydney, and he had an apron of sacking up to his chin, a big whip in his hand. A wagon-driver. Glad to do anything not to starve. That's what he had come down to.

'However, there he was, with his head inside the door, on the girl's shoulder as likely as not – officer of the watch! The helmsman, on giving his evidence afterwards, said that he shouted several times that the binnacle lamp had gone out. It didn't matter to him, because his orders were to "sail her close." "I thought it funny," he said, "that the ship should keep on falling off in squalls, but I luffed her up every time as close as I was able. It was so dark I couldn't see my hand before my face, and the rain came in bucketsful on my head."

'The truth was that at every squall the wind hauled aft a little, till gradually the ship came to be heading straight for the coast, without a single soul in her being aware of it. Wilmot himself confessed that he had not been near the standard compass for an hour. He might well have confessed! The first thing he knew was the man on the look-out shouting blue murder forward there.

'He tore his neck free, he says, and yelled back at him: "What do you say?"

' "I think I hear breakers ahead, sir," howled the man, and came rushing aft with the rest of the watch, in the "awfullest blinding deluge that ever fell from the sky," Wilmot says. For a second or so he was so scared and bewildered that he could not remember on which side of the gulf the ship was. He wasn't a good officer, but he was a seaman all the same. He pulled himself together in a second, and the right orders sprang to his lips without thinking. They were to hard up with the helm and shiver the main and mizzen-topsails.

'It seems that the sails actually fluttered. He couldn't see them, but he heard them rattling and banging above his head. "No use! She was too slow in going off," he went on, his dirty face twitching, and the damn'd carter's whip shaking in his hand. "She seemed to stick fast." And then the flutter of the canvas above his head ceased. At this critical moment the wind hauled aft again with a gust, filling the sails and sending the ship with a great way upon the rocks on her lee bow. She had overreached herself in her last little game. Her time had come – the hour, the man, the black night, the treacherous gust of wind – the right woman to put an end to her. The brute deserved nothing better. Strange are the instruments of Providence. There's a sort of poetical justice –'

The man in tweeds looked hard at me.

'The first ledge she went over stripped the false keel off

her. Rip! The skipper, rushing out of his berth, found a crazy woman, in a red flannel dressing-gown, flying round and round the cuddy, screeching like a cockatoo.

'The next bump knocked her clean under the cabin table. It also started the stern-post and carried away the rudder, and then that brute ran up a shelving, rocky shore, tearing her bottom out, till she stopped short, and the foremast dropped over the bows like a gangway.'

'Anybody lost?' I asked.

'No one, unless that fellow, Wilmot,' answered the gentleman, unknown to Miss Blank, looking round for his cap. 'And his case was worse than drowning for a man. Everybody got ashore all right. Gale didn't come on till next day, dead from the West, and broke up that brute in a surprisingly short time. It was as though she had been rotten at heart.' . . . He changed his tone, 'Rain left off. I must get my bike and rush home to dinner. I live in Herne Bay – came out for a spin this morning.'

He nodded at me in a friendly way, and went out with a swagger.

'Do you know who he is, Jermyn?' I asked.

The North Sea pilot shook his head, dismally. 'Fancy losing a ship in that silly fashion! Oh, dear! oh dear!' he groaned in lugubrious tones, spreading his damp handkerchief again like a curtain before the glowing grate.

On going out I exchanged a glance and a smile (strictly proper) with the respectable Miss Blank, barmaid of the Three Crows.

THE HAUNTED 'JARVEE'

William Hope Hodgson

'Seen anything of Carnacki lately?' I asked Arkright when we met in the City.

'No,' he replied. 'He's probably off on one of his jaunts. We'll be having a card one of these days inviting us to No 472, Cheyne Walk, and then we'll hear all about it. Queer chap that.'

He nodded, and went on his way. It was some months now since we four – Jessop, Arkright, Taylor and myself – had received the usual summons to drop in at No 472 and hear Carnacki's story of his latest case. What talks they were! Stories of all kinds and true in every word, yet full of weird and extraordinary incidents that held one silent and awed until he had finished.

Strangely enough, the following morning brought me a curtly worded card telling me to be at No 472 at seven o'clock promptly. I was the first to arrive, Jessop and Taylor soon followed and just before dinner was announced Arkright came in.

Dinner over, Carnacki as usual passed round his smokes, snuggled himself down luxuriously in his favourite armchair and went straight to the story we knew he had invited us to hear.

'I've been on a trip in one of the real old-time sailing ships,' he said without any preliminary remarks. 'The *Jarvee*, owned by my old friend Captain Thompson. I went on the voyage primarily for my health, but I picked on the old *Jarvee* because Captain Thompson had often told me there was something queer about her. I used to ask him up here whenever he came ashore and try to get him to tell me more about it, you know; but the funny thing was he never could tell me anything definite concerning her queerness. He seemed always to *know* but when it came to putting his knowledge into words it was as if he found that the reality melted out of it. He would end up usually by saying that you saw things and then he would wave his hands vaguely, but further than that he never seemed able to pass on the knowledge of something strange which he had noticed about the ship, except odd outside details.

' "Can't keep men in her no-how," he often told me. "They get frightened and they see things and they feel things. An' I've lost a power o' men out of her. Fallen from aloft, you know. She's getting a bad name." And then he'd shake his head very solemnly.

'Old Thompson was a brick in every way. When I got aboard I found that he had given me the use of a whole empty cabin opening off my own as my laboratory and workshop. He gave the carpenter orders to fit up the empty cabin with shelves and other conveniences according to my directions and in a couple of days I had all the apparatus, both mechanical and electric with which I had conducted my other ghost-hunts, neatly and safely stowed away, for I took a great deal of gear with me as I intended to interest myself by examining thoroughly into the mystery about which the captain was at once so positive and so vague.

'During the first fortnight out I followed my usual methods of making a thorough and exhaustive search. This I did with the most scrupulous care, but found nothing abnormal of any kind in the whole vessel. She was an old wooden ship and I took care to sound and measure every casement and bulkhead, to examine every exit from the holds and to seal all the hatches. These and many other precautions I took, but at the end of the fortnight I had neither seen anything nor found anything.

'The old barque was just, to all seeming, a healthy, average old-timer jogging along comfortably from one port to another. And save for an indefinable sense of what I could now describe as "abnormal peace" about the ship I could find nothing to justify the old captain's solemn and frequent assurances that I would see soon enough for myself. This he would say often as we walked the poop together; afterwards stopping to take a long, expectant, half-fearful look at the immensity of the sea around.

'Then on the eighteenth day something truly happened. I had been pacing the poop as usual with old Thompson when suddenly he stopped and looked up at the mizzen royal which had just begun to flap against the mast. He glanced at the wind-vane near him, then ruffled his hat back and stared at the sea.

' "Wind's droppin', mister. There'll be trouble to-night," he said. "D'you see yon?" And he pointed away to windward.

' "What?" I asked, staring with a curious little thrill that was due to more than curiosity. "Where?"

' "Right off the beam," he said. "Comin' from under the sun."

' "I don't see anything," I explained after a long stare at the wide-spreading silence of the sea that was already glassing into a dead calm surface now that the wind had died.

' "Yon shadow fixin'," said the old man, reaching for his glasses.

'He focussed them and took a long look, then passed them across to me and pointed with his finger. "Just under the sun," he repeated. "Comin' towards us at the rate o' knots." He was curiously calm and matter-of-fact and yet I felt that a certain excitement had him in the throat; so that I took the glasses eagerly and stared according to his directions.

'After a minute I saw it – a vague shadow upon the still surface of the sea that seemed to move towards us as I stared. For a moment I gazed fascinated, yet ready every moment to swear that I saw nothing and in the same instant to be assured that there was truly *something* out there upon the water, apparently coming towards the ship.

' "It's only a shadow, captain," I said at length.

' "Just so, mister," he replied simply. "Have a look over the stern to the norrard." He spoke in the quietest way, as a man speaks who is sure of all his facts and who is facing an experience he has faced before, yet who salts his natural matter-of-factness with a deep and constant excitement.

'At the captain's hint I turned about and directed the glasses to the northward. For a while I searched, sweeping my aided vision to and fro over the greying arc of the sea.

'Then I saw the thing plain in the field of the glass – a vague something, a shadow upon the water and the shadow seemed to be moving towards the ship.

' "That's queer," I muttered with a funny little stirring at the back of my throat.

' "Now to the west'ard, mister," said the captain, still speaking in his peculiar level way.

'I looked to the westward and in a minute I picked up the

thing – a third shadow that seemed to move across the sea as I watched it.

' "My God, captain," I exclaimed, "what does it mean?"

' "That's just what I want to know, mister," said the captain. "I've seen 'em before and thought sometimes I must be going mad. Sometimes they're plain an' sometimes they're scarce to be seen, an' sometimes they're like livin' things, an' sometimes they're like nought at all but silly fancies. D'you wonder I couldn't name 'em proper to you?"

'I did not answer for I was staring now expectantly towards the south along the length of the barque. Afar off on the horizon my glasses picked up something dark and vague upon the surface of the sea, a shadow it seemed which grew plainer.

' "My God!" I muttered again. "This is real. This –" I turned again to the eastward.

' "Comin' in from the four points, ain't they," said Captain Thompson and he blew his whistle.

' "Take them three r'yals off her," he told the mate, "an' tell one of the boys to shove lanterns up on the sherpoles. Get the men down smart before dark," he concluded as the mate moved off to see the orders carried out.

' "I'm sendin' no men aloft to-night," he said to me. "I've lost enough that way."

' "They may be only shadows, captain, after all," I said,

still looking earnestly at that far-off grey vagueness on the eastward sea. "Bit of mist or cloud floating low." Yet though I said this I had no belief that it was so. And as for old Captain Thompson, he never even took the trouble to answer, but reached for his glasses which I passed to him.

' "Gettin' thin an' disappearin' as they come near," he said presently. "I know, I've seen 'em do that oft an' plenty before. They'll be close round the ship soon but you nor me won't see them, nor no one else, but they'll be there. I wish 'twas mornin'. I do that!"

'He had handed the glasses back to me and I had been staring at each of the oncoming shadows in turn. It was as Captain Thompson had said. As they drew nearer they seemed to spread and thin out and presently to become dissipated into the grey of the gloaming so that I could easily have imagined that I watched merely four little portions of grey cloud, expanding naturally into impalpableness and invisibility.

' "Wish I'd took them t'gallants off her while I was about it," remarked the old man presently. "Can't think to send no one off the decks to-night, not unless there's real need." He slipped away from me and peered at the aneroid in the skylight. "Glass steady, anyhow," he muttered as he came away, seeming more satisfied.

'By this time the men had all returned to the decks and

the night was down upon us so that I could watch the queer, dissolving shadows which approached the ship.

'Yet as I walked the poop with old Captain Thompson, you can imagine how I grew to feel. Often I found myself looking over my shoulder with quick, jerky glances; for it seemed to me that in the curtains of gloom that hung just beyond the rails there must be a vague, incredible thing looking inboard.

'I questioned the captain in a thousand ways, but could get little out of him beyond what I knew. It was as if he had no power to convey to another the knowledge which he possessed and I could ask no one else, for every other man in the ship was newly signed on, including the mates, which was in itself a significant fact.

' "You'll see for yourself, mister," was the refrain with which the captain parried my questions, so that it began to seem as if he almost *feared* to put anything he knew into words. Yet once, when I had jerked round with a nervous feeling that something was at my back he said calmly enough: "Naught to fear, mister, whilst you're in the light and on the decks." His attitude was extraordinary in the way in which he *accepted* the situation. He appeared to have no personal fear.

'The night passed quietly until about eleven o'clock when suddenly and without one atom of warning a furious squall burst on the vessel. There was something monstrous and abnormal in the wind; it was as if some power were using the elements to an infernal purpose. Yet the captain met the situation calmly. The helm was put down and the sails shaken while the three t'gallants were lowered. Then the three upper topsails. Yet still the breeze roared over us, almost drowning the thunder which the sails were making in the night.

' "Split 'em to ribbons!" the captain yelled in my ear above the noise of the wind. "Can't help it. I ain't sendin' no men aloft to-night unless she seems like to shake the sticks out of her. That's what bothers me."

'For nearly an hour after that, until eight bells went at midnight, the wind showed no signs of easing, but breezed up harder than ever. And all the while the skipper and I walked the poop, he ever and again peering up anxiously through the darkness at the banging and thrashing sails.

'For my part I could do nothing except stare round and round at the extraordinarily dark night in which the ship seemed to be embedded solidly. The very feel and sound of the wind gave me a sort of constant horror, for there seemed to be an unnaturalness rampant in the atmosphere. But how much this was the effect of my over-strung nerves and excited imagination, I cannot say. Certainly, in all my experiences I had never come across anything just like what I felt and endured through that peculiar squall.

'At eight bells when the other watch came on deck the

captain was forced to send all hands aloft to make the canvas fast, as he had begun to fear that he would actually lose his masts if he delayed longer. This was done and the barque snugged right down.

'Yet, though the work was done successfully, the captain's fears were justified in a sufficiently horrible way, for as the men were beginning to make their way in off the wards there was a loud crying and shouting aloft and immediately afterwards a crash down on the main deck, followed instantly by a second crash.

' "My God! Two of 'em!" shouted the skipper as he snatched a lamp from the forrard binnacle. Then down on to the main deck. It was as he had said. Two of the men had fallen, or – as the thought came to me – been thrown from aloft and were lying silent on the deck. Above us in the darkness I heard a few vague shouts followed by a curious quiet, save for the constant blast of the wind whose whistling and howling in the rigging seemed but to accentuate the complete and frightened silence of the men aloft. Then I was aware that the men were coming down swiftly and presently one after the other came with a quick leap out of the rigging and stood about the two fallen men with odd exclamations and questions which always merged off instantly into new silence.

'And all the time I was conscious of a most extraordinary

sense of oppression and frightened distress and fearful expectation, for it seemed to me, standing there near the dead in that unnatural wind that a power of evil filled all the night about the ship and that some fresh horror was imminent.

'The following morning there was a solemn little service, very rough and crude, but undertaken with a nice reverence and the two men who had fallen were tilted off from a hatch-cover and plunged suddenly out of sight. As I watched them vanish in the deep blue of the water an idea came to me and I spent part of the afternoon talking it over with the captain, after which I passed the rest of the time until sunset was upon us in arranging and fitting up a part of my electrical apparatus. Then I went on deck and had a good look round. The evening was beautifully calm and ideal for the experiment which I had in mind, for the wind had died away with a peculiar suddenness after the death of the two men and all that day the sea had been like glass.

'To a certain extent I believed that I comprehended the primary cause of the vague but peculiar manifestations which I had witnessed the previous evening and which Captain Thompson believed implicitly to be intimately connected with the death of the two sailormen.

'I believed the origin of the happenings to lie in a strange but perfectly understandable cause, *i.e.*, in that phenomenon known technically as "attractive-vibrations." Harzam, in his monograph on "Induced Hauntings," points out that such are invariably produced by "induced vibrations," that is, by temporary vibrations set up by some outside cause.

'This is somewhat abstruse to follow out in a story of this kind, but it was on a long consideration of these points that I had resolved to make experiments to see whether I could not produce a counter or "repellent" vibration, a thing which Harzam had succeeded in producing on three occasions, and in which I have had a partial success once, failing only because of the imperfectness of the apparatus I had aboard.

'As I have said, I can scarcely follow the reasoning further in a brief record such as this, neither do I think it would be of interest to you who are interested only in the startling and weird side of my investigations. Yet I have told you sufficient to show you the germ of my reasonings and to enable you to follow intelligently my hopes and expectations in sending out what I hoped would prove "repellent" vibrations.

'Therefore it was that when the sun had descended to within ten degrees of the visible horizon the captain and I began to watch for the appearance of the shadows. Presently, under the sun, I discovered the same peculiar appearance of a moving greyness which I had seen on the preceding night and almost immediately Captain Thompson told me that he saw the same to the south.

'To the north and east we perceived the same extraordinary thing and I at once set my electric apparatus at work, sending out the strange repelling force to the dim, far shadows of mystery which moved steadily out of the distance towards the vessel.

'Earlier in the evening the captain had snugged the barque right down to her topsails, for as he said, until the calm went he would risk nothing. According to him it was always during calm weather that the extraordinary manifestations occurred. In this case he was certainly justified, for a most tremendous squall struck the ship in the middle watch, taking the fore upper topsail right out of the ropes.

'At the time when it came I was lying down on a locker in the saloon, but I ran up on to the poop as the vessel canted under the enormous force of the wind. Here I found the air pressure tremendous and the noise of the squall stunning. And over it all and through it all I was conscious of something abnormal and threatening that set my nerves uncomfortably acute. The thing was not natural.

'Yet, despite the carrying away of the topsail, not a man was sent aloft.

' "Let 'em all go!" said old Captain Thompson. "I'd have shortened her down to the bare sticks if I'd done all I wanted!"

'About two a.m. the squall passed with astonishing

suddenness and the night showed clear above the vessel. From then onward I paced the poop with the skipper, often pausing at the break to look along the lighted main deck. It was on one of these occasions that I saw something peculiar. It was like a vague flitting of an impossible shadow between me and the whiteness of the well-scrubbed decks. Yet, even as I stared, the thing was gone and I could not say with surety that I had seen anything.

' "Pretty plain to see, mister," said the captain's voice at my elbow. "I've only seen that once before an' we lost half of the hands that trip. We'd better be at 'ome, I'm thinkin'. It'll end in scrappin' her, sure."

'The old man's calmness bewildered me almost as much as the confirmation his remark gave that I had really seen something abnormal floating between me and the deck eight feet below us.

' "Good lord, Captain Thompson," I exclaimed, 'this is simply infernal!'

' "Just that," he agreed. "I said, mister, you'd see if you'd wait. And this ain't the half. You wait till you sees 'em looking like little black clouds all over the sea round the ship and movin' steady with the ship. All the same, I ain't seen 'em aboard but the once. Guess we're in for it."

' "How do you mean?" I asked. But though I questioned him in every way I could get nothing satisfactory out of him.

' "You'll see, mister. You wait an' see. She's a queer un." And that was about the extent of his further efforts and methods of enlightening me.

'From then on through the rest of the watch I leaned over the break of the poop, staring down at the maindeck and odd whiles taking quick glances to the rear. The skipper had resumed his steady pacing of the poop, but now and again he would come to a pause beside me and ask calmly enough whether I had seen any more of "them there."

'Several times I saw the vagueness of something drifting in the lights of the lanterns and a sort of wavering in the air in this place and that, as if it might be an attenuated something having movement, that was half-seen for a moment and then gone before my brain could record anything definite.

'Towards the end of the watch, however, both the captain and I saw something very extraordinary. He had just come beside me and was leaning over the rail across the break. "Another of 'em there," he remarked in his calm way, giving me a gentle nudge and nodding his head towards the port side of the maindeck, a yard or two to our left.

'In the place he had indicated there was a faint, dull shadowy spot seeming suspended about a foot above the deck. This grew more visible and there was movement in it and a constant, oily-seeming whirling from the centre outwards.

The thing expanded to several feet across, with the lighted planks of the deck showing vaguely through. The movement from the centre outwards was now becoming very distinct, till the whole strange shape blackened and grew more dense, so that the deck below was hidden.

'Then as I stared with the most intense interest there went a thinning movement over the thing and almost directly it had dissolved so that there was nothing more to be seen than a vague rounded shape of shadow, hovering and convoluting dimly between us and the deck below. This gradually thinned out and vanished and we were both of us left staring down at a piece of the decks where the planking and pitched seams showed plain and distinct in the light from the lamps that were now hung nightly on the sherpoles.

' "Mighty queer that, mister," said the captain meditatively as he fumbled for his pipe. "Mighty queer." Then he lit his pipe and began again his pacing of the poop.

'The calm lasted for a week with the sea like glass and every night without warning there was a repetition of the extraordinary squall, so that the captain had everything made fast at dusk and waited patiently for a trade wind.

'Each evening I experimented further with my attempts to set up "repellent" vibrations, but without result. I am not sure whether I ought to say that my meddling produced *no* result; for the calm gradually assumed a more unnatural permanent aspect whilst the sea looked more than ever like a plain of glass, bulged anon with the low oily roll of some deep swell. For the rest, there was by day a silence so profound as to give a sense of unrealness, for never a sea-bird hove in sight whilst the movement of the vessel was so slight as scarce to keep up the constant creak, of spars and gear, which is the ordinary accompaniment of a calm.

'The sea, appeared to have become an emblem of desolation and freeness, so that it seemed to me at last there there was no more any known world, but just one great ocean going on for ever into the far distances in every direction. At night the strange squalls assumed a far greater violence so that sometimes it seemed as if the very spars would be ripped and twisted out of the vessel, yet fortunately no harm came in that wise.

'As the days passed I became convinced at last that my experiments were producing very distinct results, though the opposite to those which I hoped to produce, for now at each sunset a sort of grey cloud resembling light smoke would appear far away in every quarter almost immediately upon the commencement of the vibrations, with the effect that I desisted from any prolonged attempt and became more tentative in my experiments.

'At last, however, when we had endured this condition of affairs for a week, I had a long talk with old Captain Thompson and he agreed to let me carry out a bold experiment to its conclusion. It was to keep the vibrations going steadily at full power from a little before sunset until the dawn and to take careful notes of the results.

'With this in view, all was made ready. The royal and t'gallant yards were sent down, all the sails stowed and everything about the decks made fast. A sea anchor was rigged out over the bows and a long line of cable veered away. This was to ensure the vessel coming head to wind should one of those strange squalls strike us from any quarter during the night.

'Late in the afternoon the men were sent into the fo'c'sle and told that they might please themselves and turn in or do anything they liked, but that they were not to come on deck during the night whatever happened. To ensure this the port and starboard doors were padlocked. Afterwards I made the first and the eighth signs of the Saaamaaa Ritual opposite each door-post, connecting them with triple lines crossed at every seventh inch. You've dipped deeper into the science of magic than I have, Arkright, and you will know what that means. Following this I ran a wire entirely around the outside of the fo'c'sle and connected it up with my machinery, which I had erected in the sail-locker aft.

' "In any case," I explained to the captain, "they run practically no risk other than the general risk which we may expect in the form of a terrific storm-burst. The real danger will be to those who are 'meddling.' The 'path of the vibrations' will make a kind of 'halo' round the apparatus. I shall have to be there to control and I'm willing to risk it, but you'd better get into your cabin and the three mates must do the same."

'This the old captain refused to do and the three mates begged to be allowed to stay and "see the fun." I warned them very seriously that there might be a very disagreeable and unavoidable danger, but they agreed to risk it and I can tell you I was not sorry to have their companionship.

'I set to work then, making them help where I needed help, and so presently I had all my gear in order. Then I led my wires up through the skylight from the cabin and set the vibrator dial and trembler-box level, screwing them solidly down to the poop-deck, in the clear space that lay between the foreside of the skylight and the lid of the sail locker.

'I got the three mates and the captain to take their places close together and I warned them not to move whatever happened. I set to work then, alone, and chalked a temporary pentacle about the whole lot of us, including the apparatus. Afterwards I made haste to get the tubes of my electric pentacle fitted all about us, for it was getting on to dusk. As soon as this was done I switched on the current into the vacuum tubes and immediately the pale sickly glare shone dull all about us, seeming cold and unreal in the last light of the evening.

'Immediately afterwards I set the vibrations beating out into all space and then I took my seat beside the control board. Here I had a few words with the others, warning them again whatever they might hear or see not to leave the pentacle, as they valued their lives. They nodded to this and I knew that they were fully impressed with the possibility of the unknown danger that we were meddling with.

'Then we settled down to watch. We were all in our oilskins, for I expected the experiment to include some very peculiar behaviour on the part of the elements and so we were ready to face the night. One other thing I was careful to do and that was to confiscate all matches so that no one should forgetfully light his pipe, for the light rays are "paths" to certain of the Forces.

'With a pair of marine glasses I was staring round at the horizon. All around, but miles away in the greying of the evening, there seemed to be a strange, vague darkening of the surface of the sea. This became more distinct and it seemed to me presently that it might be a slight, slow-lying mist far away about the ship. I watched it very intently and the captain and the three mates were doing likewise through their glasses.

' "Coming in on us at the rate o' knots, mister," said the

old man in a low voice. "This is what I call playin' with 'ell. I only hope it'll all come right." That was all he said and afterwards there was absolute silence from him and the others through the strange hours that followed.

'As the night stole down upon the sea we lost sight of the peculiar incoming circle of mist and there was a period of the most intense and oppressive silence to the five of us, sitting there watchful and quiet within the pale glow of the electric pentacle.

'A while later there came a sort of strange, noiseless lightning. By noiseless I mean that while the flashes appeared to be near at hand and lit up all the vague sea around, yet there was no thunder; neither, so it appeared to me, did there seem to be any *reality* in the flashes. This is a queer thing to say but it describes my impressions. It was as if I saw a representation of lightning rather than the physical electricity itself. No, of course, I am not pretending to use the word in its technical sense.

'Abruptly a strange quivering went through the vessel from end to end and died away. I looked fore and aft and then glanced at the four men who stared back at me with a sort of dumb and half-frightened wonder, but no one said anything. About five minutes passed with no sound anywhere except the faint buzz of the apparatus and nothing visible anywhere except the noiseless lightning which came down, flash after flash, lighting the sea all around the vessel.

'Then a most extraordinary thing happened. The peculiar quivering passed again through the ship and died away. It was followed immediately by a kind of undulation of the vessel, first fore and aft and then from side to side. I can give you no better illustration of the strangeness of the movement on that glass-like sea than to say that it was just such a movement as might have been given her had an invisible giant hand lifted her and toyed with her, canting her this way and that with a certain curious and rather sickening rhythm of movement. This appeared to last about two minutes, so far as I can guess, and ended with the ship being shaken up and down several times, after which there came again the quivering and then quietness.

'A full hour must have passed during which I observed nothing except that twice the vessel was faintly shaken and the second time this was followed by a slight repetition of the curious undulations. This, however, lasted but a few seconds and afterwards there was only the abnormal and oppressive silence of the night, punctured time after time by these noiseless flashes of lightning. All the time I did my best to study the appearance of the sea and atmosphere around the ship.

'One thing was apparent, that the surrounding wall of vagueness had drawn in more upon the ship, so that the brightest flashes now showed me no more than about a clear quarter of a mile of ocean around us, after which the sight was just lost in trying to penetrate a kind of shadowy distance that yet had no depth in it, but which still lacked any power to arrest the vision at any particular point so that one could not know definitely whether there was anything there or not, but only that one's sight was limited by some phenomenon which hid all the distant sea. Do I make this clear?

'The strange, noiseless lightning increased in vividness and the flashes began to come more frequently. This went on till they were almost continuous, so that all the near sea could be watched with scarce an intermission. Yet the brightness of the flashes seemed to have no power to dull the pale light of the curious detached glows that circled in silent multitudes about us.

'About this time I became aware of a strange sense of breathlessness. Each breath seemed to be drawn with a difficulty and presently with a sense of positive distress. The three mates and the captain were breathing with curious little gasps and the faint buzz of the vibrator seemed to come from a great distance away. For the rest there was such a silence as made itself known like a dull, numbing ache upon the brain.

'The minutes passed slowly and then, abruptly I saw

something new. There were grey things floating in the air about the ship which were so vague and attenuated that at first I could not be sure that I saw anything, but in a while there could be no doubt that they were there.

'They began to show plainer in the constant glare of the quiet lightning and growing darker and darker they increased visibly in size. They appeared to be but a few feet above the level of the sea and they began to assume humped shapes.

'For quite half an hour, which seemed infinitely longer, I watched those strange humps like little hills of blackness floating just above the surface of the water and moving round and round the vessel with a slow, everlasting circling that produced on my eyes the feeling that it was all a dream.

'It was later still that I discovered still another thing. Each of those great vague mounds had begun to oscillate as it circled round about us. I was conscious at the same time that there was communicated to the vessel the beginning of a similar oscillating movement, so very slight at first that I could scarcely be sure she so much as moved.

'The movement of the ship grew with a steady oscillation, the bows lifting first and then the stern, as if she were pivoted amidships. This ceased and she settled down on to a level keel with a series of queer jerks as if her weight were being slowly lowered again to the buoying of the water.

'Suddenly there came a cessation of the extraordinary

lightning and we were in an absolute blackness with only the pale sickly glow of the electric pentacle above us and the faint buzz of the apparatus seeming far away in the night. Can you picture it all? The five of us there, tense and watchful and wondering what was going to happen.

'The thing began gently – a little jerk upward of the starboard side of the vessel, then a second jerk, then a third and the whole ship was canted distinctly to port. It continued in a kind of slow rhythmic tilting with curious time pauses between the jerks and suddenly, you know, I saw that we were in absolute danger, for the vessel was being capsized by some enormous Force in the utter silence and blackness of that night.

' "My God, mister, stop it!" came the captain's voice, quick and very hoarse. "She'll be gone in a moment! She'll be gone!"

'He had got on to his knees and was staring round and gripping at the deck. The three mates were also gripping at the deck with their palms to stop them from sliding down the violent slope. In that moment came a final tilting of the side of the vessel and the deck rose up almost like a wall. I snatched at the lever of the vibrator and switched it over.

'Instantly the angle of the deck decreased as the vessel righted several feet with a jerk. The righting movement continued with little rhythmic jerks until the ship was once more on an even keel.

'And even as she righted I was aware of an alteration in the tenseness of the atmosphere and a great noise far off to starboard. It was the roaring of wind. A huge flash of lightning was followed by others and the thunder crashed continually overhead. The noise of the wind to starboard rose to a loud screaming and drove towards us through the night. Then the lightning ceased and the deep roll of the thunder was lost in the nearer sound of the wind which was now within a mile of us and making a most hideous, bellowing scream. The shrill howling came at us out of the dark and covered every other sound. It was as if all the night on that side were a vast cliff, sending down high and monstrous echoes upon us. This is a queer thing to say, I know, but it may help you to get the feeling of the thing; for that just describes exactly how it felt to me at the time – that queer, echoing, empty sense above us in the night, yet all the emptiness filled with sound on high. Do you get it? It was most extraordinary and there was a grand something about it all as if one had come suddenly upon the steeps of some monstrous lost world.

'Then the wind rushed out at us and stunned us with its sound and force and fury. We were smothered and half-stunned. The vessel went over on to her port side merely from pressure of the wind on her naked spars and side. The whole night seemed one yell and the foam roared and snowed over us in countless tons. I have never known anything like it. We were all splayed about the poop, holding on to anything we could, while the pentacle was smashed to atoms so that we were in complete darkness. The storm-burst had come down on us.

'Towards morning the storm calmed and by evening we were running before a fine breeze; yet the pumps had to be kept going steadily for we had sprung a pretty bad leak, which proved so serious that we had to take to the boats two days later. However, we were picked up that night so that we had only a short time of it. As for the *Jarvee*, she is now safely at the bottom of the Atlantic, where she had better remain for ever.'

Carnacki came to an end and tapped out his pipe.

'But you haven't explained,' I remonstrated. 'What made her like that? What made her different from other ships? Why did those shadows and things come to her? What's your idea?'

'Well,' replied Carnacki, 'in my opinion she was a *focus*. That is a technical term which I can best explain by saying that she possessed the "attractive vibration" – that is the power to draw to her any psychic waves in the vicinity, much in the way of a medium. The way in which the "vibration" is acquired – to use a technical term again – is, of course, purely a matter for supposition. She may have developed it during the years, owing to a suitability of conditions or it may have been in her ("of her" is a better term) from the very day her keel was laid. I mean the direction in which she lay, the condition of the atmosphere, the state of the "electric tensions," the very blows of the hammers and the accidental combining of materials suited to such an end – all might tend to such a thing. And this is only to speak of the *known*. The vast *unknown* it is vain to speculate upon in a brief chatter like this.

'I would like to remind you here of that idea of mine that certain forms of so-called "hauntings" may have their cause in the "attractive vibrations." A building or a ship – just as I have indicated – may develop "vibrations," even as certain materials in combination under the proper conditions will certainly develop an electric current.

'To say more in a talk of this scope is useless. I am more inclined to remind you of the glass which will vibrate to a certain note struck upon a piano and to silence all your worrying questions with that simple little unanswered one: What *is* electricity? When we've got that clear it will be time to take the next step in a more dogmatic fashion. We are but speculating on the coasts of a strange country of mystery. In this case, I think the next best step for you all will be home and bed.'

And with this terse ending, in the most genial way possible,

Carnacki ushered us out presently on to the quiet chill of the Embankment, replying heartily to our various good-nights.

THE CREW OF THE 'FLYING DUTCHMAN'

Henry A. Hering

I

On a bright summer day in the year of grace sixteen hundred and sixty-two the Reverend Richard Waddilove, A.M., Vicar of Bridlington Keye, was enjoying his mid-day meal, when his serving-girl brought him word that Reuben Oram wished to speak with him.

'Bid him come in, Letty,' said the worthy clergyman, who was busily engaged with the breast of a chicken, provided by some thoughtful parishioner.

'Your pardon, Parson,' said the new-comer, hesitating on the threshold.

'Come in, Reuben, come in. The clergy need to eat and drink as well as the laity – and I for one don't attempt to disguise it.'

The Vicar's heavy paunch and rubicund nose bore evidence to the truth of his assertion.

'Take a seat, Reuben,' the clergyman went on. 'They tell me you have been across to the Low Countries. How did you find the Hollanders? Are they rearing a second Van Tromp to sweep us off the seas?'

As there was no answer, the Vicar put down the tankard he was raising to his lips and looked at his visitor. Only then did he note his troubled appearance. In the past Oram had been as cheery and hearty in his manner as his fellows, but now he sat with care and anxiety written on every feature, and nervousness in every movement.

'What ails you, Reuben?' asked the Vicar kindly. 'Are you in trouble?'

But the sailor sat there twirling his cap and shuffling his feet. His lips moved, but no words came.

'Tut, tut, man. Tell me all about it. Is the wife ill, or the bairns?'

'No, your worship. Would to God it were no worse than that.'

'I am not married myself, Reuben Oram,' said the clergyman gravely, 'but your words sound somewhat unkindly.'

'Parson,' cried Oram, springing to his feet and walking to and fro like a caged animal – 'Parson, I don't know what I am saying. I don't know what I am doing. All I know is that I am damned – damned till the day of Judgment, and after maybe.'

Parson Waddilove rose in his turn to his feet. He put his

hands on the shoulders of the other and looked quietly into his face. There was a great pity in his little ferret eyes.

'Sit down, Reuben. Damned most of us deserve to be, but God is merciful unto all men. Your sin must be great indeed if He cannot pardon you. What have you done?'

'Nothing that could deserve punishment such as mine. Parson, is there no hope for me?'

'Surely, lad, there is hope for the worst of us. But tell me what troubles you, and it may be that I can ease your mind.'

'Would that were possible, sir! But listen, and you may judge.'

'One minute, lad. October ale hath many uses. At a pinch it is of service as a poultice; but when a man has a tale to tell its value increases ten-fold. Drink, man,' and Parson Waddilove reached him the tankard he himself had intended to drain.

Oram took a long pull, and then with firmer voice began:

'It all happened long ago, Parson – fifteen years ago at least – five before I settled here. It was my last long voyage. Vanderdecken was owner and skipper. Wind and weather were with us. We had a quick run out to the eastern seas, and for once in a way the captain seemed passably well pleased with things. The cargo was bartered to some advantage, and we were returning with a rich store of elephants' teeth, camphor, gum, and wax; and it was said the heavy cases in the supercargo's cabin held gold. But from the day we left Java, homeward bound, everything went wrong, and the skipper's temper tallied with our luck. For whole weeks we lay becalmed, and when the wind did come it either came in squalls or blew from the wrong quarter. We held on as best we could till Madagascar was sighted, and then we ran into a couple of pirates, who shot our masts down and bored holes in us from bow to stern. We careened at Table Bay, and put to sea once more with a ship and a skipper the worse for wear. Next day we lay becalmed off the coast, and three greasy Hottentot heathens put off in a dug-out to barter some skins with us. They were down below when the breeze freshened, and out of pure devilment the skipper plied them with drink, and carried them and their craft to sea with us. When they came to, they found themselves in irons. They nearly went mad; and that night one of them managed to get free, and was found trying to lower their cockle-shell. The captain was on deck at the time or no one would have stopped him. As it was, the whole three of them, bound hand and foot, were put in the boat and dropped astern. Then Vanderdecken went aft and fired at them with his carbine and pistols. Each time he shot he hit a helpless victim; and he fired five times before that boat with its cargo of horrors drifted away into the darkness.'

Parson Waddilove gave a gasp of horror.

'And you called yourselves men and allowed this infamy to happen!'

'A skipper does as he likes on his own ship, sir,' said Oram doggedly. 'Brands did tell him what the rest of us only dared think, and the next day he was keel-hauled for mutiny. We all gave the captain a wide berth, but few of us escaped his heavy hand, and never a week passed without one or another of us feeling the irons or the cat. Off the Azores we sprung a leak. The cargo – even the coffers of gold – had to go overboard, and then the pumps only just managed to keep the ship afloat. It was with a mutinous crew, a rotten ship, and the temper of the devil that Vanderdecken entered the port of Amsterdam, and when we were safely moored off the Waser Keye there was not one of us but swore he would see the skipper down with Davy Jones before he would sail with him again.'

'I should think so indeed,' cried the Parson. 'Wild beasts were the fit companions of such a monster.'

'And yet, sir, when he was ready for his next voyage six of us went back on our oath. He had always had an evil reputation, and the report of his last devilries had increased it, and he couldn't make up a crew without us. He offered us, his old hands, double wage and money down before we sailed, and for the sake of the gold we took our kits into his fo'c's'le – Heckhausen, Bergh, Jansen, Krantz, Hans Biebrich and myself. We soon found out our mistake. As the skipper had paid us double wages he thought he had the right to treat us doubly ill, and nothing we did found favour with him. He came across Heckhausen staggering forrard to his bunk after a dirty night's watch in the Channel, and told him he was drunk. Heckhausen gave him the lie, and had his head broken in with Vanderdecken's speaking-trumpet. He made me, master-gunner though I was, clean every blessed weapon on board as they never had been cleaned before. The nine-pounders, the cohorns and patteraroes, every popgun on board was overhauled as if we were going to tackle the whole Spanish fleet, and the skipper stood over me blasting me for a lazy land-lubber the while. Jansen had too much schnapps one day – there was no doubt about that – but he got three dozen with the cat for it. Sooner than finish the voyage with that hell-hound – begging your worship's pardon – the six of us deserted when the ship ran into Lisbon river, and Vanderdecken sailed without us.

'Your worship knows the story of that last voyage of his – how the ship was beaten back again and again; how the captain heaved the pilot overboard in a fit of blind passion; how in his blasphemy he swore by the sacred cross that he would double the Cape, though he had to sail till the last day to do it; how God doomed him to fulfil his vow; and how, as a spectre ship, the vessel is still seen carrying out the decree of the Almighty, while the vessel that sees her battling against the adverse winds and weather with which she is eternally surrounded is herself doomed to destruction.'

The clergyman nodded.

'Yes, I have heard the story of the *Flying Dutchman*.'

'Then perhaps your worship can tell me why God should punish an innocent crew for the skipper's faults? He damned them both equally, and to a plain sailor like myself it doesn't seem right.'

'It is simply a sailor's yarn, Reuben. The whole story is a mere legend – a myth.'

'There, by your leave, sir, you are wrong. But we'll come back to that. Well, we didn't hang together long when we deserted, and after some years of wandering up and down, I came over here, herring-fishing with Hans Biebrich, when I chanced to meet my Sally, as bonny a lass as I had ever clapped eyes on. We agreed to hitch up together, and as you know, Parson, I married and setded here, and have lived an honest life, at peace with my neighbours, and I hope with God.'

'Yes, Reuben,' said the clergyman, 'I know nothing to your detriment, and I have even pointed you out as a model for others to imitate.'

'God forbid, sir, any man should wish to live my life. Well, Parson, so I lived, happy and contented, until a month or so ago, when I took the opportunity of running over to Amsterdam with a fleet of returning schuyts, to see how it fared with old shipmates there. I found Hans, but he was in great distress. He was expecting a letter.'

'Who from?'

'From the skipper – Vanderdecken.'

'But according to you, Vanderdecken exists no longer in the flesh.'

'That is so, sir, and that is why the letter troubled Hans. It was a summons he expected, and it would have to be obeyed.'

'But why? Spirits cannot compel attendance, can they?' said the Parson lightly.

Oram shook his head.

'There were four deserters besides Hans and myself, and he told me that Heckhausen, Bergh, Jansen, and Krantz had each received the summons in their turn, and had died mysteriously soon afterwards. Biebrich was expecting his summons when I left him.'

'Tut, tut, man,' said the other. 'He and his mates were no doubt overwrought by the thought of Vanderdecken and his supposed fate. If the others have met with sudden and even mysterious deaths it is a coincidence only, and in no way to be connected with your captain.'

'There was the summons, sir – a written summons to each man.'

Parson Waddilove laughed.

'Reuben Oram, I gave you credit for more sense. It's astonishing what you sailors will believe. Just look the facts calmly in the face and see what grounds you have for crediting this devilish story. After you deserted, Vanderdecken proceeded on his course, and the ship was probably lost off the Cape. The captain would have to answer the Almighty in another world for his wicked deeds. What evidence have you that his vessel was ever seen as a spectre ship? You as a sailor know of what are called mirages – optical delusions whereby objects at a far distance are sometimes apparent near at hand. What is there to prevent the appearance in the southern seas of a mirage of some vessel – not unlike Vanderdecken's – surrounded by stormy seas, and maybe buffeted by adverse winds? Having heard of the legend of the spectre ship, the crew at once conclude they have indeed seen that vessel, and should ill-fortune meet them afterwards, they readily ascribe their troubles to it. Come, Reuben, you must admit that this is reasonable. The Romanists are ready and even wishful to believe in these tales of marvel. Cannot we of the true Church teach them a lesson, and refuse to accept their childish legends?'

'But what of the written summons, sir?'

'What of it, indeed? Your mates were, like yourself, much influenced by their connection with Vanderdecken and on the look out for further supernatural events. Any ill-natured wag might play on their feelings, and if someone chose to perpetrate this sorry joke, they would readily believe it to be a letter from the ill-fated captain himself. Much brooding over it might well hasten their end, as it may do yours. Why even now you told me that Biebrich was expecting the summons when you left. That proves my words. He doesn't even wait for its coming. He anticipates it. Small wonder if some wag should take advantage of his weakness – no doubt well known.'

Oram listened attentively to the clergyman as he spoke.

'I wish I could believe it so, sir,' he said, 'for what you say sounds indeed reasonable enough; but I cannot, I cannot. Parson, I am in earnest. Am I a man likely to be frightened by some old woman's tale? There is in my heart that which tells me it is all true, and that my summons will come in its turn, maybe before Hans gets his. Only one thing can I do that may avert it. I spent every guilder of Vanderdecken's gold before I knew of the curse that might attach of it, and as I received it for services I did not render, I ought not to have touched it. But I can make restitution. See, sir, here is the amount in full – something over maybe. It was put by for the wife in case anything should happen to me, but if it saves her husband's soul she would not think it misspent. Take it, sir. Give it to the service of God, and I may yet be saved.'

The Parson looked longingly at the glittering heap of silver and gold. The church bell, long cracked, was now broken and useless; the pulpit was shaky in its foundations; the church roof leaked; windows were broken beyond patching, and the poor were ever at his doors. Yet he dared not, without authority, take the money for these purposes.

'I will refer the matter to his Grace the Archbishop,' said he with a sigh, for he much feared the needs of the diocese would prove greater than those of the parish; 'but you may rely upon it, Reuben, that the money will indeed be devoted to the service of God, and if this is the only link that binds you to a spectre captain, you need fear no molestation from him.'

Oram seemed greatly relieved, and the clergyman did his best to deepen the impression he had made.

'Now, Reuben,' said he, 'bury your past. Lose yourself in gratitude to God that you are well and strong, blessed with a good wife and bonny children. Work for them and think of them, and banish for ever all thoughts of spectre ships and spectre captains, and all will yet go well with you.'

Oram took the clergyman's proffered hand respectfully,

thanked him for his consolation, and returned home with a lighter heart than he had known for many a long day.

'A strange tale,' Parson Waddilove muttered as he gathered the coins and deposited them in an old teapot on his top shelf. 'A strange tale indeed. I like it not. Such things have been.'

II

Some two months after the above, Reuben Oram returned home one evening after a hard day's toil. Fish had been plentiful of late; rarely he cast anchor but his coble was filled to the thwarts with codling, whiting, or other spoil, and he now knew that, despite his donation to the Vicar, he had laid by enough to see him through the winter months. An enterprising tradesman had recently set up a shop in the village, and Oram had had one or two long consultations with him. To-day he stepped inside again, and when he left the shop his pockets bulged out suspiciously.

The children met him at the gate of his few yards of garden, for they had been on the watch for him, and his wife greeted him on the doorstep. No sooner inside than, with great importance, Reuben produced a little packet.

'Lass, this is for you,' he said to his wife. 'It's no great thing, but I have thought for a long time past you sadly needed something like it.'

Mistress Oram gave her man a hearty kiss before she opened it.

'It's downright good of you, Reuben, to have thought of me. Well, I do declare – a brooch that looks like real gold, and glass the image of diamonds! I shall look grand in it, Reuben, on Sundays. And won't Mary Proctor envy me! Here's another kiss, lad.'

The children gathered round the trinket, and eyed it with awe. The glass flashed bravely in the light, and the metal shone with fine determination to ape its betters.

'And now, lassie, what's in this parcel, I wonder?' said Oram, producing a larger and bulkier package.

The little mite seized it eagerly, and with hands trembling with excitement untied the string and unwrapped the paper.

'A baby! a baby, mother! Isn't she a beauty – and look at her hair – and hasn't she rosy cheeks!' and the child took the doll in her arms and crooned over it with delight.

'I wonder if there's anything for Tom,' said the father when he had taken his fill of his bairn's joy; 'I wonder now,' and he dived into various pockets with a fine pretence of search.

The lad was all agog with excitement, and when the parcel at length came to light and the paper was unwrapped and a glorious cockle boat, painted in brilliant hues, was disclosed to view, he gave vent to his unbounded satisfaction.

'And now, lad,' said Mistress Oram, beaming with importance, 'presents all round to-day. I've got something for you. Not that I bought it, but it came, and I've the giving of it. See here,' and she produced something from under the table-cloth. 'A letter,' she said, 'from Lunnon.'

Letters were few and far between in those days, and this was the first which had ever reached this humble household.

'A letter – for me?' said Oram in a strange, harsh voice.

'Yes, it's been waiting at York this week past. Cockles the carrier brought it to-day, and there's a whole shilling to pay on it.'

Oram did not hear her. The blood had gone from his face, and his hands trembled as he clutched it.

'Why, what ails you, lad?' cried the woman.

'It's nothing – nothing – I'm only tired,' said Reuben, as he gazed mechanically at his wife's present; 'I think I'll take a turn outside. Bide indoors, Sally, till I comeback.'

His wife gazed at him with anxious wonder as he left the house. She watched him to the corner of the road and then turned from the window. The brooch was on the table, but the mock diamond seemed to have lost its lustre and the would-be gold looked tarnished; but the children were happy with their toys.

Parson Waddilove was preparing his sermon when he was disturbed, and he left his manuscript with a sigh.

'What is it, Reuben?' he said.

'Parson,' he cried with a world of agony in his voice. 'Parson, it's come – the summons. Here it is.'

The clergyman took the letter and read the superscription:

TO REUBEN ORAM
mariner,
at the Bridlington Keye,
hard by York,
England.

'Well, what is this? An unopened letter. From some old shipmate, doubtless. The summons? Pshaw! Reuben, I'm ashamed of you and your old dames' fears.'

'For God's sake read it, Parson. You'll see who's right then,' and, with nails clenched into the palms of his hands and teeth biting his lips till the blood came, he stood over the clergyman as he broke the wafers and unfolded the letter.

One glance sufficed, and the Vicar sat bolt upright in his chair with a startled look.

Oram turned round and faced the window. Even at that terrible moment he did not care that Parson Waddilove should see his face.

'Read it, sir,' he said firmly, after a moment's silence.
The Parson read:

TO REUBEN ORAM.

The Captain is short handed and summons deserters; so make ready. Heckhausen, Bergh, Jansen, Kranz and Biebrich are on board. You will join the first day of December.

VANDERDECKEN

There was a long pause.

'Do you believe me now, sir?' said Oram with a bitter smile, turning round at length.

'Lad,' said the clergyman gravely, 'the letter – summons, as you call it – is here undoubtedly; but I am still of the mind it is some scurvy trick played upon you as upon the others.'

'Summons or trick, they all died soon afterwards,' said Oram doggedly.

'Then make up your mind to live, Reuben. If you determine you are going to die on the day named – December first – then die you may, but if you trust in God and defy the power of the evil one to reach you, then you will live.'

'That cursed gold,' muttered Oram.

'No longer cursed, Reuben. Only to-day I received a letter

from our good Archbishop. He hath been pleased to allow your money to go to the purchasing of our new church bell. December first is yet a month ahead. I will journey this week to York and arrange for the bell to be delivered and fixed by then; and that shall be the date of its consecration. As it rings out its sacred notes you shall know that the money has lost its curse by being devoted to the service of the Almighty, and that by its agency, for generations yet to come, shall souls be saved from eternal punishment, and not lost.'

For the moment the Parson's words brought a ray of hope to Oram's heart; but at each step nearer home his spirits sank. The bell might ring – but the summons had come.

III

The days passed, and the summons was never out of Oram's mind. He brooded over it by day and dreamed of it at night. He lost flesh and became a mass of nerves. His wife was much alarmed at his altered condition, but Oram, though he gave her many reasons for it, withheld the true cause. She divined it had some connection with the letter, but the very mention of it distressed her husband so much that she dared not refer to it again. She did her best to cheer and comfort him, but she was hurt he should wish to hide anything from her. His neighbours and mates were quick to note the change in his manner and appearance, and many were the explanations offered. Of course it was known he had received a letter, and soon the rumour spread that it was from a former wife, who threatened an immediate descent on his present household. Oram vouchsafed no information: he rarely spoke to anyone now. He grew surly and neglected his work. And so the month wore on.

It was the last day of November. The whole day Oram had wandered about in a fever of unrest and anxiety. The morrow was the date fixed by the summons – what it would bring him the wretched man scarcely dared think of. Was he to die as the others had died? Had the consecration of the money defeated Vanderdecken's fell purpose? Or was it all a fable and a myth, as Parson Waddilove had urged? To-morrow at this time he would know. Dusk was falling, night was gathering in, as Reuben Oram, filled with these unhappy thoughts, was making his way homewards. His cottage was now in view: the light streaming from the window and the open door. That, at any rate, was his haven for to-night. Let to-morrow – Good God! what was that? His eyes had glanced seawards, and suddenly he stopped as though rooted to the ground. The blood ran cold in his veins; his eyes started from their sockets; his very heart seemed to stand still, while his limbs trembled as though he were palsy-stricken.

There were others looking seawards that evening, and they afterwards declared they saw nothing unusual; there was the little fishing fleet at anchor – that was all. But Oram saw something more than this.

With her sails set dead against the wind he saw the Spectre Ship enter the bay.

'My God,' he cried, 'the captain's come for me!'

There was a pause. By the second hand of your watch you could have counted twelve, and then, looking neither to the right nor to the left, and with steady feet, Reuben Oram walked to his home.

The children were in bed, but he roused them from their slumbers. With one perched on either knee and his wife in the ingle-nook, he sat before his untouched supper and talked and laughed as he had used to. He sang them songs, he told them wondrous tales; and the youngsters crowed with glee, while their mother smiled happily upon them. The cloud had passed; her goodman was himself again. Then the bairns fell asleep in his arms and he put them to bed himself, and kissed them – and then – and then he turned to his wife – and told her all.

There was no sleep for man or woman in the cottage that night, and when the sun was high in the heavens there they still sat, hand in hand, waiting for the end.

The gate creaked on its hinges, footsteps were heard outside, and a knock came at the door.

'Reuben, Reuben,' said a well-known voice.

'It's only the Parson, lad,' said the wife, and she rose and unbarred the door.

'Well, good folk,' said the cheery clergyman. 'This is a nice time to be abed. Why, how's this?' as his eye caught the ashes of yesterday's fire, yesterday's meal untouched, the bed unslept in.

Oram muttered something unintelligible, while his wife caught up the children from their cot, and took them into the wash-house to dress. Oram and the Parson were left alone together.

'Reuben, I've bad news for you. The bell was fixed yestere'en and all seemed well. Overnight one of the beams on which it was hung gave way, for it seems the strain was too great. The bell crashed through the floor below and is broken.'

Oram laughed. 'A good omen, sir, for to-day. But what matters it? Do you think the ringing of a bell would keep the devil away? You should try candle and censer and say mass. The Romanists have more powerful weapons, Parson.'

'Reuben, Reuben,' said the clergyman, greatly shocked, 'these words become you not.'

Again the man laughed – a hideous laugh. 'They'll become me right enough to-morrow, Parson, when I am damned. Vanderdecken is here. The foul ship came last night with her cargo of spectres. There would have been a choir full of them for the consecration, and the skipper could have sounded his speaking trumpet right merrily; no doubt they had a fine time of it in the belfry last night.'

Parson Waddilove stared at the sailor in silent horror. He was evidently going mad.

'Parson,' he went on with terrible earnestness, 'you'll see to Sally and the bairns after – after to-day. Here's money,' and he opened a chest and produced a bag therefrom. 'Here's money that will see them through the winter – then God help them, for I cannot. You'll look after them, sir? The lass might go as a serving wench when she is old enough, and the lad must be a sailor, I trow. But, Parson, tell him never to sail in a ship bound for the Cape. Merciful heaven! to think of him meeting his father's ship and being doomed to perish.

Make him swear it, sir, by all that's holy. And the wife – my Sally – oh, God! how can I talk of these things – it's worse than death itself –' and the man broke down and hid his face in his arms.

Suddenly he started up, pale and ashy as death.

'Hark!' said he, with 'That's the captain's voice,' and he stared at the door with deadly terror written on his face.

He rose to his feet, swaying to and fro like a drunken man and holding on to the table for support.

'I am ready, skipper,' he said.

The clergyman followed the direction of his eyes, but he saw nothing unwonted in the room. There was no one there but themselves.

Oram made one or two steps forward as though following an invisible guide – then he trotted and fell to the floor, insensible.

'Mistress Oram! Mistress Oram!' cried the clergyman as he bent over the sailor; and the affrighted woman rushed in. Together they lifted him on the bed; and, leaving the wife chafing his hands and bathing his head, the Vicar ran off to procure what medical assistance the village afforded.

It was some hours before Parson Waddilove finally left the cottage. He waited till the leech arrived and the patient had been bled, and consciousness had returned; he called again in the afternoon, and once more late at night to see how he was progressing. He left him fast asleep under the influence of a potent drug the apothecary had been obliged to administer.

The clergyman left the house about eleven o'clock. He was much distressed by the events of the day, and now he determined to take a walk on the cliffs to compose himself.

The night was fine, and there was a glorious moon shining on the water. All looked peaceful and calm; and a sudden desire seized the Parson to have a short pull. Despite his increasing years and weight, he often took a boat out when the tide was favourable and the water calm; and it was so now. It was almost the bottom of the ebb; in half an hour the tide would turn and bring him back. He made his way down the cliffs to the little landing stage, alongside which the boats were moored, and chose one – Oram's – he knew of old. He hunted for a pair of blades, and, having found them, cast off from the mooring ring and pulled out into the bay.

In five minutes or so he rested. His mind was too busy for physical exertion. His thoughts persisted in turning to Oram.

'His mind must have become unhinged by much brooding over the letter,' said the Parson to himself; 'and last night he said he saw the Sceptre Ship. As if such a thing were possible –' Then he stopped. His heart beat as though he had heard the first trump of Judgment; his scalp tightened; the blood curdled in his veins.

There, not fifty yards away, lay the weird semblance of a vessel, a three-masted merchantman. There was hurrying to and fro on board, for she was preparing to sail, but not a sound was audible. Shapes of men were straddling on the foot-ropes of the topsail yards, loosing the canvas out of the gaskets. There was a capstan on the high forecastle head, the bars manned and the cable already hove short. There was a filmy fiddler on the capstan top, fiddling a soundless tune. By the high poop lanterns stood the phantom captain, with his speaking trumpet under his arm, shouting orders unheard. There she lay, in outward form a vessel; but there was no colour, no substance. She was white; impalpable as a shadow, vague as a dream – in truth a Spectre Ship.

Parson Waddilove gazed at the white glare in spellbound horror. Ha! what is that? A boat swings up and out from the booms, and is lowered. Four sailors climb down, and with noiseless strokes put off and pull towards him, shorewards. Nearer, nearer they come, and he is fascinated by their approach. He tries to shout a warning, but the words stick in his throat. They are but a boat length away. Now they are on him, right amidships. He waits for the crash.

A shadow flits by. They are gone.

His eyes follow. Unheedingly they are pulling to the shore. A cloud passes over the moon and they are lost. The

Parson strains his senses, listening and watching in breathless suspense. Not a sound is to be heard, save the faint clash of the sea breaking out on the weed-wrack and shingle. Ha! there they are again. Great God! what is that?

There are now five men in the boat!

On they come, the fifth man holding the tiller. They pass the Parson's boat scarce a dozen yards off. That fifth shadow – that ghostly semblance of a man – *it is Reuben Oram.*

They pull to the vessel, climb on board, the boat is hauled up, and the anchor broken out of the ground. One by one the sails unfold and, straining at their sheets and bolt ropes, belly out in the breezeless tide, surges away to sea.

The crew of the *Flying Dutchman* was complete.

THE FRINGE OF CALAMITY

Victor MacClure

The general cargo steamer *Bertha* wallowed in the troughs of lead-coloured waves. Her engines were silent. Down in the engine-room the black squad sweated and panted in the stifling heart, while MacCormick, the ready-fisted Scots chief, drove them like slaves to the task of the replacing of a fractured rod.

The *Bertha* took way enough from the hastily rigged try-sail to keep her steady, but the wind was rising rapidly, and the glass was falling in jerks, and never a soul aboard but knew that an anxious time was coming. When the blow came the try-sail would be useless. All the chances were that it would be ripped to rags, for the tarpaulin was perished, as was to be expected on a not altogether well-found ship.

The crew, working resentfully through the dog-watches, had done what they could to make all snug; and a rough-looking framework of spars and canvas lay spread on the forecastle, with a length of stout cable made fast to it. The other end of the cable was bent to the forecastle bitts, and the sea-anchor, for that is what the rough framework was, lay ready to cast overside.

Two seamen sprawled on the cover of the forward hatch, and they cursed the heat with fluent and varied profanity. They were meagrely clad. One wore a battered bowler and a pair of dungaree trousers which had been clipped in the legs until they were like running shorts – and, except for a sweat-rag round his neck, that was the sum of his costume. The other, bosun's mate of the *Bertha*, upheld the dignity of his position in a thin singlet, armless and ragged, dingy duck trousers, and a deep-sea cap, of which the peak was not the only shiny part.

The seaman – called 'Nobby' for the plain reason that his name was entered as 'Clark' on the ship's books – ran his hand down his arm, and let the collected perspiration drip from his fingers on the deck.

'Gosh!' he exclaimed to the quartermaster. 'This perishin' 'eat! Wot d'ye say now to walkin' down the Mile End Road, stoppin' at any pub you liked, an' 'aving a few pints drawed mild?'

'Stow it, Nobby,' returned the quartermaster. 'Wot's the good o' fond reckerlectin'? Beer! Lumme, I'd pour it all over me! You shut your face, son. Wotcher got to mention it for? Perisher!'

'The Mile End Road! 'Streuth!' said Nobby, in an agony of

remembrance. 'W'y can't it blow cold for a change?'

'It don't blow cold much in them seas. An' there's a typhoon-blowin' up, wind about two hundred knots. Even in the thick of it, it won't blow cold –'

'Chuck it, Bill,' expostulated Nobby. 'Two 'undred knots! W'y –'

'You don't know them seas, Nobby,' said the quartermaster, calmly. 'The glass was droppin' and bucketin' about just like this when the *Minnie* went ashore on the Low Islands. Gosh! That was a blow! Two hundred knots was nothing like it. The ship's boats was held out on the falls like that much buntin' before they blowed away. You don't know them seas, Nobby.'

'No,' said Nobby. 'An' once I gets out o' them you don't find me back in them. That's wot! A cool little pub in the Mile End Road,' he broke off. 'That's my mark.'

'I wisht you'd shut up about the Mile End Road,' said Bill Somers pathetically. 'You make me that thirsty, an' I don't want to crawl forrard for a drink o' look-warm water. Smoke ain't no good to you, neither. Makes it wuss.'

He lapsed into silence, and for a while the querulous Nobby shared the quiet. But his distinctly Cockney temperament could not endure the lack of conversation for long. He had to speak.

'Funny thing old Sam Farquhar gettin' religion,'

he ventured.

Bill swabbed his face with the sweat-rag that was round his neck.

'You'd think it funnier if you'd known Sam as long as I have,' he said. 'I've been to sea for nigh on twenty years now, an' I've seen a few rips in my time – but 'streuth, I've never met one that could hold a candle to old Sam. 'E was a one, and no mistake. The blind-ohs! The general cussing around, booze, gambling, wimmen! Lumme –'

'Bad, was 'e?'

'Bad? I believe you,' breathed Bill. 'I mind once in the *Sarah Good*, it was sixteen 'undred tons out o' Liverpool – we lay off Rosario. One night I saw Sam go off with three dago wimmen. Gosh, a fair corker was Sam. Broke ship, 'e did, an' we found 'im two days after, playin' casino with a blinkin' dago on one of them wimmen's naked bellies. There was a knife fight before we got 'im away. Mad drunk!'

'Coo!' said Nobby. 'Them rips is the wust w'en it comes to gettin' religion. Seen it often at sea. An' them Scotchies is wuss than any, if you asks me. They gets religion awful bad.'

'You said an earful then, son,' Bill agreed. 'Wot's the old perisher doin' now?'

'Talkin' 'ell and brimstone to them card-players in the fo'c'sle,' yawned Nobby. 'Irritatin' old perisher. As if it wasn't 'ot enough already. Enough to drive you dotty, 'e is.'

'Funny how them religious blokes can't keep it to themselves,' said Bill. ''Ullo! 'Ere comes old Ollsen. Wotcher, Nils?'

A tall Scandinavian dropped on the hatch-cover beside the other two seamen.

'Too pretty dam' hot,' he remarked. 'Presently he blows hard. You wait!'

'Let it blow,' said Nobby. 'Maybe it'll cool the air a bit.'

'Don't talk so ignorant, Nobby!' Bill Somers said crossly. 'You'll wish you were out o' wot's coming to us before it's over. Won't 'e, Nils?'

'Sure,' Ollsen agreed; 'there won't be much left on deck. An' it won't blow cold, neither. Like the stokehold.'

'Cheerful lot o' perishers, you are,' Nobby said, 'I don't think!'

Silence fell upon the group. The wind was rising steadily, but it whipped no spume from the oily looking sea. The hummocks of water rose and fell unbroken, the colour of dirty lead, and the sky seemed almost coppery green in the intensity of the sub-tropical heat. The men on the hatch lay supine, ever and again raising a tired arm to wipe the beads of sweat from their eyes with the sweat-rags they wore round their necks. A lanky young seaman strolled up to the three, and looked down upon them morosely, his hands dug deep in his trouser pockets. His shadow fell on Bill Somers, and that seaman shaded his eyes to look for the cause.

'Wotcher, Joe?' he remarked.

' 'Cher Bill,' came the reply. Then, after a pause, 'Do you believe in 'ell, Bill?'

'Eh?' said Bill. 'Wot's that you say?'

'Do you believe in 'ell?'

Bill sat up. So did the others, for a religious question will always attract the sailor for the first moment.

'I dunno,' said Bill. 'I suppose I do.'

'If 'ell's any 'otter than them seas,' Nobby interposed, 'it can't be much –'

Joe shook his head irritably.

'Do you believe, Bill, that everybody's doomed to hell – even kids that's just been borned?' he asked.

'Lor' love you, no,' said Bill. 'W'y? 'Oo said they was?'

'Old Sam Farquhar,' replied Joe. ' 'E ses every sailorman's doomed. 'E ses even babies is doomed before their mothers 'as them –'

This idea struck Nobby as being rank blasphemy.

'Wot? – babies!' he exclaimed. 'The old perisher! Don't you believe it, Joe. 'E's off 'is rocker –'

' 'E read it out of a book – a printed book – not the Bible,' Joe explained in a hollow voice, 'the other – *The Doctryne of Pre* – somethink – *Pre-destitut-ion.*'

'The perishin' old blighter!' exclaimed Nobby. 'It would be in print –'

'Print ain't all gospel,' growled Bill. 'I shouldn't worry if I was you, Joe.'

'I ain't worried,' said Joe fretfully. 'I was only askin' of yer.'

He sat on the edge of the hatch and stared sullenly at his feet.

'Wot a ship! Wot a ship!' breathed Nobby. 'Wot with the 'eat, an' a wind that don't cool you, an' a set o' blurry Salvationists! Lumme, I wish I was back in the Mile End Road!'

'I wish I could 'ear them engines beginnin' to turn over,' grunted Bill. 'The blow'll be on us in 'arf a pig's whisper. I don't fancy ridin' an 'urricane with a sea anchor!'

'I 'eard the Chief tell the Old Man 'e expected steam about eight bells,'said Nobby.

'I 'ope 'e's right,' grunted Bill. 'The Old Man looks fair grey in the chops. I don't blame 'im, with the bottom droppin' out o' the barrowmeter.'

'It will blow for sure!'croaked Ollsen. 'A big blow, Iknow.'

'You needn't make po'try about it, Nils,' grinned Nobby.

By this time the wind was singing steadily through the rigging, and the sky had taken on a colour of livid pink.

The men on the hatch lay cursing the heat with versatility. Suddenly the big Scandinavian sat up, and raised a warning finger.

'Can't you not hear it?' he demanded.

' 'Ear wot?' someone asked sleepily.

'Can't you not hear a bell?'

The seamen listened intently, but one by one fell to shaking their heads in negation.

'There ain't no bell, Nils,' said Bill Somers. 'Where'd there be a bell? This course is off the track o' ships, an' besides young 'Orricks is on the look out. 'E'd have spotted anything in sight. Wot you've 'eard, Nils, is something clinking in the engine-room.'

'It was a bell,' said Nils positively. 'I'm sure I heard a bell.'

He lapsed into silence but with an intent look in his blue eyes. Presently he tapped the quartermaster on the arm gendy.

'Listen,' he said. 'Can't you not hear it now?'

Once more the group fell to listening. They held their breaths to listen, but they heard no sound.

'Look at the thing reasonable, Nils,' argued Bill. 'There's three 'ere can't 'ear no bell. Young 'Orricks ain't sung out. The sun's in your 'ead, chum, and your ears is singing. Go forrard and 'ave a swig of water. Do you good.'

Ollsen rose slowly to his feet, but shook his head unconvinced. He walked slowly to the faucet by the forecastle entrance.

'Old Nils 'as got 'em,' said Nobby sympathetically. ' 'Ow should 'e 'ear a bell? Everybody knows them Scans ain't got no earsight. Their eyes is fine – none better – but I never met a Scan yet that was quick of 'earing.'

'I believe you,' Bill agreed. 'But Scans is good sailormen.'

'You bet they are,' said Nobby. Then he allowed his jaw to drop. 'I believe – I believe,' he said slowly, 'I can 'ear a bell!'

' 'Ow, chuck it –'

'There's a bell all right,'said Joe.

' 'Arf a mo!' Bill said testily. 'Yus,' he decided, 'I believe you're right. Mysterious blinkin' thing!'

The voice of the mate sung out from the bridge.

'Any of you down there hear a bell?'

'Yus, sir,' they chorused. 'We all can 'ear it – faintlike.'

'I wonder what it is?' came the mate's voice querulously. 'Where'd you reckon it came from, Somers?'

'Down the wind, sir.'

'It's ahead,' said Nobby softly.

'Garni'Joe corrected scathingly. 'It's on the port quarter –'

'Quiet, you men!' came the mate's voice. 'Darn funny thing!'

Ollsen joined the group.

'I told you there was a bell,' he said with melancholy triumph.

'Nip aloft, one of you – you, Ollsen,' ordered the mate, 'and see what there is in sight.'

'Dodge up to the fo'c'sle, Joe,' Bill supplemented, 'an' 'ave a squint along of 'Orricks.'

Ollsen shinned up the ratlines, while Joe mounted the forecastle. Bill and Nobby looked up at the Scan open-mouthed. There was a period of silence.

'Anything doing, Ollsen?' the mate shouted.

'Nothing in sight, sir,' came the reply. 'It's too dark to see properly.'

'Come on deck, then.'

Ollsen descended the ratlines and landed nimbly on deck. It was, as he had said, too dark to see properly. It was as if the sun had been plunged in thick smoke. The wind was moaning in long gusts. Now it was difficult to move about the decks, and Joe crept back from the forecastle as if he were pushing an invisible but heavy barrow.

'Not a blinkin' thing!' he shouted. 'That ain't no 'uman bell!'

'He is right,' Ollsen said. 'The bell is not a real bell – it comes from a ghost ship. Two – three watches more and we shall be under the sea – all of us.'

'Wotcher mean, Nils?' asked Bill. 'Mean it's the *Flyin'
Dutchman?*'

'Yes. Fokke of the *Lily*. Presently we shall see the old ship,
and the sea through it. Grey men will stare down on us from
over the sides. Grey men, dead for years. And at the tiller
you will see Fokke, the cursed of God! He will glare at us –
and we will soon be wrecked –'

Joe's teeth were frankly chattering, and Nobby's eyes were
wide. But Bill Somers was hardier, and though his hair
seemed to prickle he gave tongue to his scepticism.

'Chuck it, Nils,' he said. 'You don't believe that yarn, do
you?'

'My father saw him once in a ship, and twelve hours after
his ship was wrecked. Only he and two men were saved. I
know. I tell you true.'

'Oh, that be shot for a yarn!' exclaimed Bill. 'Wot do you
think, Nobby?'

'I think it's a mighty queer thing, that bell.'

'It is a ghost bell,' Nils Ollsen said doggedly. He plunged
into tales of the sea, eerie tales of phantom ships, of men
drowned mysteriously. Young Joe's teeth rattled so much
that he had to put his neck-rag between them, and Nobby,
perky Cockney though he was, found his heart sinking.
Through the voice of Nils, as a weird accompaniment, came
the 'Tinka-ting, tinka-ting!' of the bell.

Suddenly, in the midst of one hair-raising tale, there came a noise like the cracking of a mighty whip followed by a great fluttering.

'Gosh! Wot's that?' Joe exclaimed, startled nearly out of his wits.

'The sail's gone! Step lively, some of you men – cut it adrift and let go the sea-anchor!' Thus the voice of the mate.

The four men got hastily to their feet, and ran to help others on the forecastle. With the way off her, the ship drifted broadside to the wind, heeling over in sickening fashion as the rollers took her. It was dangerous work cutting away the makeshift sail, for it was parted from the mast at its peak, and was flopping about wildly over the forecastle rail. Bill Somers darted in and cut it loose, but in parting it whipped the sheath-knife from his hands. When they set about casting the big framework of spars and canvas overside the wind saved them the trouble of lifting it, raising it like a huge kite over the rail and dropping it into the sea. Presently the steamer felt the drag of it, and her bows swung slowly into the wind.

'Phew!' Bill breathed. 'Don't want much o' that in this 'eat! 'Earken to that blinkin' bell!'

They fought their way back to the hatch, leaning against the force of the wind. It was difficult to resist being flung aft violently, so great was the pressure behind them. The commotion of the flapping sail and of getting the anchor overboard had brought on deck some of the watch below, and a new group was clinging to the hatch. The men from below were discussing the mysterious bell, now closer at hand and more insistent. Some ventured into theories, but it was plain that they were concerned and as nearly frightened as a British sailor will allow himself.

One by one they crept back to the forecastle. It would be time enough to face the hurricane when the call came for 'All hands on deck!' Until that time duty lay with the watch led by Bill Somers, and the fo'c'sle offered at least shelter from the wind. Only one man remained of the watch below, a bearded man with a deep-lined face and a gaunt and powerful figure. He clung to the hatch and stared over the sea with a fixed glare in his deep-set eyes. This was Sam Farquhar, the one-time 'Rip,' now repentant.

'Wotcher, Sam?' Bill gave his usual greeting.

The Scot did not take his mad-looking eyes from the sea.

'Many are called,' he muttered, 'but few are chosen!'

'Wot say!'

'Fools!' cried Farquhar. 'Fools that ask for a sign — yet when it is given them close their eyes!'

'Blimey!' whispered Bill, and cast a queer look at the Scot.

'The peril of the wrath of God moves upon the waters.

He has sent a bell to move men to repentance. Who on the stricken earth so worthy to repent as they who go down to the sea in ships? Listen, listen to the bell, Bill Somers!'

'No need to listen,' said Bill, 'the blinkin' thing's there all right.'

'It is the voice of God.'

The Scot turned flaming eyes to the quartermaster.

'Ow, chuck it, Sam!' exclaimed Nobby. 'Wot's the good o' talking like that?'

'Repent ye, repent ye, for Judgment is at hand!' the voice rose to a shout. 'I heard a voice from Heaven –'

'You'll 'ear a voice from the bridge in a minute,' said Bill. 'The Old Man won't stand for that racket.'

'I never see such an old 'owler,' Nobby chipped in. 'Wot a ship! Wot a perishin' crew! An' listen to that blinkin' bell!'

'It is a warning to repentance. God calls to sinful men that they should repent while there is yet time –'

'Well, I can't stick this,' Bill Somers exclaimed suddenly.

He turned with a spasm of rage to Nils Ollsen, who was lying stretched out on the hatch-cover with his face in his hands.

'Here you, Ollsen,' he ordered. 'Nip along to the lamprocker an' get a glim. Lash it to the bracket 'ere. You go an' give 'im a 'and, Nobby!'

Casting a contemptuous look at Farquhar, Somers strolled

off, almost sitting on the wind. As he looked about him finally to see that all was snug, irritation grew within him. The bell seemed nearer, the wind more powerful and the heat more intense than ever. He climbed the ladder to the boat-deck, and took a casual glance down to the engine-room. Seaman-like, he was no judge of the progress the perspiring engineers were making, but he saw that they were busy enough. Yet his irritation was such that he muttered down the hatch, 'Get a move on, cuss ye!' Then he laughed at himself grimly for his petulance.

He slid down the ladder to re-examine the hatches, then crept back to the lee of the boat-deck, where he stood for a while gazing out over the darkened sea. It seemed to him that the noise of the bell was all round the ship.

On the forward hatch, young Joe lay with his fingers clinging to the windmost edge, his head down on the cover. He was afraid to let his eyes meet the gaze of Farquhar. In his undeveloped mind, tags of what he had heard at the mission-school, before he ran away to sea, were ever recurrent, and he was afraid of he knew not what. Then Farquhar began to talk into his ear.

'Seek God, Joe,' urged Farquhar. 'Seek God before he seeks you! Listen to the bell, Joe. That's God's voice. He is telling you He is coming for you – for all of us. Don't die in sin, Joe. Seek repentance while you can. Soon it will be too

late, and you will go to hell – down to the burning pit, Joe
– down to eternal torment!'

'Ow, chuck it, Sam!' whined Joe, thoroughly scared.

'Cast your burden on the Lord, Joe! Repent! Repent of
your sin and perhaps God will save you from hell fire. Look
at me, I have repented. I have found grace. Once I was the
vilest thing on earth. Before God came to me I was the
greatest of sinners. I drank and I gambled. The scum of all
the seaports on the earth was where I spent my life. I wasted
the light God gave me in the arms of –'

'You didn't ought to say them things, Sam,' Joe protested
with a feeble attempt at virtue. 'It ain't decent.'

Just then Ollsen and Nobby came aft with a lamp, which
burned steadily enough. They lashed it to the bracket on the
mast, and dropped on the hatch beside Joe. Farquhar fixed
his burning eyes upon them and called upon them to repent.
Into their ears he poured his doctrine of damnation. And the
intensity of the man in his madness – it was little else – held
them fixed. Through his voice came the insistent notes of the
unseen bell, and its sound seemed to urge the Scotsman on.
The darkness of the sky, the heat, the eerie clangour which
grew more and more distinct every minute fastened upon
every grain of superstition in the minds of the three seamen.
The fear of death fell even upon the cheerful Nobby, and
Nils Ollsen, with the tatters of cold northern doctrines in his

heart, was muttering prayers in his own tongue. Farquhar laboured exultantly, and every stroke of the bell seemed to increase his fervour. Froth grew on his lips and his voice rose and fell, but mounted above the shriek of the wind.

Head down, his vest billowing out and ripping from his back, Bill Somers slid down the ladder from the boat-deck and pulled himself hand over hand along the lifeline that now was strung fore and aft. Gasping, he flung himself on the hatch and dug his fingers into the forward edge of the cover.

'Hold on! Hold on!' he shouted. 'Here's the head of it now!'

Then something almost solid seemed to strike the ship. She lifted her head high, then plunged with a sickening sideways motion into a towering wall of dark water. Something flew up with the wall of the water into the screaming air, and came crashing against the steamer's side. It was the sea-anchor, lifted clean from the water and flung like a feather. The *Bertha* heeled over until the men, clinging for dear life to the hatch-cover, thought she would turn turtle. But she slowly Tightened with every plate and beam agroan.

Then, suddenly, after an eternity of waiting, there was complete calm.

'Oh, 'streuth!' breathed Nobby. 'We're out of it!'

Over the placid sea came the sound of the bell.

'Don't you cheat yourself, Nobby,' Bill said. 'It's a double-header. The worst of it is still to come. Hang on, hang on, for heaven's sake!'

'Repent ye, repent ye! God's judgment is at hand!' came the voice of Farquhar.

Bill took a quick look round and read something in the faces of the men. Sudden rage welled up in his heart and he turned to Farquhar.

' 'Ere you,' he commanded, 'git to 'ell out of 'ere! Puttin' the fear of 'ell into the men w'en they wants all their wits! Git!'

'Listen to that bell, Bill Somers! Tremble in the face of the wrath of God!'

'Look 'ere, Sam Farquhar,' said the exasperated Bill, 'wot with the 'eat, and you and the cussed bell, I'm fit to murder you. Take yourself and your preachin' down to the fo'c'sle darn quick or I'll set about you. Git!'

The eyes of Farquhar were lambent. They seemed to burn in his head.

'Cursed be he that trampleth his neighbour's vineyard,' he said in a thick voice. 'These men are brands to pluck from the burning! You endanger their souls to the fire of hell! You thwart God's purposes – beware the instruments of his vengeance.'

Bill Somers took a step forward. His shoulders were

218

hunched forward and his jaw was thrust out menacingly.

'Git! Git! Or – by Christ I'll kill you!'

Farquhar's gaze never left the gaze of Somers. As the quartermaster thrust forward, the Scot's hand stole to the haft of his sheath-knife. And next moment the blade was deep in Bill's vitals.

There was silence broken only by the clamour of a nearby bell.

'Jesus!' whimpered Nobby. ' 'E's done in pore Bill!'

As he and the others made to scramble to their feet the mate came clattering across the deck, revolver in hand.

'Put up your hands, Farquhar!' he ordered. 'Drop that knife!'

The maniac lifted his burning eyes from his victim and rested them on the mate. He took a step forward.

'Shoot, Smithers, shoot! He's mad!' came the skipper's voice from the bridge.

Then, as Farquhar appeared to bunch for a spring, the mate shot from his hip, and the Scot fell across the man he had murdered.

'Hold on, hold on, for God's sake, fore and aft!' the voice of the skipper thundered.

The mate took a quick glance seaward, and cast himself on the hatch-cover, beside the bewildered men. High above the ship towered a dark mountain of water, and the *Bertha* seemed to plunge right into it to hide from the screaming air.

The green mass, tons and tons of water, swept over her, and it seemed as if she would never see the light of day again. She did right after a fashion, and when she righted, the bodies of Farquhar and Somers were gone.

High above the shriek of the wind came the clamour of the bell. And it sounded as if with the next wave it would descend upon the stricken steamer.

'It's on top of us,' moaned Nobby.

He raised his eyes, and there, spinning past the ship's side, was an old bell-buoy, rusty and barnacled, on the side of which he could dimly discern this inscription:

P-RT-FLO-D-N
346.

He touched the three men beside him rapidly, so that they all looked up and followed with their gaze his pointing finger. Into the faces of all three came a look of relief. And as the clanging of the bell swept away on the wind, a new sound and a new vibration filled the ship. MacCormick, the chief, had got steam in the *Bertha*'s engines.

THE FINISH OF THE 'FLYING DUTCHMAN'

C. J. Cutcliffe Hyne

'That brass belaying-pin you're handling,' said Mr McTodd, 'came from the main fife-rail of Captain George Vanderdecken's ship, *Flying Dutchman*. I helped myself to it. I now use it, as you see, as a paper weight on my desk.'

The wireless had been playing *Fliegende Holländer*, as we discovered from the programme in *The Scotsman*, and I suppose it was the tune and my action in using his paper weight to stamp out the smoulder from a pipe-dottel of his Ballindrochater grocer's abominable tobacco in the ash-tray, where it was smelling noisily, that brought the subject into conversation. Certainly the belaying-pin was of brass; it was extremely battered; it was of ancient vintage; and it was stamped G. van V. in ancient lettering.

'I do not,' said Mr McTodd, sitting back in his red plush chair, 'I do not see the connection between that tune and the windjammer our Chief boarded off San Thomé and which the old man said was the *Flying Dutchman*. Not that I ought to grumble, seeing that the Chief didn't come back to our packet, and being second, I was given the engine-room, though I'll admit I don't carry a Chief's ticket.' Mr McTodd poured whisky for himself, had an idea of passing me the bottle, but thought better of it. 'I'm a fully qualified engineer, ye'll understand, and was the pride of the Clydebank shops where I'd served my time, but when it comes to written examinations, the Board of Trade always dislikes my spelling.'

At this point the ex-mess-room steward, who was butler, cook, housemaid and general factotum of Mr McTodd's establishment, announced dinner, and we stepped across the room, swung our chairs on their pivots, and swivelled in to face our food. The table, which was of enduring mahogany, had a coaming round its edge, and was bolted sturdily to the floor; so were the chairs; and the mahogany panelling of the room was (as the furnishing people say) *en suite*. The whole scheme of the room was reminiscent of marine engineers' quarters afloat, and indeed had been bought, ready to install, from the shipbreakers' yard at Morecambe. It was built on the purest mid-Victorian lines, and though re-upholstered by its new owner in the richest red plush, still carried out its original scheme of offensive solidity.

We started dinner with some good rasping pea-soup, fragrant of the salt pork which formed its basis. Course number two was a rhombohedron of the salt pork, the aforesaid, garnished with boiled suet dumplings that would have pierced armour plate, and assisted by potatoes and tinned beans. A virgin Dutch cheese followed, blushing with rude health, but as it seemed a pity to cut into it when there were only two of us, we didn't.

A jar of pickled onions, hospitably uncorked, stood on the table's white oilcloth cover within easy fork reach of both of us, as did also a bottle of Mr McTodd's home-made whisky. But though I, like my host, strongly object to being robbed by the excise parasites of my country to the tune of eight-and-six a bottle, the McTodd brew is a few degrees above my capacity. I am a Sassenach, and lack the copper stomach of the hardy Scot.

'Three years this pork's been in barrel,' said the engineer. 'Fine stuff. If you'll pour a little of the pickle vinegar on to it with your onions, you'll find it brightens the flavour. Watch me.'

Part of the Vanderdecken yarn I had already picked up from Brabazon, who at the time had been master of the tramp S.S. *Betty Bedford*, from East India ports for Liverpool with rice cargo. Captain Brabazon did not call Mr McTodd blessed, but admitted that he was capable. His chief engineer, Mr Augustus Pighills, a member of the well-known Goole marine engineering family, was a trial.

'Pighills,' Captain Brabazon told me, 'could not be relied

on to go straight any of the time, and could be guaranteed to go crooked most of the time. The way that fat man soaked the chandlers for cumshaw on his engine-room stores was chronic, and the rake-off he got on bunkers made me blush. He wouldn't hand out my share, either. He was a dour, hard-hearted teetotaller on the top of it all, and boasted that when he was back on the beach at Goole he'd a good practice as a Methody Dick. He was the one and only inventor, so he said, of the Converted Engineer's Revivalist Mission. He told me there was far more in that than he bagged in royalties for his patent davit and releasing gear. Now I came across another of the Pighills engineering crowd that was chief on a little coaster in West Scotland, that was a decent man, barring that he carried a weak stomach. The *Bride of Dunvegan* she was, 183 tons –'

'Yes, but Augustus?' said I. 'The yarn goes that he transhipped from your *Betty Bedford* to Captain Vanderdecken's *Flying Dutchman*. You've told me just now I was no sailor when I said I thought the gyroscopic compass was a good idea, but you admitted I seemed to have an interest in the sea and sailormen. Just get back, skipper, please, to plump Mr Chief Engineer Augustus Pighills.'

Captain Brabazon twisted a length of string into the bore of his pipe, and drew out horrors. 'The fellow was pushed on to me by the shore superintendent, and I said from the moment I clapped eyes on him he'd never make a comfortable shipmate. But he'd all the proper certificates, and testimonials, and office pull, and what not, and so they signed him on in spite of me. Little tubby chap he was, and I disliked him in the engine-room from the minute we cast off our wires from the quay in Bramley Moor dock. I may not be fond of the Scotch, but they've a right over ship's engine-rooms, and you feel unhomey when you've a foreigner like a Kelly from Cork or a Pighills from Goole taking their places. At least I am, and I never feel safe with them either. They bring in gadgets of their own, and inventions they want to try out, and before you're seven days at sea there's a tube burst, or a gauge-glass blown, and a half-boiled fireman for the old man and the steward to mend. He treated us to one of his smashes just after I'd brought up to an anchor off San Thomé.'

'Why disturb the San Thomé sea floor? Had you put in there to make sure the equator was carrying on with its job?'

Captain Brabazon regarded me with a sour eye. 'I'd gone in there to pick up a cable, as per instructions. That was before the days of wireless, and the charterers naturally wouldn't make up their minds till the last moment where my rice cargo was going to. Very tricky thing the rice market. Beats rubber, so they say. I pushed off to the beach myself. I always like San Thomé.'

'That's a very splendid building, the old amber-coloured Portuguese cathedral.'

'Well, Mister, my pub's round the North corner of it, and I tell you the lady who runs it is just fifteen-stone of all right, though I'll admit she does lay on that blue face powder too thick, and it's apt to get into your mouth. Teresa her name is, as you'll remember, though as I'm an old friend she answers to Tessa. My trouble was that our Mr Augustus Pighills came off to collect me. You see, there had been a delay in getting the reply cable, and my mate was a bit young, and –'

'Captain Brabazon, I OK every word of it. The cable station is disgustingly slow, and in my case there was a bad beach when the message did come through, and the surf-boat couldn't get off for another twenty-four hours. Besides, whatever else may be wrong with the equator since Einstein tampered with it, even the Astronomer Royal can't deny it raises a thirst.'

'It's pleasant not to be misunderstood for once. Our Mr Pighills had a song about a shark or a barracouta or something like that jammed in the weed filter of his condensers, and thought he'd like a couple more days for repairs. But I know my duty to owners as well as any shipmaster afloat, and naturally told him off in style, and in three hours it was up-hook from San Thomé bay, and off. But did that beastly mechanic clear his tubes, or whatever it was, and give me my lawful eight knots? He did not. He kept throttling down, presumably to pick chunks of fish out of his machinery, and then just as an ugly water-spout was bearing down on me, up comes one of his dirty coal heavers, chewing his sweat-rag, and giving me "Chief's comps, sir, and in three minutes main engines is going to stop for a three-hours repair." Now I ask you?'

'Probably genuine-to-goodness Act o' God, skipper. You mustn't book it all up to Goole. Besides, you had one Scot with your machinery, and whatever else N. A. McTodd may be, he's a capable engineer.'

'He is, Mister, though thirsty. But he and Pighills had been having a disagreement over a professional matter, connected with the thrust blocks, and Augustus had hit first with a cast-iron slush-lamp, and had sent the remains to his room. The slush-lamp I saw by the repairs-list was entered as "smashed – useless." But McTodd was put to sleep for eight hours.'

'Very creditable to Goole, if you come to think of it. I'll pull Mr McTodd's leg about that some day.'

'That wobble-kneed water-spout cruised down on us in style, and I tell you, with no weigh on I was frightened. The spout looked like delivering the goods fair on our starboard quarter. But it took a sheer, and swung astern, and then the top half sucked up into the black cloud above, and the bottom end boiled down, and away came a number-one-topside tornado, slewing around North-East-South before I could get my awnings furled.

'Well, of course, that was a sort of thing that might happen to anybody. But wait a minute. The air was that full of spindrift you could hardly see number two hatch from the upper bridge, and just then I heard a hand on the foredeck hailing that there was a wind-jammer trying to run us down. My eyes were feeling like pickled onions that had been well-chewed, but I slewed round to windward, and just caught the look of her. She was a rum-looking craft, barque-rigged, with single topsails, and (I'll trouble you) a lateen mizzen. She'd a high poop with funny kind of street lamps at the butt end of it, and forrard she'd a beak and a bowsprit stuck up at an angle of forty-five, with a pocket handkerchief of a square-s'l pulling like a bull-dog on the under side of it. She was pierced for about a dozen guns, but they were all in-board, and well-secured. She was steered by a tiller, and had four hands on the relieving taykles, regular Drake, and kids' books, and Armada style. Of course Mister, you'll say she couldn't have been, and I'd not got over that San Thomé jag at Teresa's. But there she was, blowing through it, slap athwart my bows, at a good nine-point-five, pushing her old bows into it to above the knight-heads.'

'One does meet funny kind of craft south of the line,' I

admitted. 'There are similar nautical survivals up White Sea way.'

'Let me get a word in edgeways, Mister. This prehistoric freak cleared us to leeward, and then I'm hanged if she didn't go about, and flatten her sheets, and come sailing back again nearer to the wind's eye than a racing cutter. A great clumsy apple-bowed tub she was, just like one of those Armada pictures, and if you'd asked me, never went to windward in her life without the help of a tug and a tow rope. She rolled like a palm oil puncheon being hauled off a surf beach.

'Mark you it was blowing too; the wind was an equatorial tornado, running all-out; and it had eased my *Betty Bedford* of both quarterboats, all awnings, and everything else that would shift. Old-fashioned single-topsails she had, as I told you, and they went out when I was a boy. But she'd both fore and main set, and courses with never a reef tied down, and her big lateen mizzen was pushing away on the poop with the yard bending and whipping like a fishing rod. I tell you the quartermaster was nearly kicked away from her tiller at every second, but the four blokes on the relieving taykle knew their job, and amongst them they steered her as cleverly as those sharps in the fancy jerseys you see racing at Cowes.'

'Fine sailor-men, Captain.'

'The best that are left outside the churchyards,' Captain

Brabazon admitted. 'Well, the old galleon, or whatever she was, made a short board of it, and rounded up and hove-to, main topsail aback, and then I'm hanged if hands didn't lay aloft, and rig whips to her yardarms, and start to hoist out a clumsy tub of a boat she carried in chocks on her deck amidships.

'It's my belief if they'd got her into the water she'd have blown away like a chip, but the breeze began to ease then, as is the way with these tropical blows, and though of course a hell of a sea got up in no time, that didn't seem to worry the ancient mariners worth a cent. Whiskers they had, all of them, most yellow-white, and they wore short P-jackets, and petticoats, and high sea-boots like the parties in the kid's pirate yarns I've been telling you about. The sour smell of her came down to us in waves: it was like the frowst in the bird-house in the Antwerp Zoo, Mister, if you've ever tried that.

'They hove up their boat off the chocks, bowsted her overside, and dropped her into the water. A clumsy clinker-built brute she was, a bit on the North Sea trawler's dinghy lines, only more so, and I don't suppose she'd have stove-in if she'd hit Mount Ararat. Four of those whiskered mariners tumbled in to her off the starboard main channels, and then an officer who looked a thousand went aboard and shipped a steering sweep. He'd pistols in his belt. All five of them had cutlasses strapped on. They were got up in regular kid-book buccaneer rig as I keep on telling you. But they were boatmen: I give them that. I'd no hands aboard the *Betty Bedford* that could have kept even one of my lifeboats afloat in a sea like what was running then.

'Then up on to the top of the fiddley climbs my fat Mr Pighills to see about a ventilator that had jammed, and "My Christmas!" says he. "Captain, but that's the *Flying Dutchman.*"

' "I thought," said I, "you were teetotal."

'He didn't even trouble to answer that. He just climbed over on to my upper bridge without invitation. "Man, Captain," says he, "here's a legend come true. That boat's coming off to ask you to take letters to Holland. Don't take 'em. It means big danger, and the old *Betty* will sink soon enough without your helping her. She's just rotten. The main condensers are a comic opera, and though I called our Mr McTodd a liar over what he said about our thrust-block holding down bolts, I'll admit to you that half of them are stripped. But that packet of Captain Vanderdecken's immortal – up to a point, and if I can board her, and bring her people round to the True Faith, and let their weary bodies die comfortable like, I've got the best point any Revivalist Missionary ever had in this competitive world. Man, Captain, it's a thing I can retire on into a house of my own, with an institute attached, and very likely a two-seater. If you'll help me and don't balk things, I'll see you have your proper rake-off. Captain, think: this chance may mean a ten-pun note to you, or at the lowest seven pounds five".'

'Seems to be a man who was used to big figures, your stout Mr Augustus Pighills,' said I.

'Well, Mister, money continues to talk, and the master of an old 800-ton tramp like the *Betty Bedford* sees mighty little of it. I guess I fell to our Mr Pighills' blan-dish-what-you-calls like a Krooboy fades to gin. I ordered the mate to rig a guess-warp, but to put over no ladder, and Captain Vanderdecken, if that was old white whiskers at the steer oar, comes alongside like a *pukka* sailor, and bawls up to me in what was perhaps Dutch.

' "No savvy," I sang down to him. "Can do dago or pigeon".'

' "Can do," said he, and spouted a stream of what I recognised was French. But his Dutch accent was beyond me, mine, being the pure Marseilles variety. Then our Mr McTodd came out on deck and took over. He was still a bit what the doctors call whambly from that bash on the head with the cast-iron slush-lamp, but he'd the gift of tongues all right, though it struck me most was cross-bred Coocaddens and Clydebank.

' "Here you Dutchman, Captain Vanderdecken!" said

McTodd. "Whit d'ye mean by being in these latitudes? You were doomed to roam in the Indian Ocean because you swore you'd tack board and board off the Cape till you weathered it on the passage westward, or hell froze over. You guaranteed to carry on along those lines, Captain, and that's why you were allowed to become a ghost. But now you have brought your packet round the bottom corner of Africa, and are doing naval manoeuvres off San Thomé. Captain, you've dirtied your ghost's ticket, and it's my idea you've been disrated, and are once more plain meat and bones seaman. That may not be the best Free Kirk theology, which my father who was minister of that body in Ballindrochater tried to ram into my heid. But it's common sense, which is a thing even the Churches in these modern times have to accept. Get me?"

' "*Ja*," said old hairy at the boat's steering sweep, and rather drooped, "Ja, *Mynheer*, I bin feel a change."

' "You'll not, during the time you been ghosts, have broached many stores, Captain?"

' "No," says Cappy Vanderdecken, "we don' eat nothing. Don' seem to have no appetite."

' "Nor drink?" says McTodd, sort of what you might call prophetic and eager.

' "Well, *Mynheer*, I keep the key of the spirit room hung to this chain round my neck – *so* – and so de schnaps ha'n't been touched."

' "Salt beef gone to mahogany," says McTodd. "Salt pork soaked into the barrel staves, hard-bread mere weevil-dust, but schnaps as bright as ever. Does schnaps improve like Madeira, Captain, by being carried round the Cape in a windjammer? I've never tried any; I've taken most of my spiritual refreshments hot from the still; but it shall never be said of me that I'm above being lairned. Couldn't you bring us off an anker of that old matured schnaps for this packet to drink your health in?"

' "Eet is cargo, and I could not in faith to my owners geef it to another."

' "Of course you couldn't, Cappie. My mistake. But I take it yours isn't a long ship?"

' "Pardon, but I do not get?"

' "Long ship: craft where it's a long time between drinks."

' "No, *Mynheer*. I am old, if you like, but I am Hollander, and in my country we keep the guest's cup full."

' "Man," said McTodd, "you almost persuade me to change my nationality. I'm Scotch, myself, though I'm sure you'd never guess it of me. Hand that boat along the guess-warp a bit further aft, and I'll board her through the well-deck gangway!" '

Captain Brabazon's account of proceedings was fairly

good up to this, but faded off afterwards into wishes that he had accepted Teresa's invitation, and settled down in a partnership in the little restaurant at the back of the ivory-coloured cathedral in equatorial San Thomé. So after that sumptuous and succulent dinner in Mr McTodd's house at Ballindrochater, I applied to him for further details. I used tact, and avoided any reference to the slush-lamp, which would have hurt his professional feelings. 'You were in your room, I believe, with a dose of malaria, when old Captain Vanderdecken came alongside the *Betty Bedford*?'

'Malaria was the currse, with all its distressing symptoms. But the emergency re-recuperated me. I'm a scientific observer, ye'll mind. I felt I'd a mission to note conditions, sanitary and otherwise, in that pre-historic windjammer, and so I tumbled into the boat, and told the hands to let go the guess-warp, and push off home. Unfortunately Pighills, who had been misrated as our packet's chief, insisted on coming also. The man was a poor engineer, with the most faulty theories on the lubricants needed for steam engines that have ever drifted to sea, and he was also a schismatic of the most poisonous school. He was worse than a UP. I warned him that trouble would come of it if he insisted on boarding the old windjammer, and sure enough as we were being ferried across, a six-inch flying fish shot out of the water, and bobbed into his fat mouth which he had open for convenience in cursing me. But, like a good many other unbelievers, he wouldn't be told. *Hinc* – you'll pardon me: I meant that – *hinc lachrimae*.

'For the sake of experience, and no' because I was forced, ye'll understand, I've signed on in some of the worst engine-rooms that have been carried across the wa'er. But never have I set foot on a worse sea-ruin than yon *Flying Dutchman*. She'd not a bit of wire on her. Her rigging was all hemp, stretched to the limit, and with the tar bleached out till it was white as a laundry show. Her decks had spewed their oakum, and were like sponge to the foot, and she hadn't a winch or a windlass about her. She'd capstans and pulley-haul taykles from her heavy lifts, and enough brass pins in her fiferails to make teeth for a saw. Think on to make me tell you about those belaying pins later. You've seen one of them.'

'I'm going to crack some of your walnuts with it now,' said I. '*G. van V.* are the initials on it, I see.'

'Well, Mister, teetotallers I hear drink port with walnuts. You stick to the sound home-brewed whisky you'll find in that bottle, and you'll live longer. Help 'self. G.W.V. stands for George William Vanderbilt, the party that had the extravagant yacht with the silver door-handles which old Pirrie bought and then sold to the breaking yard at Morecambe. I had thought of buying some of her cabin fixtures to add to the furniture of this room. But when it came to the point, I looked around me, and refrained. It's pairfect, just pairfect, as it stands: best engineer's mess-room style: and if you can tell me people with better taste, I'd like to hear about them. That yacht stuff, when you came to look it over next morning, was a wee meretricious –'

'Was old Cappie Vanderdecken's packet a dry ship after all? Or perhaps you weren't invited below?'

'Invited? Lord help you, Mister, a quartermaster and one of the mates did the hall-porter business of bowing me to the door in the poop half-deck that led to the main cabin, and inside there was a steward with bunches of ragged riband at the knees of his plus-fours that nearly did a curtsey at the sight of me. That fat little Augustus Pighills came puffing along in my wake, but I suppose they'd got used to the look of sea-going engineers by then, because they took little enough notice of him.

'There was only five foot of head-room except between deck beams, which were frequent, so once inside I stayed sat, and that, Mister, as you'll know for yourself, is a bad observation point for a gentleman who is apt at times to exceed his high co-efficient of absorption. The schnaps when it came was a thing to make hymns about. Bit varnishy, of course, like all those Hollander drinks, but smooth as best tinned milk, and milk as a virgin's prayer. There are whiles, ye'll note, I drop into poetry. A ship-mate I sailed with, one Kettle, had the habit, and I caught it of him.

'The schnaps was in none of your nasty little bottles; the old Father Christmas steward in his doddering plus-fours with the swanky-bows served it out of a wicker-covered demi-john, no less, and though we supped it from horns that carried the taste of the last eighteen drinks they'd been used for, I doff my hat to Cappie Vanderdecken's cellar.

'Pighills was the blot on the cabin. Pighills is teetotal, and like all his breed always had to go around shouting about it. I personally dislike the Hun liver sausage; it always provides me with returrns; but do I make a song and dance about it? I do not, and put out my fork into the next dish as a gentleman should. Old Captain Vanderdecken was a gentleman, and forgave much to a guest. But I could see his mossy whiskers begin to bristle and twist at Pighills' cant and clack about the sin of swigging schnaps and the advantages of his conventicle down Goole way.

'But Pighills, with his two elbows locked in the standing fiddles of the black oak table, preached away without a break, and I just carried on with the wicker-covered demi-john to prevent further waste. Man, it was sinful to think of that beautiful schnaps being carried all those years uselessly about the stormy oceans.

'The row came when Cappie Vanderdecken produced his packet of letters. There must have been forty of them in the bundle, which was lashed up with spun-y'n. They were yellow and sea-stained, and tattered at the angles, ye'll mind that according to the histories they'd been hunting a mail-boat for 200 years.

'Mossy whiskers had got tired of being the pleasant landlord, and was now all captain. He tackled me first. "You," he said, "will take charge of these letters to our friends at home in Holland, and see that they are delivered."

'I disliked his tone. It had the regular deck bark that we in the engine-room always get narky over. But he was an old, old man, and I was grateful for his beautiful schnaps, and it had maybe softened some of my asperities. So I just said, "Captain, I'm not a postman. Moreover, mail carrying is a monopoly of the Government, and ships' officers on pain of keel-hauling and a fine not exceeding £1 sterling and costs are forbidden to carry other folks' letters. See 7 Vic. cap 22 *et seq*. Ye'll see my attitude?"

'My Law talk, translated into Dutch, was a wee above his heid, which was my intention. It was a pairfect bit of tact. The Old Man waved me back to the demi-john, and tackled Pighills, and there was an opportunity to Pighills' taste. I've always disliked the English in engine-rooms, especially when they are preachers, and Captain Vanderdecken shared my dislike.

'I can't report how the dispute went on, for after the first five minutes of it I slept. We'd been having a strenuous time on the *Betty*'s machinery since leaving San Thomé, nothing of course out of the way to a highly skilled engineer like myself, but I'll admit tiring. So I slept, with my head jammed down in the fiddle that held that wicker-covered gallon bottle.

'I was woke by a man falling over my back. Nothing in that, you'll say, Mister. It's a thing, as *you* know, that's happening every day in seaports all over the world. But this man started to cuff me over the heid on a spot where a few hours before I'd had a wee abrasion from a lump of cast iron. That woke me, and I found myself scrapping with that octogenarium in the plus-fours and the ribbon-bunches who had been acting pot-man. I'd respect for his years, and put him to the deck with a touch an angel might have envied.

'But that steward carried a bo's'n's whistle, which by sea law he'd no right to, and he put it in his gums, and blew as loud a call as a man with teeth could manage. All the petticoated sea-booted ship's company came pouring into the cabin off the main deck, smelling noisily, and I saw we were in for one of those little disturbances which you and I know so well, Mister.

'Pighills and Captain Vanderdecken were having a private dog-fight of their own on the floor, and, being a Scottish gentleman, of course I didn't interfere with them. But that frowsty Dutch crew started attending to me; they looked really mean and ugly; and that low-roofed cabin with only five-foot head room under the deck beams was no place for a man who knows how to use his hands to get in real artistic work. So I broke through – and left casualties.

'For a windjammer of some 300 tons to-day, even with single topsails if you can imagine such freaks doing work on the seas now, we'd have a skipper and a mate and perhaps three deckhands. The cook would be on the head sheets. *Flying Dutchman* must have had seventy of a crew, and where they stowed below, the good Lord, who had presumably the freedom of the forecastle, knows. I was not invited there, and am ignorant of the way it was packed. The deck area was cluttered with gun carriages and chicken crates, and every kind of dunnage, and those Dutch could not all get on to me at once. But enough did, and they must have been bonny fighting men 200 years earlier. You may think tiredness and the malaria I told you about handicapped me, and perhaps they did a bit. But the three-quarter gallon of that pairfect schnaps that I'd put under hatches merely made me vivacious. Still, I'm free to admit to you, Mister, that I picked a brass belaying pin out of the main fife-rail to help put in the proper accents on my conversations. The pin's the one you're now stopping down the tobacco in your pipe with – and I always like to see friends load freely when they use my pouch. It's marked *G. van V.* Don't mind leaning back in that chair. The antimacassar will keep the grease in your heid from spoiling my red plush seating.'

'So they hove you overboard?' I suggested.

'Well,' said Mr McTodd thoughtfully, 'as the late Lord Balfour said in his *Essay on Philosophic Doubt*, weight tells. The Earl was a man who lived near Ballindrochater when he wasn't away earning his living in Parliament. I always wanted to meet him over a dram and drum into him my views on Empire politics, but I'll never have the opportunity now – in this world at any rate. It will be a satisfaction to him at this moment, if he's listening in from wherever he may be, to lairn that he's the weight of my opinion, based, mark you, on experience, on the theory of this thesis being correct. As a convinced metaphysician myself –'

'I tapped the table with the brass belaying pin. 'Drop politics, man, and get back to *Der Fliegende Holländer.*'

'I didn't know you'd the gift of tongues like that, Mister. But I wish you'd stop beating up my furniture. That last bat dinged the coaming. Better try a stand-easy on the home-brewed. This timber's best bay-wood mahogany as specified by the Shore Superintendents for marine engineers' mess-rooms. As regards those Dutch deck hands, as I've admitted already, numbers told. I can tackle seven any day and enjoy the job. But offer seventy, and you see me beat. I put in some good useful work with that brass pin you're handling, and brought it home with me. *Spolia opima*, and it's not one professional soldier out of a thousand that can point to those on his walls. But at last they hove me neck and crop into their clumsy clinker-built dinghy that was bumping against the old ship's bilge-streak, and it took thirty-seven of it to do the job. Also I'll admit that thairty of them had picked out those brass belaying pins, and each had given me the maximum bat over the heid permitted to his years.

'You've said, Mister, most injuriously, that in your opinion I'm all bone above the ears. But for that ancestral protection my brain would have been spread like a ham sandwich on my shoulder blades after the way those *Flying Dutchman* deck-hands battered at me. With the – the reinforcement aforesaid, and possibly a skinful of that pairfectly matured schnaps acting as a resilient, I escaped with nothing worse than a concussion, which, added on to the bat with the cast-iron – as-you-were – added on to the malarial symptoms I have spoken about already, made me a very interesting subject for enquiry for any young coroner who was whipping up a practice. Luckily the *Betty Bedford's* old man, Brabazon his name was, had seen similar cases previously in his sea career. He had me picked out of the old windjammer's quarter-boat when it blew in against his packet, and taken to my room, and laid out on my bunk, and covered with two blankets. He omitted the restorative of a second-mate's tot of whisky as by Board of Trade ordained for those apparently knocked-out. If I've not mentioned it before, I'll state now, the skipper was English, and therefore by nature thrifty about such important matters.

'What? No, Mister, I didn't see our Mr. Augustus Pighills again. He and Cappie Vanderdecken were enjoying a dog-fight on the cabin floor when I pulled out from that department for the more spacious main deck, and the last I saw was Cappie trying to ram his tattered packet of yellow mail with the spun-y'n lashing on it down the neck of my chief's dungaree overalls. He may have done it. I suspect he did, because getting someone to take off their mail was the one way of breaking the curse which lay on the *Flying Dutchman*; and even whilst I was enjoying that scrap I was telling you about on the main deck, with my back to the fife-rail I couldn't help but see that at every roll she brought up a bit lower in the water than she did the roll before.

'Of course, with Pighills "missing: believed drowned" the Old Man was pairfectly correct in promoting me Chief, though I'll admit that, thanks to the Board of Trade's beastly requirement in the way of spelling, I've never bothered to take out a Chief's ticket. The *Betty* didn't carry a third, so the donkeyman was promoted to that elevation, and he, feeling his new responsibility, got the condenser intake cleared – which was the cause of our stoppage – whilst I was confined to my room, and when I came-to there was the old girl grinding off her eight-point five, with donkey and a fireman standing watch and watch in the machine shop and calling themselves Second and Third Engineers, I'll trouble you, – the unqualified sons of perdition.

' "Missing; believed drowned," was the best we could send home to Goole to the relations and friends of Mr Augustus Pighills.

' "I didn't want you to push off to that couldn't-happen old windjammer as you know, Mr McTodd," says our *Betty Bedford's* old man. "But you being somewhat dazed with that knock" – "Malaria" said I – "dazed with any old thing you like, and hooked it without leave. So did the chief. It was your funeral. I saw you both board her, and those frosty-whiskered Santa Claus pirates bow at you arrival. I saw you both go below. Then for half an hour it was as-you-were, although the damned old ruin got in the trough and tried to roll herself over. But she kept afloat though scuppers spouted, and I wondered what kind of anti-sea-sick mixture they were giving you in the cuddy.

' "Pighills," Captain Brabazon goes on, "I never saw after he went below. But you shot out on to the well deck after about a two-hour wait with a fine tumult at your heels. It looked to me the old tub was settling in the water. But that didn't seem to impede your efforts. You put up a dandy scrap, Mac, and when in the finish they rushed you, and held an inquest, you didn't seem sufficiently dead to suit them. So they hove you over into the boat that was riding alongside, and you wagged hell back at them with that brass belaying pin that you have brought back on board of me here. The *Flying Dutchman* settled down out of sight by the time you'd drifted alongside me. We saw her mast trucks pulled under. I logged her as 'sailing ship, name unknown, sunk with all hands.' "

'There you have it, Mister. Captain Brabazon of the *Betty Bedford* was a man I never liked, he having, like Captain Vanderdecken, too much of the deck manner for the engine-room officer to really cotton to. But there was his evidence hot and new. He saw this brass belaying pin marked *G. van V.* brought aboard the *Betty Bedford*. Here it is now in my best mahogany and panelled parlour in Ballindrochater. What more do you want?'

'Was that the real end of the *Flying Dutchman*?' I asked.

'Do you read Lloyd's shipping list?' Mr McTodd asked.

'Not regularly,' I admitted.

'Well, read it, Mister, and next time you see "*Flying Dutchman*, G. Vanderdecken, Master," reported in those pages, you apply to me, and I will send you three dozen of my best home-brewed whisky. And, Mister, I don't give away valuable liquor like that unless I'm forced, being Scottish myself.'

I had to leave the brass pin marked *G. van V.* behind me, though I tried to annex it. A horrid thought hung in my head all through Mr McTodd's yarn that the master of the *Flying Dutchman* was named *van Straaten*, and I wanted to see if the people at the British Museum could connect that up with the *G. van V.* on the battered belaying pin.

BY THE LIGHT OF THE LANTERNS

Pierre MacOrlan

I

The first lantern scooted over the ship's bridge as though borne on invisible and diminutive legs, for the form of the one who carried it, mingled with the pitch-black of the sky, was indistinguishable. A torch caught up the fugitive gleam, and its light revealed the lantern-bearer as a huge, emaciated figure, whose smoke-dried visage displayed three terrifying apertures, two eyes and a mouth. The nose, so thin as to be imperceptible, appeared to have been eaten away by some abominable malady.

The lantern-bearer raised his light, so that it fell on the one with the torch, and the face of the latter was seen to be very much like that of the other. The three tremendous gaps in each face gave the two a common cadaverous likeness.

By the poop-deck, an ancient structure if there ever was one, other lanterns were changing place, like goblin lights at the entrance of a cemetery. In the starless sky, sombre masses of sails bent over the silent ship like clouds puffed by a tempest. The plash of the ship's stem, ploughing its way, was distinctly audibly. A confused sound of bare feet, their whereabouts revealed by chiefly thuds along the rigging, preceded a sudden flaring of the lanterns, which lighted up, one by one, like luminous flowers in the black fields on the borders of Acheron.

By the light of the lanterns, the night watch was hoisting the rigging and running about in shrouds. This strange spectacle might have passed as a funereal amusement in the land of dead souls. The uproar increased, and the grinding of pulleys mingled confusedly with the cries of curlews, skimming the silvered crest of the restless void.

In order to facilitate the activity of this maritime hive, a seaman raised his torch at arms' length; its gleam rode against the black sky and, on the bridge, cut to shreds the immense and comical shadows which, suddenly elongated, suddenly shortened, gave rise to a fantasy that made it impossible to identify the owner of any shadow – who was, after all, perhaps, but the shadow of his shadow. Occasionally, a bright-coloured cloth, yellow as butter, enveloping a carronade, would light up in a swift flash the brass work of cannon, rudely covered by a tarpaulin. At the foot of the main-mast, a tremulous, broken voice arose. It was that of a man singing:

When I adjusted your cockade
And turned your black neck round,
It was because I then was bound
To see Camarde, the naughty maid.

He stopped short, like a machine that had run down, and another, behind a lantern, chuckled. In a weak voice, the man finished the song.

The little laughter of the old men, like the sound of grain being shelled, spread among the shrouds, from group to group about the cannonry, then in process of being polished.

A commandant with a speaking trumpet was endeavouring to bring order out of the confusion, but on account of the wind, which sang melodiously through the rigging, the only sound to be made out was a sort of 'Oua, oua, ouao.' The boatswain's whistle resembled the lanterns, some of which had gone out. On the horizon, a narrow band of livid light indicated the line of separation between the blackness of sky and sea.

A thin, broken voice, which might have been that of the previous singer, stammered: 'L-l-larboard watch a-a-head.'

There was only one lantern left on the bridge. A man's voice spoke: 'It's another day.'

The glimmer of sunrise and that of a lamp were striving with each other in the cabin of the *Flying Dutchman*. The night watch already had betaken themselves to sleep, now that the sun had come once more to diffuse the gliding rays of the great and ambulant mystery.

Well steered by its masters against those rapid currents which lose themselves about the poles, the big ship, an eternal wanderer, now made for unknown seas, far from the frequented paths of men, in order that its crew might enjoy a daytime repose without being on the alert and without having to listen for the unpleasant sound of a trumpet, calling the dead to their post of combat.

The sailors aboard this good ship, the hardened wood of which had stood the test of time, owed allegiance to a certain perjured captain, who, like the land-holder, Juan Espera-en-Dios or Bouttedieu, roamed the seas, the paths across the plains, the woods and villages of the world with no new sight ever to greet his eye.

The captain bore the name of Peter Maus. He was a native of Düsseldorf and had been immobilized by death under the aspect of a skeleton-like old dotard, wearing for two hundred years the identical costume he had worn as a living being, at the time he had traded for Holland. He had been a good spender, then, with the sons of Amsterdam, who were skilled in the practice of a wholesome and peaceable debauchery, accompanied by numerous divertissements of a more or less gross nature.

The love of women, so far from being able to save him from his destiny, had not been able to triumph over that other destiny which impelled him incessantly toward new adventures, which he always hoped would be more thrilling than any gone before; and now, alone with his secret, in the company of his crew, he was sailing the seas with a hundred outlawed rascals and a handful of imbeciles who had been shanghaied aboard the big ship freighted with despair.

The lieutenant belonged to the same generation as the captain. He was a Norman of Dieppe, Pierre Radet by name, commonly known as Little Pierre. He knew Peter Maus' secret and, like the latter, aspired feverishly to a repose for which he dared not hope. In the solitude of the cabin, populated with world-maps and compasses of a form long since fallen into desuetude, these two would sit, their heads between their hands, studying the charts and keeping a sharp lookout for the reef they longed to strike, which should plunge them once more into a real death, a death which should be no mere legend but an eternal rest. But in spite of the precision of their manoeuvrings, the bewitched currents always kept the *Flying Dutchman* far from shipwreck and destruction.

The day watch having been told off, while the remainder of the crew took such repose as they could in the ship's broadsides, under the pale light of the northern sun, which spread a great cloth of golden spangles over the sea, Peter Maus and Little Pierre would experience an envious desire to eat and drink. Their mummified organisms, however, could serve them no longer; their needs did not correspond to their desires. They were animated by a ferocious hatred of the earth and of the old life they had led among the living; and accordingly, they would clench their fists and amuse themselves in the patient and edifying contemplation of the punishments which they proposed to visit upon the living, if, some day, divine grace should permit them to share once more in life.

In their sacrilegious ignorance, these two old madmen, without being aware of the fact, would be praying to heaven.

'O God,' they would groan, 'grant that we may meet upon our way but one living being, fat and chubby, and grant, in thy all-powerful kindness, that we may torture him and make him suffer to suit our pleasure.'

And they would add, childishly: 'Grant, O God, that we may make a meal of bread and sausages, just once more.'

Then, Pierre Radet, known as Little Pierre, would take from the cupboard an empty bottle and two glasses. He would place them dreamily on the table, brushing them off with the flap of his round-jacket. Then he would go through the motions of pouring wine, and first one and then the other would put the glass to his withered old lips and pretend to drink.

Madness would shake them, suddenly, and the bottle would be hurled to the floor. The bottle would break.

Little Pierre would lament his luck and begin whimpering: 'Don't break the damned bottle, for the love of God. Soon, or we shan't have any more bottles, and then, we'll not be able to pretend that we're drinking.'

Sometimes they would suck on a long empty white-clay pipe, and then, with their eyes sunken in their emaciated sockets, they would recall the good old days and hate life to their hearts' content, that life so fertile in pleasures, that life the gestures of which they sought, in their distress, to reconstruct by means of a sterile and imaginative parody.

'After thinking it over well,' said Little Pierre, 'it is better to be dead. For the weak point with us, when we were sailors, was putting into port; in one night, the result of six or seven months' labour would run aground in the purse of Ninon la Bretonne.'

'You forget Angela Cecchi of Palerma,' said Peter Maus.

'Ah, yes, Angela Cecchi and her little place at the foot of the Pellegrino.'

Once more, they would plunge into their memories. Each

of them, in his fleshless head, under its cover of dried skin, would launch forth upon a weird sea of images, at once naïve and perverse, at times vague, at times endowed with the perfection of absolute design.

'There is a God,' Peter Maus would declare. 'Who could doubt it, seeing that we have been damned by Him for all eternity? It was different when I was a child – I don't care to recall how many years ago that was – I believed in God then, all right, but I wasn't sure of anything. I said my prayers like the other children, as a matter of precaution, and in order to put all the chances on my side. Since then, I have acquired the absolute certainty of a divine providence.'

'Well, Maus,' Little Pierre would speak up in his turn, 'does that mean that we're going to have to sail the long stretch without putting in for all eternity?'

'I could eat an orange,' Maus would remark, clacking his skinny mouth, which was like an old leather purse.

'Imbecile,' Little Pierre would reply, shrugging his shoulders.

He would reach out his hand for the bottle, and the two again would go through the motions of drinking. Their shoulders would shake in foolish laughter. Clinking their glasses, they would repeat a tremulous toast:

'Here's to you, youngster.'

'Same to you, sailor.'

Whereupon, Little Pierre would arise and, stumbling like a drunken man, would begin to curse roundly the sea, mankind, and everything under the sun.

In the broadsides, the crew listened with the smiles of veteran connoisseurs to the vociferations of the two old dotards. Swinging in their hammocks, they were not asleep. They, too, pretended – pretended to sleep, though sleep was an unimportant matter to them, since they were dead; all day long, they dreamed madly, haunted by life-like images of unfulfilled desires.

The sun dived once more into the cold waters of the Antarctic sea, and with the first stars, the watch came down. Their coarse boots clattered on the gunroom ladder, and the night life of the ship began again. As a precaution against meeting a vessel manned by living beings, the tarpaulins covering the cannon were removed, and, on the bridge at the foot of the mainmast, guns and long-bladed knives with handles of rough wood were stacked. A whistle from the captain of the watch called the men to their posts. Some of the crew, who were little more than skeletons, hardly could stand against the wind, which filled the sails like leather bags, while others, twisted into pitiful shapes, looked like grapevines in a storm.

Towards midnight, the blind lookout, who had been stationed at his post as a jest, gave a long raucous blast upon his horn. Already, however, the crew of the *Flying Dutchman* were leaning over the gunrails, regarding with open mouths a terrifying and luminous apparition, which was bearing down upon them with the regular, rhythmic breathing of a good healthy beast.

A long row of lamps adorned the sombre mass of an enormous vessel. The crew of the *Flying Dutchman* contemplated, without a word, this magnificent craft, which was, perhaps, to be their liberator, and which seemed even more phantom-like than their own.

'It's the end!' cried Peter Maus, all of a sudden. 'Lads, we're really going to die this time. Down on your knees, lads, and thank God, as you see me doing.'

All fell to their knees and beat their heads on the deck, in the hope of a catastrophe which should put an end to their cruise.

They did not raise their heads at the sound of a distant and rather dull detonation. Suddenly, a great sheaf of flames spurted up from the brilliantly lighted vessel, and a shower of débris of all sorts fell on the deck of the *Flying Dutchman*. Instinctively, since they had nothing to fear, the crew raised their elbows, protectingly.

When they opened their eyes, the sea was deserted. In place of the huge ship, there was nothing but an expanse of smooth water.

Peter Maus shook his fist in the face of heaven, and the blind lookout, high among the shrouds, laughed.

It was then that a feeble cry from the sea caused every mother's son to pick up his ears. It was, without doubt, the wail of a little child. The voice was small and hoarse. One could picture a baby, with its wry and rumpled face, shaking its chubby fists and kicking up its little feet.

'Let down the long boat,' ordered Peter Maus.

The ancient pulleys groaned, as, not far away on the bosom of the sea, the cry of an infant arose, unmistakably, on the air.

II

In a violent odour of iodine, seaweed, and wet wood, the long boat was drawn up, and with it, a very small baby in a three-piece hood, with a red face and little fingers perpetually in motion. It might have been some ten or twelve months old. Its big round eyes surveyed without fright the funereal visages of the dead seamen who crowded about it.

'Faith,' said Little Pierre, 'it's really a live baby. It is round and well formed.'

All about the infant, the ghostly figures pressed, gazing upon their prey with eager eyes. They examined it with great exaltation, but their glances revealed nothing of what was in their inmost thoughts.

At daybreak, Peter Maus and Little Pierre, who had installed the child in the ship's cabin, began considering how they were going to contrive to bring it up. A ship peopled by dead men who did not eat naturally contained no provisions.

'This child is alive,' said Peter Maus. 'There can be no doubt of that. Can a live being go on living among dead men? I do not think so. We might kill the brat, and perhaps, a little dead one like him would liven things up a bit aboard ship, with his pretty little ways and all that sort of thing, which one expects to find in a child of good bringing-up.'

'This child is too small to give us much amusement,'

replied Little Pierre. "Let's bring him up till he's ten; at that age, on the day of his first communion' (and Little Pierre crossed himself) 'we will kill him; and then, we shall have a little dead cabin boy to lighten our labours.'

'Your plan is adopted,' said Peter Maus, 'and we shall look about among the hulks of this craft we have frightened into shipwreck to see if we can find some sort of nourishment for this little milk-lapper.'

A leading French newspaper carried in its columns the following information, which is curious enough in its way:

Shanghai, July 10, 1921.

The Japanese cruiser, *Nogi*, returning from target practice, recently encountered, in the offing of the bay of Along, a vessel which, with its fires extinguished, was making in a southerly direction. Having given the usual signals, the commodore gave the order to stop the ship and fitted out a whale-boat to board the mysterious craft.

It was found that the vessel in question, a Swedish freighter, had been completely plundered and abandoned. It contained no provisions of any sort. There was one curious detail. In the officers' cabin, the cover had been laid, and a few morsels of food were in the last stages of putrefaction.

It is difficult to imagine the motives which had forced the crew of this ship instantly to abandon their occupations. The affair has the appearance of a Bolshevik atrocity.

This dispatch, read by thousands, did not catch the attention of the crowd. It conveyed a superficial hint of romantic adventures, but it was not detailed enough to be highly interesting. Strictly speaking, the discovery made by the cruiser, *Nogi*, had in it the elements of a romance of rare perversity, but one, of course, which could lay no claim to the approving interest of serious folk.

There was no one in the world, not even the most credulous sailor, but would have had his doubts, had he been told that at the bottom of this mysterious drama was to be found a tiny infant, picked up by one of the crew of damned souls aboard the eternal *Phantom Ship*. One survivor of the adventure there was who, after a few glasses in a tavern swept by seaside breezes, had a tale to tell: of how, one night in the Pacific, his ship had been assailed by an invisible crew, by the light of innumerable lanterns. His tale was listened to with the respect commonly accorded a *raconteur* of quality, without any one's believing a word of the narrative.

The *Flying Dutchman*, commanded by its skipper, Peter Maus, continued on its endless tack and ran up the black flag in place of the one it originally had flown. Frequently, in the middle of the night, the harsh sound of a trumpet would give the signal to clear the decks for action, and fifty lanterns would scamper over the bridge. And the *Flying Dutchman*, rising in all its haughtiness out of the darkness, would hurl forth its adventurers to plunder the goods of the living.

The child prospered among the dead. Little Pierre patiently fattened it up with the aid of bottles of preserved milk. Sometimes, they would spread a coverlet on the bridge, and every one would come to look at the baby, wallowing in its bed of soft wool. The dead men, clustered about the rosy infant, would take on the appearance of stones and old marbles. Part of their skeletons at times showed through their dry, cracked skins. They called the child 'the Rosy King'; and as a matter of fact, he did resemble those roses, at once fragile and robust, which flourish in little village churchyards.

The Rosy King grew and learned to repeat docilely the words which were taught him. He expressed himself a little in all languages, speaking all of them in an antiquated form.

During the night, he would play about, leaping like a familiar demon over the lanterns and climbing up to the lookout to tease the blind old salt who was always so restless. He would roll on his back like a cat, catching the dead men round their pins and crying: 'Come on, now, you old beast, give me my stick.' And the crew would find much amusement in it all, and think, 'What a pretty little dead boy Rosy King will make. For all eternity, we shall be able to refresh our souls with his gestures, his words, his cries and his little hurts.'

In the cabin, between the map of the world and the maritime charts, among the piles of preserve-bottles and biscuit-packages, which had been taken aboard from plundered cargoes, the young Rosy King would listen benevolently, with his knees on a stool, to the monotonous counsels of the captain and the second officer.

'How is it,' the child would ask, 'that you are so different from me? And besides, you have such a funny odour. And you don't eat like me nor drink milk and sweet water.'

'That,' Peter Maus would reply, 'is because you are now living in the kingdom of the dead. Here, on this ship, we are all dead ones.'

'What is a dead one?' Rosy King would inquire.

'You don't understand.'

'Ah, I want to be dead like you, like Little Pierre, like Gruida, the boatswain, and like Loiselet who plays the flute. I want to be dead like you, so I can have a pretty brown skin, and so I can crack the bones in my hands. I'd like to run over the bridge with a little lantern.'

'We were just like you, fat and chubby youngsters, when we were alive.'

'Where do the alive people live,' the child would ask, 'on the English coast?'

Peter Maus gave up trying to explain the double mystery

of life and death, but each day, Rosy King would listen to the former's curses against those enigmatic beings, the living, whom the captain held responsible for his own damnation.

Certain nights, under the diabolical light of the lanterns, the dead crew would dance, hurling abominable threats at the living. Having gone through the motions of drinking, they would imitate the excesses of drunken men; and then, they would light a fire in their empty pipe-bowls, and their mouths would suck in, voluptuously, the green and yellow flames.

The young Rosy King was now twelve years old. He presided at these celebrations, playing horseback with a cannon. He would clap his hands, ravished by the spectacle, which for him was the most amusing one he could dream of.

'One day, I shall be dead like them,' he thought, and his little bosom would heave with pride.

III

Clad in a coat of scarlet cloth, which formerly had belonged to Peter Maus, and which an ingenious spectre had retailored, after a half-way fashion, Rosy King had further obtained from Little Pierre, who was inclined to spoil the child, a tiny lantern, which he would brandish by night as he galloped over the worm-eaten deck of the *Flying Dutchman*.

He loved this life by one's wits aboard the famous ghost-ship, and he was vastly amused by the terror-stricken faces of poor mariners, surprised in mid-sea by the rapid passage of the vessel, the crew of which were the victims of so wondrous a punishment. But he loved, above all, to stand against the poop-house and listen to the dead as they took vengeance on the living. The child had come to consider these living beings as mysterious, cruel, perverted in character, and with unsavoury pasts behind them – as a people from whom he must guard himself at all costs.

Later, thanks to the conversation of Little Pierre, he had created for himself a conception of life that was all his own, one that the infernal environment in which he had been reared only tended to strengthen. Life impressed him as being a distant catastrophe, so distant that he was unable precisely to estimate its dimensions; but he had a frightful chill, every time he thought of it at all attentively. His youth, however, did not permit of any but the briefest meditations. And so, he grew up, in the broadsides of this legendary ship, without any point of comparison which would give him a chance for a reasonable appraisement of his exceptional situation.

Then, one day, Peter Maus, contemplating the childish grace of the lad, who had grown to quite a size on a diet of fishes, which he now caught with considerable skill, conceived the idea of redeeming past sins by one good deed. So he said to Little Pierre:

'Lieutenant, the more I think of it, the more I am struck with the idea that Providence, in sending us, upon a wreck, this little living creature, was merely trying us out. Don't you believe that we would be acting in accordance with the ends of Providence, if we were to give the child back to life? True enough, the presence among us to a little rascal of a dead lad could not help relieving the bitterness of our fate; but I do not think that God has placed him in the path of the *Flying Dutchman* to meet that same fate. What do you think?'

Little Pierre brought the long bones of his hands together over his knees.

'I think the same as you,' he replied, 'that it would be best to set the child ashore; and perhaps, if we did so, it would bring us a little divine favour.'

'Very well, we'll set him ashore, along the coast, tomorrow night; yes, we'll set him ashore along the Breton coast, near Auray, on holy ground. Let's be sure to put all the chances on our side.'

'You old villain,' remarked Little Pierre.

Whereupon, Peter Maus straightened himself and yelped: 'Cross yourself! You swine! Cross yourself! You blasphemer! You Judas, you! You Judas!'

They fought, and the clashing of their arms was like the sound of wooden sticks.

The following day, shortly before nightfall, Peter Maus called Rosy King to him and, pointing out with one finger a grey band on the horizon, said to him: 'There is the land from which you came to which you are going to return. You cannot stay with us any longer. God will not permit it . . . I have spoken to you angrily about God sometimes, but I was wrong; I spoke as all the damned do, as you will understand, too late, if you ever come to this state . . . Almighty God has given you life, and we cannot make a dead one out of you.'

The child began to cry: 'Let me die by your side, O Peter Maus, and I will make you laugh by imitating old Gruida when he plays the flute.'

But Peter Maus shook his head, and the lad, shrivelled up with despair, threw himself down on the bridge and set up a weird wail that was enough to tear the heart out of any man.

'Of course, you couldn't have avoided this,' grumbled

Little Pierre. 'It would have been better to set him ashore without telling him all that.'

Night came, and the Southern Cross shone in the sky. With all sails filled, the *Flying Dutchman* soon left the tropics behind, in a supernatural effort to take advantage of the favouring winds. Soon, the quiet harbours of old Europe hove into view.

The skeleton crew, drawn up on deck, gazed at the lad as he stood, shivering with fright, in his scarlet coat of ancient cut. The lanterns on the bridge outlined the dark shadow of each man, but all the light streamed on Rosy King's white face and chattering teeth. Then, there came a noise like the rustling of wings, and the sound of the yawl, brushing the ship's sides, was heard.

'Come, Rosy King,' said the captain, 'say good-bye and pray for us. Here's a little silver to buy candles. The first woman you meet will tell you what you should do for the repose of our souls.'

'I don't want to live!' screamed Rosy King. 'Let me be, Peter Maus, let me be!'

They lowered the lad down into the yawl, and Peter Maus took the tiller. The oars ground in their tholes. Soon, a black line hollowed itself out into a semi-circle.

'Attention,' commanded Peter Maus, 'back water all around.'

The yawl snapped throughout its frame.

'Pull to the larboard,' directed Peter Maus.

The bottom of the yawl grated on the shingles, and Peter Maus carefully stepped overboard. The water came up to his thighs. He took Rosy King in his arms and made for land.

A frightful whistling filled the night.

'Don't be afraid,' said Peter Maus, 'it's only the wind in the trees!'

He deposited Rosy King at the foot of a white path that ran back into the land; then, with great strides, he regained the long boat.

Rosy King, paralyzed with fright, stood still, without a whimper; but as the long boat receded farther and farther from shore, in order to regain the *Flying Dutchman* as quickly as possible, as is the law of dead souls, the cry of a child might have been heard. It was the cry of a dying soul, lamenting its fate.

'Good-bye, Rosy King,' cried Peter Maus once more, from the long boat.

TRAIN FOR FLUSHING

Malcolm Jameson

'They ought never to have hired that man. Even the most stupid of personnel managers should have seen at a glance that he was mad. Perhaps it is too much to expect such efficiency these days – in *my* time a thing like this could not have happened. They would have known the fellow was under a curse! It only shows what the world has come to. But I can tell you that if we ever do get off this crazy runaway car, I intend to turn the Interboro wrongside out. They needn't think because I am an old man and retired that I am a nobody they can push around. My son Henry, the Lawyer one, will build a fire under them – he knows people in this town.

'And I am not the only victim of the maniac. There is a pleasant, elderly woman here in the car with me. She was much frightened at first, but she had recognized me for a solid man, and now she stays close to me all the time. She is a Mrs Herrick, and a quite nice woman. It was her idea that I write this down – it will help us refresh our memories when we come to testify.

'Just at the moment, we are speeding atrociously *downtown* along the Seventh Avenue line of the subway – but we are on the *uptown* express track! The first few times we tore through those other trains it was terrible – I thought we were sure to be killed – and even if we were not, I have to think of my heart. Dr Steinback told me only last week how careful I should be. Mrs Herrick has been very brave about it, but it is a scandalous thing to subject anyone to, above all such a kindly little person.

'The madman who seems to be directing us (if charging wildly up and down these tracks implied *direction*), is now looking out the front door, staring horribly at the gloom rushing at us. He is a big man and heavy-set, very weathered and tough-looking. I am nearing eighty and slight.

'There is nothing I can do but wait for the final crash; for crash we must, sooner or later, unless some Interboro official has brains enough to shut off the current to stop us. If *he* escapes the crash, the police will know him by his heavy red beard and tattooing on the backs of his hands. The beard is square-cut and there cannot be another one like it in all New York.

'But I notice I have failed to put down how this insane ride began. My granddaughter, Mrs Charles L. Terneck, wanted me to see the World's Fair, and was to come in from

Great Neck and meet me at the subway station. I will say that she insisted someone come with me, but I can take care of myself – I always have – even if my eyes and ears are not what they used to be.

'The train was crowded, but somebody gave me a seat in a corner. Just before we reached the stop, the woman next to me, this Mrs Herrick, had asked if I knew how to get to Whitestone from Flushing. It was while I was telling her what I knew about the buses, that the train stopped and let everybody off the car but us. I was somewhat irritated at missing the station, but knew that all I had to do was stay on the car, go to Flushing and return. It was then that the maniac guard came in and behaved so queerly.

'This car was the last one in the train, and the guard had been standing where he belongs, on the platform. But he came into the car, walking with a curious rolling walk (but I do not mean to imply he was drunk, for I do not think so) and his manner was what you might call masterful, almost overbearing. He stopped at the middle door and looked very intently out to the north, at the sound.

' "*That* is not the Scheldt!" he called out, angrily, with a thick, foreign accent, and then he said "Bah!" loudly, in a tone of disgusted disillusionment.

'He seemed of a sudden to fly into a great fury. The train was just making its stop at the end of the line, in Flushing.

He rushed to the forward platform and somehow broke the coupling. At the same moment, the car began running backward along the track by which we had come. There was no chance for us to get off, even if we had been young and active. The doors were not opened, it happened so quickly.

'Then he came into the car, muttering to himself. His eye caught the sign of painted tin they put in the windows to show the destination of the trains. He snatched the plate lettered "Flushing" and tore it to bits with his rough hands, as if it had been cardboard, throwing the pieces down and stamping on them.

' "That is not Flushing! Not *my* Flushing – not *Vlissingenl* But I will find it. I will go there, and not all the devils in Hell! Nor the angels in Heaven shall stop me!"

'He glowered at us, beating his breast with his clenched fists, as if angry and resentful at us for having deceived him in some manner. It was then that Mrs Herrick stooped over and took my hand. We had gotten up close to the door to step out at the World's Fair station, but the car did not stop. It continued its wild career straight on, at dizzy speed.

' "*Rugwaartsch*!" he shouted, or something equally unintelligible. "*Back* I must go, like always, but yet will I find my Vlissingen!"

'Then followed the horror of pitching headlong into those trains! The first one we saw coming, Mrs Herrick screamed. I put my arm around her and braced myself as best I could with my cane. But there was no crash, just a blinding succession of lights and colours, in quick winks. We seemed to go straight through that train, from end to end, at lightning speed, but there was not even a jar. I do not understand that, for I saw it coming, clearly. Since, there have been many others. I have lost count now, we meet so many, and swing from one track to another so giddily at the end of runs.

'But we have learned, Mrs Herrick and I, not to dread the collision − or say, passage − so much. We are much afraid of what the bearded ruffian who dominates this car will do next − surely we cannot go on this way much longer, it has already been many, many hours. I cannot comprehend why the stupid people who run the Interboro do not do something to stop us, so that the police could subdue this maniac and I can have Henry take me to the District Attorney.'

So read the first few pages of the notebook turned over to me by the Missing Persons Bureau. Neither Mrs Herrick, nor Mr Dennison, whose handwriting it is, has been found yet, nor the guard he mentions. In contradiction, the Interboro insists no guard employed by them is unaccounted for, and further, that they never had had a man of the above description on their payrolls.

On the other hand, they have as yet produced no

satisfactory explanation of how the car broke loose from the train at Flushing.

I agree with the police that this notebook contains matter that may have some bearing on the disappearance of these two unfortunate citizens; yet here in the Psychiatric Clinic we are by no means agreed as to the interpretation of this provocative and baffling diary.

The portion I have just quoted was written with a fountain pen in a crabbed, tremulous hand, quite exactly corresponding to the latest examples of old Mr Dennison's writing. Then we find a score or more of pages torn out, and a resumption of the record in indelible pencil. The handwriting here is considerably stronger and more assured, yet unmistakably that of the same person. Farther on, there are other places where pages have been torn from the book, and evidence that the journal was but intermittently kept. I quote now all that is legible of the remainder of it:

'Judging by the alternations of the cold and hot seasons, we have now been on this weird and pointless journey for more than ten years. Oddly enough, we do not suffer physically, although the interminable rushing up and down these caverns under the streets becomes boring. The ordinary wants of the body are strangely absent, or dulled. We sense heat and cold, for example, but do not find their extremes particularly uncomfortable, while food has become an item of far distant memory. I imagine, though, we must sleep a good deal.

'The guard has very little to do with us, ignoring us most of the time as if we did not exist. He spends his days sitting brooding at the far end of the car, staring at the floor, mumbling in his wild, red beard. On other days he will get up and peer fixedly ahead, as if seeking something. Again, he will pace the aisle in obvious anguish, flinging his outlandish curses over his shoulder as he goes. "*Verdoemd*" and "*verwenscht*" are the commonest ones – we have learned to recognize them – and he tears his hair in frenzy whenever he pronounces them. His name, he says, is Van Der Dechen, and we find it politic to call him "Captain".

'I have destroyed what I wrote during the early years (all but the account of the very first day); it seems rather querulous and hysterical now. I was not in good health then, I think, but I have improved noticeably here, and that without medical care. Much of my stiffness, due to a recent arthritis, has left me, and I seem to hear better.

'Mrs Herrick and I have long since become accustomed to our forced companionship, and we have learned much about each other. At first, we both worried a good deal over our families' concern about our absence. But when this odd and purposeless kidnapping occurred, we were already so nearly to the end of life (being of about the same age) that we finally concluded our children and grand-children must have been prepared for our going soon, in any event. It left us only with the problem of enduring the tedium of the interminable rolling through the tubes of the Interboro.

'In the pages I have deleted, I made much of the annoyance we experienced during the early weeks due to flickering through oncoming trains. That soon came to be so commonplace, occurring as it did every few minutes, that it became as unnoticeable as our breathing. As we lost the fear of imminent disaster, our riding became more and more burdensome through the deadly monotony of the tunnels.

'Mrs Herrick and I diverted ourselves by talking (and to think that in my earlier entries in this journal I complained of her garrulousness!) or by trying to guess at what was going on in the city above us by watching the crowds on the station platforms. That is a difficult game, because we are running so swiftly, and there are frequent intervening trains. A thing that has caused us much speculation and discussion is the changing type of advertising on the bill-posters. Nowadays they are featuring the old favourites – many of the newer toothpastes and medicines seem to have been withdrawn. Did they fail, or has a wave of conservative reaction overwhelmed the country?

'Another marvel in the weird life we lead is the juvenescence of our home, the runaway car we are confined to. In spite of its unremitting use, always at top speed, it has become steadily brighter, more new-looking. Today it has the appearance of having been recently delivered from the builders' shops.

'I learned half a century ago that having nothing to do, and all the time in the world to do it in, is the surest way to get nothing done. In looking in this book, I find it has been ten years since I made an entry! It is a fair indication of the idle, routine life in this wandering car. The very invariableness of our existence has discouraged keeping notes. But recent developments are beginning to force me to face a situation that has been growing ever more obvious. The cumulative evidence is by now almost overwhelming that this state of ours as a meaning – has an explanation. Yet I dread to think the thing through – to call its name! Because there will be two ways to interpret it. Either it *is* as I am driven to conclude, or else I . . .

'I must talk it over frankly with Nellie Herrick. She is remarkably poised and level-headed, and understanding. She and I have matured a delightful friendship.

'What disturbs me more than anything is the trend in advertising. They are selling products again that were popular so long ago that I had actually forgotten them. And the appeals are made in the idiom of years ago. Lately it has been hard to see the posters, the station platforms are so full. In the crowds are many uniforms, soldiers and sailors. We infer from that there is another war – but the awful question is, "What war?"

'Those are some of the things we can observe in the world over there. In our own little fleeting world, things have developed even more inexplicably. My health and appearance, notably. My hair is no longer white! It is turning dark again in the back, and on top. And the same is true of Nellie's. There are other similar changes for the better. I see much more clearly and my hearing is practically perfect.

'The culmination of these disturbing signals of retrogression has come with the newest posters. It is their appearance that forces me to face the facts. Behind the crowds we glimpse new appeals, many and insistent – "BUY VICTORY LOAN BONDS!" From the number of them to be seen, one would think we were back in the happy days of 1919, when the soldiers were coming home from the World War.

'My talk with Nellie has been most comforting and reassuring. It is hardly like that we should both be insane and have identical symptoms. The inescapable conclusion that I dreaded to put into words is *so* – it must be so. In some unaccountable manner, we are *unliving* life! Time is going backward! "*Rugwaartsch*," the mad Dutchman said that first day when he turned back from Flushing; "we will go backward" – to *his* Flushing, the one he knew. Who knows what Flushing he knew? It must be the Flushing of another age, or else why should the deranged wizard (if it is he who has thus reversed time) choose a path through time itself? Helpless, we can only wait and see how far he will take us.

'We are not wholly satisfied with our new theory. Everything does not go backward; otherwise how could it be possible for me to write these lines? I think we are like flies crawling up the walls of an elevator cab while it is in full descent. Their own proper movements, relative to their environment, are upward, but all the while they are being carried relentlessly downward. It is a sobering thought. Yet we are both relieved that we should have been able to speak it. Nellie admits that she has been troubled for some time, hesitating to voice the thought. She called my attention to the subtle way in which our clothing has been changing, an almost imperceptible de-evolution in style.

'We are now on the lookout for ways in which to date ourselves in this headlong plunging into the past. Shortly after writing the above, we were favoured with one opportunity not to be mistaken. It was the night of the Armistice. What a night in the subway! Then followed, in inverse order, the various issues of the Liberty Bonds. Over forty years ago – counting time both ways, forward, then again backward – *I* was up there, a dollar-a-year man, selling them on the streets. Now we suffer a new anguish, imprisoned down here in this racing subway car. The evidence all around us brings a nostalgia that is almost intolerable. None of us knows how perfect his memory is until it is thus prompted. But we cannot go up there, we an only guess at what is going on above us.

'The realization of what is really happening to us has caused us to be less antagonistic to our conductor. His sullen brooding makes us wonder whether he is not a fellow victim, rather than our abductor, he seems so unaware of us usually. At other times, we regard him as the principal in this drama of the gods and are bewildered at the curious twist of Fate that has entangled us with the destiny of the unhappy Van Der Dechen, for unhappy he certainly is. Our anger at his arrogant behaviour has long since died away. We can see that some secret sorrow gnaws continually at his heart.

' "There is *een vloek* over me," he said gravely, one day, halting unexpectedly before us in the midst of one of his agitated pacings of the aisle. He seemed to be trying to explain – apologize for, if you will – our situation. "Accursed I am, damned!' He drew a great breath, looking at us appealingly. Then his black mood came back on him with a rush, and he strode away growling mighty Dutch oaths. "But I will best them – God Himself shall not prevent me – not if it takes all eternity!"

'Our orbit is growing more restricted. It is a long time now since we went to Brooklyn, and only the other day we swerved suddenly at Times Square and cut through to Grand Central. Considering this circumstance, the type of car we are in now, and our costumes, we must be in 1905 or thereabouts. That is a year I remember with great vividness. It was the year I first came to New York. I keep speculating on what will become of us. In another year we will have plummeted the full history of the subway. What then? Will that be the end?

'Nellie is the soul of patience. It is a piece of great fortune, a blessing, that since we were doomed to this wild ride, we happened in it together. Our friendship has ripened into a warm affection that lightens the gloom of this tedious wandering.

'It must have been last night that we emerged from the caves of Manhattan. Thirty-four years of darkness is ended. We are now out in the country, going west. Our vehicle is not the same, it is an old-fashioned day coach, and ahead is a small locomotive. We cannot see engineer or fireman, but Van Der Dechen frequently ventures across the swaying, open platform and mounts the tender, where he stands firmly with wide-spread legs, scanning the country ahead through an old brass long-glass. His uniform is more nautical than railroadish – it took the sunlight to show that to us. There was always the hint of salt air about him. We should have shown who he was from his insistence on being addressed as Captain.

'The outside world *is* moving backward! When we look closely at the wagons and buggies in the muddy trails alongside the right of way fence, we can see that the horses or mules are walking or running backward. But we pass them so quickly, as a rule, that their real motion is inconspicuous. We are too grateful for the sunshine and the trees after so many years of gloom, to quibble about this topsy-turvy condition.

'Five years in the open has taught us much about Nature in reverse. There is not so much difference as one would suppose. It took us a long time to notice that the sun rose in the west and sank in the east. Summer follows winter, as it always has. It was our first spring, or rather, the season that we have come to regard as spring, that we were really disconcerted. The trees were bare, the skies cloudy, and the weather cool. We could not know, at first sight, whether we had emerged into spring or fall.

'The ground was wet, and gradually white patches of snow were forming. Soon, the snow covered everything. The sky darkened and the snow began to flurry, drifting and swirling upward, out of sight. Later we saw the ground covered with dead leaves, so we thought it must be fall. Then a few of the trees were seen to have leaves, then fall. Soon the forests were in the full glory of red and brown autumn leaves, but in a few weeks those colours turned gradually through oranges and yellows to dark greens, and we were in full summer. Our fall, which succeeded the summer, was almost normal, except towards the end, when the leaves brightened into paler greens, dwindled little by little to mere buds and then disappeared within the trees.

'The passage of a troop train, its windows crowded with campaign-hatted heads and waving arms tells us another war has begun (or more properly, ended). The soldiers are returning from Cuba. *Our* wars, in this backward way by which we approach them, begin with victory celebrations and end in anxiety! More nostalgia – I finished that war as a major. I keep looking eagerly at the throngs on the platforms of the railroad stations as we sweep by them, hoping to sight a familiar face among the yellow-legged cavalry. More than eighty years ago it was, as I reckon it, forty years of it spent on the road to senility and another forty back to the prime of life.

'Somewhere among those blue-uniformed veterans am I, in my original phase, I cannot know just where, because my memory is vague as to the dates. I have caught myself entertaining the idea of stopping this giddy flight into the past, of getting out and finding my way to my former home. Only, if I could, I would be creating tremendous problems – there would have to be some sort of mutual accommodation between my *alter ego* and me. It looks impossible, and there are no precedents to guide us.

'Then, all my affairs have become complicated by the existence of Nell. She and I have had many talks about this strange state of affairs, but they are rarely conclusive. I think I must have over-estimated her judgment a little in the beginning. But it really doesn't matter. She has developed into a stunning woman and her quick, ready sympathy makes up for her lack in that direction. I glory particularly in her hair, which she lets down some days. It is thick and long and beautifully wavy, as hair should be. We often sit on the back platform and she allows it to blow free in the breeze, all the time laughing at me because I adore it so.

'Captain Van Der Dechen notices us not at all, unless in scorn. His mind, his whole being, is centred on getting back to Flushing – *his* Flushing, that he calls Vlissingen – wherever that may be in time or space. Well, it appears that he is taking us back, too, but it is backward in time for us. As for him, time seems meaningless. He is unchangeable. Not a single hair of that piratical beard has altered since that far-future day of long ago when he broke our car away from the Interboro train in Queens. Perhaps he suffers from the same sort of unpleasant immortality the mythical Wandering Jew is said to be afflicted with – otherwise why should he complain so bitterly of the curse he says is upon him?

'Nowadays he talks to himself much of the time, mainly about his ship. It is that which he hopes to find since the Flushing beyond New York proved not to be the one he strove for. He says he left it cruising along a rocky coast. He has either forgotten where he left it or it is no longer there, for we have gone to all the coastal points touched by the railroads. Each failure brings fresh storms of rage and blasphemy; not even perpetual frustration seems to abate the man's determination or capacity for fury.

'That Dutchman has switched trains on us again! This one hasn't even Pintsch gas, nothing but coal oil. It is smoky and it stinks. The engine is a wood-burner with a balloon stack. The sparks are very bad and we cough a lot.

'I went last night when the Dutchman wasn't looking and took a look into the cab of the engine. There is no crew and I found the throttle closed. A few years back that would have struck me as odd, but now I have to accept it. I did mean to stop the train so I could take Nell off, but there is no way to stop it. It just goes along, I don't know how.

'On the way back I met the Dutchman, shouting and swearing the way he does, on the forward platform. I tried to throw him off the train. I am as big and strong as he is and I don't see why I should put up with his overbearing ways. But when I went to grab him, my hands closed right through. The man is not real! It is strange I never noticed that before.

Maybe that is why there is no way to stop the train, and why nobody ever seems to notice us. Maybe the train is not real, either. I must look tomorrow and see whether it casts a shadow. Perhaps even *we* are not . . .

'But Nell is real. I *know* that.

'The other night we passed a depot platform where there was a political rally – a torchlight parade. They were carrying banners, "Garfield for President." If we are ever to get off this train, we must do it soon

'Nell says no, it would be embarrassing. I try to talk seriously to her about us, but she just laughs and kisses me and says let well enough alone. I wouldn't mind starting life over again, even if these towns do look pretty rough. But Nell says that she was brought up on a Kansas farm by a step-mother and she would rather go on to the end and vanish, if need be, than go back to it.

'That thing about the end troubles me a lot, and I wish she wouldn't keep mentioning it. It was only lately that I thought about it much, and it worries me more than death ever did in the old days. *We know when it will be*! 1860 for me – on the third day of August. The last ten years will be terrible – getting smaller, weaker, more helpless all the time, and winding up as a messy, squally baby. Why, that means I have only about ten more years that are fit to live; when I was this young before, I had a lifetime ahead. It's not right!

And now *she* has made a silly little vow – "Until birth do us part!" – and made me say it with her!

'It is too crowded in here, and it jolts awfully. Nell and I are cooped up in the front seats and the Captain stays in the back part – the quarterdeck, he calls it. Sometimes he opens the door and climbs up into the driver's seat. There is no driver, but we have a four-horse team and they gallop all the time, day and night. The Captain says we must use a stagecoach, because he has tried all the railroad tracks and none of them is right. He wants to get back to the sea he came from and to his ship. He is not afraid that is has been stolen, for he says most men are afraid of it – it is a haunted ship, it appears, and brings bad luck.

'We passed two men on horses this morning. One was going our way and met the other coming. The other fellow stopped him and I heard him holler, "They killed Custer and all his men!" and the man that was going the same way we were said, "The bloodthirsty heathens! I'm a-going to jine!"

'Nellie cries a lot. She's afraid of Indians. I'm not afraid of Indians. I would like to see one.

'I wish it was a boy with me, instead of this little girl. Then we could do something. All she wants to do is play with that fool dolly. We could make some bows and arrows and shoot at the buffaloes, but she says that is wicked.

'I tried to get the Captain to talk to me, but he won't. He

just laughed and laughed, and said,

‘ "*Een tijd kiezan voor – op schip!*"

'That made me mad, talking crazy talk like that, and I told him so.

‘ "Time!" he bellows, laughing like everything. " 'Twill all be right in time!" And he looks hard at me, showing his big teeth in his beard. "Four – five – six hundert years – more – it is nothing. I have all eternity! But once more on my ship, I will get there. I have sworn it! You come with me and I will show you the sea – the great Indian Sea behind the Cape of Good Hope. Then some day, if those accursed head winds abate, I will take you home with me to Flushing. That I will, though the Devil himself, or all the –" And then he went off to cursing and swearing the way he always does in his crazy Dutchman's talk.

'Nellie is mean to me. She is too bossy. She says she will not play unless I write in the book. She says I am supposed to write something in the book every day. There is not anything to put in the book. Same old stagecoach. Same old Captain. Same old everything. I do not like the Captain. He is crazy. In the night-time he points at the stars shining through the roof of the coach and laughs and laughs. Then he gets mad, and swears and curses something awful. When I get big again, I am going to kill him – I wish we could get away – I am afraid – it would be nice if we could find mama –'

This terminates the legible part of the notebook. All of the writing purporting to have been done in the stagecoach is shaky, and the letters are much larger than earlier in the script. The rest of the contents is infantile scribblings, or grotesque childish drawings. Some of them show feathered Indians drawing bows and shooting arrows. The very last one seems to represent a straight up and down cliff with wiggly lines at the bottom to suggest waves, and off a little way is a crude drawing of a galleon or other antique ship.

This notebook, together with Mr Dennison's hat and cane and Mrs Herrick's handbag, were found in the derailed car that broke away from the Flushing train and plunged off the track into the Meadows. The police are still maintaining a perfunctory hunt for the two missing persons, but I think the fact they brought this journal to us clearly indicates they consider the search hopeless. Personally, I really do not see of what help these notes can be. I fear that by now Mr Dennison and Mrs Herrick are quite inaccessible.

MAX PEMBERTON

Max Pemberton was born in London, England in 1863. He attended Caius College, Cambridge, and became involved in journalism soon after graduating. Pemberton soon became a major figure on Fleet Street, and acted as editor of boys' magazine *Chums* in what was its heyday. Between 1896 and 1906 he also edited *Cassell's Magazine*, in which capacity he published the early works of R. Austin Freeman and William Le Queux. Aside from his journalism, Pemberton published a number of novels, his most famous being *The Iron Pirate* (1893). His short story 'Wheels of Anarchy' (1910) also remains widely anthologized. In 1920, Pemberton founded the London School of Journalism. He died in 1950, aged 86.

HEINRICH HEINE

Christian Johann Heinrich Heine was born in Düsseldorf, Germany in 1797. In 1814, he attended a merchant school, and began an apprenticeship at a bank in Frankfurt. From 1819 until 1825, Heine studied law in various cities across Germany, and in 1824, during his travels through the Harz Mountains, met Johann Wolfgang von Goethe. After passing his law exam, Heine continued to travel, moving to England in 1827. Here, he began to focus seriously on writing, which had been a hobby for him throughout his youth.

In 1828, Heine's *Book of Songs* was published. The collection of bittersweet poems was highly popular, and instandy established his international literary reputation. His *Pictures of Travel* (4 vols., 1826-31), was equally popular, and in 1831 Heine moved to Paris. His political articles, many of which critiqued German conservatism, were adjudged to subversive by the German state, who sent spies to watch him. Heine's second verse collection, *New Poems* (1844), reflected his increasing interest in radical politics, and his third and final, *Romanzero* (1851), is a bleak work which some scholars consider his masterpiece. Heine died in 1856, aged 58. He is now regarded as one of Germany's great lyric poets, and a key figure in German Romanticism.

WILHELM HAUFF

Wilhelm Hauff was born in Stuttgart, Germany in 1802. In 1818, he was sent to the Klosterschule (convent school) at Blaubeuren, and in 1820 began to study at the University of Tübingen. In four years, he completed his philosophical and theological studies at the Tübinger Stift -a hall of residence and teaching previously attended by G. W F. Hegel, Friedrich Schelling and others.

Upon leaving university, Hauff became tutor to the children of the famous Württemberg minister of war, General Baron Ernst Eugen von Hugel (1774–1849), and for them wrote some of his best-known fairy tales, published in his *Märchen almanach auf das Jahr 1826* (*Fairytale Almanac of 1826*). Some of these tales – such as 'Der Zwerg Nase' (Little Longnose) and 'Das Wirtshaus im Spessart' (The Inn in the Spessart)- remain very popular in Germany to this day.

Over the rest of his somewhat brief life, Hauff was an incredibly prolific author, producing a string of novels, short stories and poems. His 1826 historical romance *Lichtenstein: Romantische Sage aus der wuerttembergischen Geschichte* (*Lichtenstein: Romantic Saga from the History of Württemberg*) was immensely popular – so much so that it inspired Duke Wilhelm of Urach to rebuild his castle in accordance with Hauffs description as laid out in the book. Critics, meanwhile, regard his masterpiece as the 1827 novella *Phantasiem im Bremer Ratskeller* (*The Wine-Ghosts of Bremen*).

In January 1827, Hauff undertook the editorship of the *Stuttgart Morgenblatt* – a popular morning newspaper – and in the following month married his cousin Luise Hauff. However, his happiness was prematurely cut short by his death from fever in November of that same year, aged just 24.

W. CLARK RUSSELL

William Clark Russell was born in New York City, USA in 1844. After finishing school, he spent eight years' service as a sailor, before becoming a journalist on the staff of the *Daily Chronicle*. During his late twenties, Russell turned to novel-writing, publishing his first work, *As Innocent as a Baby*, in 1874. Russell quickly became a hugely popular author, producing more than 40 novels over the course of his life. His best-selling work was *The Wreck of the Grosvenor* (1877), which became one of the best-read melodramas of the Victorian era, and continued to sell well long into the 20th century. Russell died in 1911, aged 66.

GEORGE GRIFFITH

George Chetwyn Griffith-Jones was born in 1857. During his twenties he became a freelance journalist, authoring a series of pamphlets on secularism and writing articles for *Pearson's Magazine*. In 1893, inspired by Philip H. Colomb's *The Great War of 1892*, he published his first novel, *The Angel of the Revolution*. A lurid tale of global dominance via airship warfare, it remains his best and most famous work. Griffith followed it with more than twenty other novels, and countless short stories – of these, *The World Peril of 1910* (1907) also remains relatively well-read. Despite being somewhat forgotten now, in his day Griffith was an extremely popular writer, and his work foreshadowed World War I and the Russian Revolution. His short story 'The Great Crellin Comet' (1897) was the first story to include a ten second countdown for a space launch. Aside from his science-fiction, Griffith was a keen traveller, completing a record-breaking voyage around the world in just 65 days and helping discover the source of the Amazon River. He died in 1906, aged 48.

JAMES BRANDER MATTHEWS

James Brander Matthews was born in New Orleans, USA in 1852. He attended Columbia College and Columbia Law School, graduating in 1873, but turned quickly to a literary career. From 1892 until 1900, he was professor at Columbia University, eventually becoming the first professor of dramatic literature in the USA. Matthews was an influential educator and scholar, drawing students from all over the country. Although he primarily wrote non-fiction, and was widely noted for works such as *The Philosophy of the Short-Story* (1901) and *The Development of the Drama* (1903), he also penned short fiction and some poetry. Matthews died in 1929, aged 77.

JOSEPH CONRAD

Joseph Conrad was born Józef Teodor Konrad Korzeniowski in Berdichev – a town in Polish Ukraine, then part of the Russian Empire – in 1857. He was left orphaned at the age of eleven, and placed in the care of his uncle in Kraków. The young Conrad found Russia oppressive, and soon after he turned sixteen, he went to Marseille, France, to begin a career as a seaman. Over the next few years, Conrad mastered the fundamentals of seamanship while voyaging to such far-flung destinations as Colombia. He also learnt French and made many acquaintances in dramatic, literary and bohemian circles.

In 1878, Conrad was wounded in the chest. Some biographers say he fought a duel in Marseille, others that he attempted suicide. Following the incident, he took service on his first British ship, landing in England later that year. By 1886, during which time he had voyaged to many other destinations, including Indonesia, Conrad was fluent in English. He gained both his Master Mariner's certificate and British citizenship, and officially changed his name to the anglicized 'Joseph Conrad'.

In 1889, in an event which would inspire his best-known novel, *Heart of Darkness*, Conrad visited the Congo Free State of Africa as captain of a steamboat. Five years after the voyage, in 1894, Conrad gave up the naval life – partly because of ill health, and partly because he was becoming increasingly interested in writing. He published his first novel, *Almayer's Folly*, in 1895, and his major productive phase spanned from 1897 to 1911, during which he penned books. However, Conrad's first major success came in 1913, with the publication of *Chance*. A commercial and critical success, the novel established Conrad as the most popular writer of his era, and saw him make the acquaintance of writers such as Henry James and Stephen Crane. He even appeared on the cover of the 7th April, 1923 edition of *Time* magazine.

Conrad died in 1924, aged 66. He is now regarded as one of the great novelists in the English language, despite the fact that he did not speak the language fluently until his twenties. Conrad's most influential work remains *Heart of Darkness* (1899), to which many have been introduced by Francis Ford Coppola's film, *Apocalypse Now* (1979). However, *Lord Jim* (1900) and *Nostromo* (1904) continue to be widely read, and *The Secret Agent* (1907) and *Under Western Eyes* (1911) are also considered fine works.

WILLIAM HOPE HODGSON

William Hope Hodgson was born in Essex, England in 1877. He began a four-year apprenticeship as a cabin boy at the age of fourteen, and spent most of his teens at sea. In 1899, having returned to Blackburn, England, he became a well-known bodybuilder, and his first writing endeavours were essays on the subject of fitness and health. He turned his attention to fiction during the early part of the 20th century, and in 1904 published his first short story, 'The Goddess of Death'. Over the next few years, his fiction spread to the American market, where his 'Sargasso Sea stories' were well-received. Hodgson wrote prolifically for the rest of his life, and is best-known nowadays for two novels – *The House on the Borderland* (1908) and *The Night Land* (1912) – and the much-anthologised stories 'The Whistling Room', 'The Voice in the Night' and 'The Shamraken Homeward-Bounder'. Hodgson was killed by an artillery shell at Ypres in April of 1918.

VICTOR MACCLURE

Victor MacClure was born in London, England in 1887. He published a good deal of short fiction, but was best known for his 1924 novel *The Ark of the Covenant*, which was later serialised in four parts in 1929. MacClure died in 1963, aged 76.

C. J. CUTCLIFFE HYNE

C. J. Cutcliffe Hyne was born in Bibury, England in 1865. Raised in Yorkshire, he attended Cambridge University, where he received both a Bachelor's and Master's degree. He started writing in his twenties, producing the popular Captain Kettle series. Kettle first appeared as a side character in *Honour of Thieves* (1895), and went on to appear as the protagonist in three sets of twelve short stories, all of which were published in *Pearson's* magazine and subsequently collected in a number of collections. However, Hyne is probably best-remembered as the author of the novel *The Lost Continent: The Story of Atlantis* (1900), considered one of the classic fictional retellings of the myth of the drowning city. Over the course of his life, he penned roughly fifty novels and a great number of short stories, as well as travelogues, essays and political commentary. He died in 1944, aged 78.